FRACTURE

Book 2 of the Resonance Tetralogy

Hugo Jackson

Inspired
Quill

Published by Inspired Quill: September 2016

First Edition

Fracture © 2016 by Hugo Jackson
Contact the author through their website: www.hugorjackson.com

Chief Editor: Sara-Jayne Slack: www.sjslack.co.uk
Cover Design: Katie Hofgard: www.katiehofgard.daportfolio.com
Typeset in Garamond

Paperback ISBN: 978-1-908600-53-0
eBook ISBN: 978-1-908600-54-7
Print Edition

Printed in the United Kingdom
1 2 3 4 5 6 7 8 9 10

Inspired Quill Publishing, UK
Business Reg. No. 7592847
www.inspired-quill.com

Praise for Hugo Jackson

"*Legacy* is very satisfying. Jackson brings a complex and colorful anthro world to life. His descriptions are full of lush detail."

— Fred Patten, *Dogpatch Press*

"I can't say enough good things about this book. The writing is great. The world is fascinating. The heroes are intriguing and lovable. The villains are terrifying, and the fight scenes are written as if by a fight choreographer. I loved it. A perfect book for adults, teens, and children alike."

— M. Shaw, *Amazon Reviewer*

"I loved it! This book honestly gave me a huge nostalgia rush – a lot happens once things start rolling. […] A fun fantasy romp with a great cast of heroes."

— David Popovich, *Bookworm Reviews (Youtube)*

"Overall, a very well written story that kept me entertained from start to finish. Every once in a while you stumble across an amazing gem, and this is one of those."

— *J. Poole, Bestselling Author of* The Bakkian Chronicles

To Alex, Toby, Vincent, Freya, Jack, James, George, Lucy, Will and Taz, Leo, and the currently-brewing child of Maggie and Dan.

You have the future. Use it well.

FRACTURE

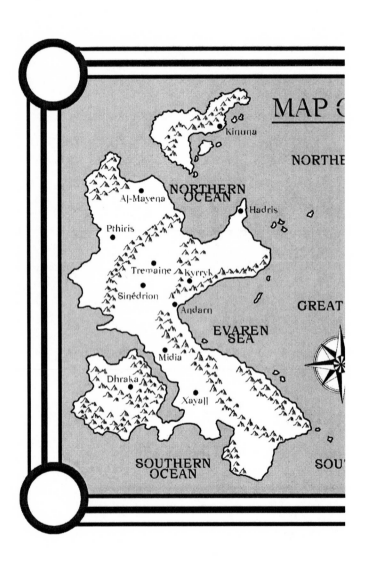

MAP O

NORTHE

NORTHERN
OCEAN

Kinuna

Al-Mayena

Hadris

Pthiris

Tremaine · Kyrryk

Sinédrion

Andarn

GREAT

EVAREN
SEA

Midia

Dhraka

Xayall

SOUTHERN
OCEAN

SOU

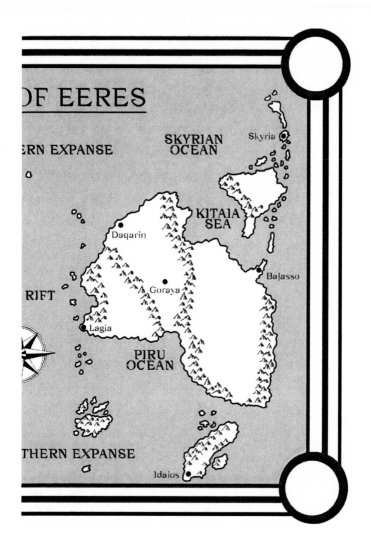

OF EERES

ERN EXPANSE

SKYRIAN OCEAN

Skyria

KITAIA SEA

Daqarin

Balasso

RIFT

Goraya

Lagia

PIRU OCEAN

THERN EXPANSE

Idaios

Prologue

The door smashed shut, splintering at its hinges. A terrified, desperate figure collapsed down the steps and into the street. He had barely hit the floor when he was up again, tearing down the dark pavement and away from his pursuer. The ragged breath cried from his throat, his feet slammed the rough stones, and he felt the electric burn of fear clambering over his shoulder. He dared not look, not for a second.

He was going to die.

The streets of Andarn listed wildly as the sleek tayra pelted from door to door, scrabbling madly at latches, casting his fists against the forbidding barriers in the hope that someone would grant him mercy. The shadows, deepened and spread by the clouded, starless sky, struck him with a lance-like fear whenever he caught sight of them.

"Please, help!"

The empty streets devoured his cry, and nobody came. Behind him, he felt his pursuer advancing quickly, too quickly. He sprinted away again, survival and sanctuary his desperate, vanishing goals.

"Guards! Someone, *please!*"

Rounding a corner too fast he listed sideways into the wall, crushing his shoulder against the brick. He wrenched himself upright, head spinning from the impact, only to have his neck slammed with choking force, pinning him to the wall. Knife-like claws sunk into his throat. He gasped and spat, tugging vainly at the assassin's grip.

"P…please… I'll get you… what… you… want…"

A smile in the darkness. Wry and sickening.

"What I want is a good death. Thank you for your assistance."

The tayra's eyes widened in horror as a blade flashed in the torchlight. The curved edge sliced from the base of his neck to his chin. His blood painted the ground, and when the cut was done, his body dropped.

Satisfied, the dark figure dipped his claw in the fresh crimson and scrawled a message on the wall. His work done, he paused only to spit on his prey before vanishing into the night.

The clouds rolled by overhead, and the city stood in cold silence.

Chapter One

For weeks it had been hard to tell if it was ash or snow falling from the bright, colourless sky above Xayall. Now, however, in the throes of winter, tiny ice flakes danced their way down to the sovereign city-state. Huddled in the centre of its wide, shallow valley, the usually vivid tapestry of rich greens surrounding the city had faded under the season's frosty restraint and lay eerily still. No gentle, rustling breeze tousled the leaves and calmed the valley with its sound, and many of the forest birds had flown to warmer climates, leaving the city in a strange, ethereal quiet.

The skies had been deep grey during the city's second brutal siege, and since then had regained no colour, only brightening with the sun's winter rise, like a sheet of rolling, translucent glass. Five months after the onslaught of Dhraka's reptilian forces, one could be forgiven for thinking Xayall was a ruin from a distance, were it not for the many plumes of smoke rising softly from its chimneys and the constant, irregular beat of city reparations. It still bore the heavy scars of conflict, and little had changed since the echoes of battle cries and clashing metal stopped ringing in the trees.

The skeleton of the metal pyramid Gargantua lay wedged against the outer wall. The giant drawbridge it had lowered for its troops to swarm into the city was twisted, partly broken during the machine's demise. Its empty cannons reached for the sky, the iron fingers of a dying giant.

Now depleted of the vicious legions and armaments within, the Gargantua was a harrowing, empty chamber, an enormous mausoleum that echoed and rumbled as the wind coursed through its desolate hallways. The hollow smell of burnt metal still hung in the air, and every so often ghostly metallic noises of decay resounded in its charred stomach.

Xayall itself, despite being in a similar condition to its deceased and rusting assailant, still held hints of the vibrant life it harboured before its ordeal under Dhrakan claws. Teams of soldiers and civilians worked diligently to clear the streets, and many smaller buildings were already mostly healed of their wounds. The once bright sandstone walls, although still riddled with scorch and pock marks where the Dhrakan bombs had spent their wrath, were patrolled by dedicated troops eager to defend against any unwanted raids. The biggest change in the city's visage, however, had been made to the central tower. Formerly the city's glimmering pinnacle, the Tor's severed column now virtually disappeared against the blanket of clouds, while the wing structures previously cradling the sky had shattered at its base when they fell, and were now solemnly being used to rebuild vital structures still suffering from damage.

"What do you see, Faria?"

The young fox jumped at the deep voice in her room and pulled the blankets around her neck. Her small, elegant frame looked even more diminutive in the hospital's generous bed, and the many bandages covering her slowly-healing wounds and burns only served to restrict her gentle body further.

She had been gazing at the city for so long that her focus had been completely removed from the immediate world around her. She turned her head to her visitor and gave him a weary smile. Every time Osiris was in the city he would come to keep up to date on her condition, both mentally and physically. If he had any concerns, the physicians were not usually far behind upon his departure.

Not prone to expressing emotion anyway, the gryphon had seemed even more guarded since Faria had been admitted to Xayall's hospital straight after her return from Nazreal. She found his stoicism sweet in a strange sort of way, but even through her tiredness, she knew he was trying to prepare her for the role she had yet to fulfil as Xayall's Empress. His aged lifespan had allowed him to oversee the construction of two different eras of their planet's history, watch countless mistakes and injustices, and witness great heroism and sacrifice. She trusted him to know what a leader should bring to the world, but the burden of that knowledge was not something she looked forward to receiving herself.

"Ah, Osiris, you startled me," she replied, shifting herself upright. "The city's rebuilding well, from what I can gather. I like picking sections to watch for a few days to see how quickly they're repaired. As for everything below the rooftops... It's hard to tell without being down there.

Damage can look worse or better from so far away, and I wouldn't like to speak for those who aren't fully recovered yet. There's still a lot to rebuild, and... I, um... need to retake my duties, eventually,"

Osiris strode to the window. His hulking avian frame would have blocked out most of the light, but his crimson armour and golden wings reflected a warm glow to the walls. His bedside manner left a lot to be desired at times. Despite his presence always being a great comfort to her, she could tell he battled with his own uncomfortable emotions, especially where she was concerned. Initially, when they returned to Xayall, he had been by her side every time she woke up, along with her wolf companions Aeryn and Kyru, but Osiris seemed to grow more pre-occupied with reparations and future issues as time passed, and the guarded care and concern that he showed her became marred with thoughts of the ongoing political and military struggles of the sovereign. She could understand why: Osiris' past was millennia long, and undoubtedly difficult. He conducted himself with an emotional mask that, to most, remained impenetrable. Faria had become one of the few who could see past it, into years of wisdom and painful memory. She had seen the same look in her father, and it saddened her greatly.

Faria worried that she would start to look the same if she were left in the hospital room by herself for too long. Here she lay, the recent inheritor of a sovereign nation's title of 'Empress' (by itself an obsolete and criticised honorific), and her greatest act so far was to secure herself a big window and a collection of blankets any avid quilter would be proud of. Even ignoring the weight of responsibilities she had not yet even shouldered, it currently took most of her strength to simply stay awake.

"Do not worry too heavily on your duties for now. I am glad to see you too," Osiris said with a slight smile. "I'm sorry I haven't been here more often, but getting the Coriolis out of the sand to the nearest ocean is proving more difficult than I expected. How are you feeling?"

She shifted in her bed, trying to force co-operation into the huge bank of pillows she'd constructed specifically against the doctors' orders so that she could see outside.

"All right," she said, stifling a yawn. "I mean… I still feel like I've been burnt inside and out, and as if my joints would snap as soon as they move. It doesn't hurt as much now, but I think there's more medicine in me than muscle. I can't even go near a crystal. My body's so weak they don't know what could happen. They say it's better for me to sleep, but it makes me sick to lie down so much."

The gryphon looked reflective for a second. She knew the look well, and she only hoped that he wouldn't draw another comparison to her father, as usually accompanied such an expression.

"You will heal, in time. I will make sure of it."

She gave a secret sigh. Every time she thought she'd come to terms with her father's absence, the feelings spilled over like water from a spring, and the pain in her hands, her whole body, would burn again. And it wasn't Osiris' responsibility for her to get well, even if he personally marshalled every doctor in the city to her bedside.

"I'm… I'm glad. At least, I hope I will. Sometimes I just…"

He turned to her expectantly as she trailed off. Feeling

defeated by an argument she didn't even know she was having with herself, she rested her head back against the pillows. Still watching the city in the middle-distance, her bright, electric blue eyes fogged with a wistful gaze.

"I don't know," she said quietly, after a time. "Everything's changed. It feels like a completely different world. But…" She looked back up at the ceiling. "More than that, I don't… I don't really know who I am at the moment. I don't know if the world's changed or if it's just me. I've lain in this bed for months barely able to move, drifting in and out of sleep while outside everything spins around me and…" She took a deep breath and held it, as if trying to compress her emotions into a smaller, more manageable form than the pulsing, sometimes violent wave of feelings that bashed at her body. "I hate it, Osiris. I… I don't even know that I'm happy to have survived some days. And I'm ashamed of that. But there's so much that I know only I can do, just so much…" She let her head fall to the side to stare at the window once again.

Osiris watched her, his calm expression betrayed by a hint of worry in his deep red eyes.

"Who would be here if you were not, Faria?"

"I don't know," she lied. It had taken her a long time to stop blaming herself for the shortcomings and losses of previous battles, and she still had days where she would do nothing but replay specific moments over and over, as if thinking about them hard enough would give her a chance to change them. So many people had sacrificed so much for her survival, in ways so great and so deep that she felt she would never be able to repay them.

"It would be poor of me to give up, wouldn't it?"

"In what sense?" he asked coolly.

She hadn't meant it as a question. "In every sense. Poor recompense to everyone, and poor strength on my part. I think…" She let out a long, heartfelt sigh. "It's about time to stop being ill, Osiris. There are a lot of people counting on me."

He let out a quiet laugh – quiet for him, anyway: being such a size and with such a commanding voice he did few things with subtlety.

"Your nobility and conscience are admirable, Faria. But do not forget, people are counting on you to recover and be yourself as much as anything else. There is more to living than duty."

"You don't seem to think so," she quipped with a sly smile, catching the gryphon completely off-guard. He cracked his shoulders indignantly, making his huge golden wings bristle. It created quite a draft, stronger since his restrictive injuries had healed.

"*My* life is best spent safeguarding Eeres' interests," he muttered, waving his claw dismissively. "You are too young to lose passion in such a cold way, and you are far kinder than I am. Do not underestimate the value of compassion, especially when times are dark. And besides, I still have the Coriolis as an escape. Which I really must return to."

Faria looked disappointed. "I'm sorry I can't help. It seems everyone who stops by has to run off and do something after visiting me. I feel useless wrapped up in bed."

Osiris flicked an imaginary speck of dust from his gleaming shoulder armour. "Resisting resonance energy strong enough to move continents is no minor task," he said with an air of light scolding. "I would always be grateful for your help, Faria." He punctuated himself with a short, frustrated breath. "And I know it would be a lot quicker with your assistance, but your absence from the task is not your fault, and we would be in a far worse situation if you had not protected us. Once the Coriolis is back in dock here, we will spend time talking about Nazreal and preparing ourselves for the journey ahead."

Faria scrunched her nose in playful disgust. "There's no getting past you, is there?"

His feathers bristled. It was a subtle dig, but she knew how hard he was trying to be both dutiful and kind. She regretted how little she could do when her mind swam in such fast rivers of thought, especially when his ship meant so much to him. In a world that knew nothing of his species or his world, this was the single piece he could still keep hold of. She would be doing the same in his position. She was lucky, albeit reluctantly so, that her world, her friends, and her city were taking care of themselves without her intervention. He stood by her bed. "I have asked Aeryn and Kyru to check in on you while I'm away. I hope that is permissible."

She nodded gratefully. "They do already, you know."

"Yes," he said bluntly, "but now I have specifically asked them to come in and see you. So I expect they will be here more often, at the very least."

Faria allowed herself a smile at Osiris' expense for his determination to trust almost no-one but himself. Without the three of them, she would have been completely alone, and she didn't believe she could have found the strength, the motivation, to survive otherwise.

"Thank you, Osiris. I'll miss you, as always. I have Bayer and Kier, too – they're very good to me. They always have been."

As hopeful as she tried to sound, she couldn't hide the sadness in her voice when her thoughts turned to one of her companions in particular.

"I did visit him before seeing you."

She swallowed and looked to her hands, wringing them in her lap. Eventually, she forced herself to reply. "And…?"

"Physically, he has healed a moderate amount, but there has been no change in his response for some time, and he will not wake yet. He needs to travel to Skyria for further attention."

She winced. Osiris' words felt so cold, so painfully distant regarding a friend who had always been so warm and kind. Many harsh memories of her struggle still lingered, but Tierenan's injuries had weighed on Faria's mind the most. Her stomach roiled and twisted whenever she relived the moment her brightest friend was struck down by Raikali. When she had insisted on seeing him after she first woke up, she needed to be led away and forced to sleep, the sight of his condition upset her so badly. The young raccoon had looked like a ghost, torn and battered, and still caked in blood, old and new. She was sure he would die. He hadn't even been moved from the Tor to the hospital; his condition was so grave that he had to be treated virtually where he lay, and monitored intensely. Still, with all of the falcon surgeon Maaka's efforts, and a great deal of unconscious strength from Tierenan himself, he held onto life with the thinnest thread. How he might recover past that, though, was still a grave uncertainty. Even for only being a few floors apart, it crushed her to know that he would not be bouncing colourfully into her room any time soon, if ever.

"I see. I want… to go with him, when he does."

Osiris nodded. "All the more reason to get the Coriolis free. I will not have you putting yourself at risk, understand?"

Faria puffed her blankets in an indignant rustle. "You sound like the physicians," she mumbled. "I had to ask for hours before they even let me near a window, and they're constantly trying to convince me I'm too cold. I already told them I have more blankets than the rest of the city put together. I want to go outside again. And I miss my real bedroom."

The gryphon scratched his beak idly. "Well, Aeryn and Kyru lack the stringency that I have, so I am sure they can aid you in breaking any rules that have been laid before you. Just be careful. Even though Raikali and Fulkore are gone, we are still vulnerable, you especially." He flicked his claw demonstratively toward her, and she answered with a reluctant nod.

"I promise, Osiris. I'll be fine," she sighed. "I've started asking for regular reports on the city's progress, but they don't always arrive." She shifted in her bed, looking embarrassed as she formed her next question: "Could you scare someone before you leave, please?"

He gave a derisive snort; she surmised it was at the lack of reports. It was an irritation guaranteed to strike an immediate nerve with Osiris.

"Of course. Is there anything else you need, Miss Empress?"

"Not right now, thank you." She shot him a warning

glare. "By the way, if you call me 'Miss Empress' or 'Your Majesty' again, I'll clip your wings. 'Faria' is fine, and most important to me."

As he swept into the corridor, she could have sworn she heard him laugh.

Chapter Two

B ayer felt the touch of the still, cold air on his body. He
felt as if the world was slowing down, an oddly familiar
sensation that he couldn't place which left him uneasy. He
had finally rid himself of the bandages that been holding his
wounds in place after the sieges, and he was eager to taste
freedom again.

Xayall barracks' arena was a modestly sized
amphitheatre with raised seats and four turrets projecting
over the central training space. Rows of heavy wooden
platforms, separated at intervals by the sandy floor, covered
trenches used in battle training. Currently, most of those
who entered the ring were small groups, the few that could
be spared from either Andarn or Xayall's troops to undergo
important briefings or training, but the regimented marches
and orientation of new recruits had ceased for some time.
Bayer had found a quiet area by one of the towers, behind
some missing platforms, distancing himself from a group of
Andarn soldiers currently undergoing drills in the centre,

their silver and white armour matching the soft skies above.

A single flake of snow drifted in front of him, landing silently on the ground, where it slowly faded to a wet shadow in the sand. He looked up as more tiny flecks drifted into view, only visible against the sand-dusted walls of the arena. It wasn't a thick snowfall, but there was something very... final about it. He shook his head.

He held his sword in both hands and brought it in front of him, porting the hilt at waist height and tilting the point forwards, as if threatening an invisible enemy with a sharp rap between the eyes. Taking a deep breath, the ocelot slid his right foot from in front to behind him, and slowly swept the sword about him at shoulder height before turning his body to follow. With a flick of his wrists the blade circled upwards and came down directly in front of him, a vertical strike, carried out with a steady, seamless flow.

As he rolled his arms to swing the blade upwards again, twisting the sword over, a jolt of pain snapped down his right arm, freezing him in position. He took a slow and deliberate breath, feeling his hackles rise, trying to lower his arm to where the pain would stop pulsing in bursts through his shoulder. Eventually he dropped the sword tip to the ground and rested his arm on the hilt, glaring at it resentfully. At least the pain came less frequently now. Raking his claws on the bound leather grip, he scowled. These injuries were nothing, he thought. He had to be stronger than this.

He glanced around the arena. It had never been a very imposing building, mainly because Xayall never had a large military force. Bayer had often wondered about that – how a city which actually needed protecting more than others could end up with so inconspicuous a guard, and he often came to disagreements with Aidan about it. The fox, Faria's father and former Emperor, had always insisted that having too large a military invited people to ask what needed protecting, and that it was better to have a smaller, better-trained group of soldiers defending what was really necessary. Hence his interest in Kier and Bayer as bodyguards for himself and Faria, Bayer supposed. For all his strengths, however, Faria's father had never been a military man, and as far as Bayer was concerned, with all that he sought to protect, Aidan had dangerously overestimated the security of his own city's walls, and mistrusted the greed of the world.

Bayer resisted the urge to call it selfish if only for the sheer power those two resonators wielded – by itself a dangerous asset to be sighted by enemies – but he felt greatly conflicted as to the damage the former Emperor's planning had done to Xayall, previously one of the finest, most open sovereigns on Eeres. He had seen enough battles to know how easily a city fell long before the Dhrakans tasted Xayall's air, and any citizen deserved protection as much as a member of royalty. He would debate the gaping holes in training or security openly with Kier often enough, and even though the fox agreed for the most part, Bayer always felt like there was some sort of secret he wasn't being let in on.

Right now, he wasn't even sure *what* he was supposed to be guarding, with his role as Faria's protector usurped by the two wolves she had brought back with her. He knew Kier suffered the same contemplations. With Aidan's death, the younger fox lost his role as the Emperor's bodyguard, and had no orders to follow until Faria decided whether he or Bayer, or both, were needed any more.

In the corner of his vision he noticed another figure enter the arena. He tensed, thinking it was Osiris, but as soon as he recognised the familiar soldier in the distance he relaxed.

Kier strode into the barracks with a great air of purpose. The fox's armour stood out bright and bold against the washed-out colours of the sandy walls: bottle green and black, with gold fittings and detailing. A short, sleeveless livery coat in ornate embroidery of the same colours, a jinbaori, tapered to his athletic frame as he marched towards the commanding officer of the Andarn troop. The officer appeared to straighten out his company and dust off his armour in a hasty effort to present himself. Perhaps not so much for the appearance of Kier himself, Bayer thought, trying not to be too dismissive of his closest friend, but the boldness of his dress and the rarity of the weapon strapped to his back gave a distinct importance to him. The blade had a long, single-edged curve. Almost Kier's height with an angular tip, the hilt was at an angle acute to the blade like a gun's handle, with a narrow crossguard that curved upwards elegantly but sharply around the base of the sword, and small scallop-shaped cup guards running alongside the hilt. It certainly was impressive, and soldiers had a habit of being drawn to tools of particular interest, especially where weapons and armour were concerned.

Not that the fox couldn't make an impression on his own, however; Kier had just made being noticed or unnoticed (dependent on his mood or need for discretion) somewhat of an art form. It always impressed Bayer how

Kier could subtly change his perception to others. The fox used his talent well.

Bayer watched the fox and the senior officer talk briefly, then exchange polite salutes. He admired the confidence the fox held himself with now, a welcome improvement to his youthful timidity. Once Kier had finished his conversation, he caught sight of Bayer and strode towards him, a more eager step than the one used entering the arena. Something in his walk put Bayer on guard; a tension and preoccupation that meant he was embroiled in something serious. He saw that too much in his friend these days.

"You look tired," Bayer called, resting the flat of the sword on his shoulder.

Kier half-smiled. "You're not exactly looking bright yourself, you know. I take it your 'physiotherapy by sword' hasn't threatened your injuries into disappearing yet?"

The ocelot's jaw tightened. "Mmm, something like that. I'm just trying to find a way to stay useful since the siege. At least you get to play Junior Representative for the time being."

Kier sighed. "Yeah, well…" He glanced behind him, towards the barrack's entrance. Some Andarn troops and a figure in gold crossed under the arched doorway, watching Kier. Bayer guessed they were the reason for the fox's disturbance. "It's not without its drawbacks. It's partly a distraction, partly… trying to find a purpose. Or keep one. Nobody really knows what to do or where we stand. There hasn't been a sovereign-against-sovereign war on this continent for over sixty years."

"*Civil* wars happen all the time, though," Bayer said irritably. "It depends on how closely you're willing to look.

Most people ignore it, but seeds of conflict lie everywhere, ready to bed themselves in people who tread on the wrong ground."

"We were *attacked*, Bayer. This wasn't just some petty escalation of insults, and we're not fighting ourselves. There's a big difference."

Receiving no reply, Kier watched Bayer for a second, and saw his expression harden. Kier gave him a sceptical eye. "Bayer, what are you thinking?"

The ocelot looked steadily ahead, fixed in a steely glare. "It's different for you. You faced this when you had the training for it. For me, this is…" He paused for a second, swallowing down the memories that he couldn't relive again. "I don't think I can stay here. I don't know that I belong."

Kier's shoulders dropped slightly, his silver eyes discerning Bayer's frustration. He set a hand on the feline's good arm. "I don't think Faria would just cast you aside."

Bayer shook his head, moving his arm away. "No, she wouldn't. I'm not talking about her. It's this city, the ruin of it… if Aidan knew Dhraka was going to attack, why didn't he do more to protect the city?"

The fox folded his arms. "Preparing for war can invite war, you know that. You should see how many spats the Representatives get into when other sovereigns build outposts or stockpile weapons." Kier wasn't trying to admonish him, but it was hard not to sound dismissive. "I'm not saying I agree with how little defence Xayall had, but Aidan didn't want to invite people to look inside our walls. He was afraid enough of Nazreal being discovered."

Bayer looked to him quickly, bitterly. "And how much did you know about that before he left? Did you know about the city, why he was trying to hide it? Didn't he understand that simply by *being here*, he was drawing attention to himself, and us? He was like a beacon for greedy opportunists. How didn't he see that?"

The fox held his hands out to calm his friend. "Settle, Bayer. I didn't know anything – I didn't even know Nazreal was right over there. I was only told that there was dangerous knowledge in Xayall, to do with Aidan, and Faria's mother. I didn't understand *how* dangerous until I found the city in flames. I just thought it had to do with their resonance." He stepped in closer, quietly trying to appeal to Bayer's reason. "You're not the only one who feels wronged by this. Aidan knew he was sticking our heads over the parapet, but… apparently he had a plan, and wanted to end it without hurting the sovereign he loved."

"Some plan. And why alone?" Bayer growled, his claw tightening on the sword hilt. "Why not inform the city, the guards, any of the Representatives, us, even Faria, of the great and dangerous secrets we were sitting on before it was too late? Did he think that we wouldn't support him? Don't you resent that, that selfish mistrust?"

Kier didn't say anything. It was true to an extent – Aidan's desire to bury time's secrets had hindered their ability to sufficiently prepare to protect themselves, but he didn't agree that it was direct mistrust. He had seen the Senate meetings, the backbiting and secret deals, and the eye-for-an-eye negotiations of the desperate and greedy. And if Aidan's own history was true, he had seen all of this before, and had been desperate to find a different path.

Bayer looked scornfully at his blade. "How many lives could have been saved, Kier? The permanence of such a mistake is too grave to bear lightly."

The fox straightened himself. "Aidan knew the value of life," he said in a quiet, determined voice. "Don't ever question that. He knew he was on borrowed time against the Dhrakans, and stirring the sovereign into a panic might have risked people running to the hills, *into* the mouth of danger. Every time a secret is told, it's one more target for torture or extortion. Given the depth of Nazreal's secrets, I know I would want to burden as few people as possible with that knowledge, if only to save them from being chased to ruin. The last thing he wanted was war."

Bayer looked to the sky and took a deep lungful of air, before letting it out in a long, tired whistle. He watched the vapour from his breath form a thin stream of mist before dissipating.

"He had a good heart, but he tried to protect too much by himself. I can't forget what I saw." He balled his fist, watching the muscles in his arm tense and tighten. "Times like this... I just feel so useless."

"Yeah," Kier sighed in agreement, still considering his friend's thoughts, wondering if something more might be at the heart of his dissent. "You're not alone. There's little any of us can do to resolve such massive upheaval, but I don't want you to tear yourself to pieces about it."

Bayer stared at the clouds. "Still my friend from the library, aren't you?" he said eventually, tilting his head to catch Kier's expression.

The fox pulled at his sleeve a little. "Yeah, of course I am," he replied quietly. He then puffed up and snapped an accusing claw at Bayer. "So don't dismiss me, you onerous cynic. I've invested years trying to make you see some kind of joy in the world, and I won't give up so easily."

Bayer laughed, the first time he had done so in a while.

"Listen," Kier said secretively, producing a scroll from within his jinbaori. "I need to find Alaris. Those soldiers at the gate have a request for his removal, and I can't shake them off. Apparently something serious is happening in Andarn. Come with me – you're not doing anyone any favours by isolating yourself."

Bayer scoffed. "You've got soldiers looking over your shoulder and you stand here listening to me moan like an old man? You're not right, Kier."

Kier smiled in return. "I don't know if there is a 'right' at the moment. Besides, I never said I'd put my duty above those I care about."

Bayer shook his head, hiding his muzzle in embarrassment. "You're insufferable."

"Only for you, Bayer. But anyway," the fox continued, "I'm trying to stall them. I don't want to lose Alaris just yet."

Despite the city's busy reparation, the streets were still bereft of their previous population, both visitors and residents alike, and the atmosphere was greatly muted. The market still ran, thankfully, but few traders had ventured back to Xayall as yet. Winters were a quiet time for trade at best anyway, but Xayall held a historic reputation for being a welcoming and bustling environment at any time of year. *Not so much now*, Bayer thought, as they marched the streets, passing soldiers distributing aid or civilians in the midst of rebuilding before the harsh cold set in around them. He kept glancing surreptitiously at the quartet of visiting guards behind them. Their leader, a surly and officious-looking otter, watched Kier vigilantly for signs of deviation. Kier hadn't been unprofessionally distracting or discourteous, but this was not the first time Alaris had been requested back and he almost always had a smokescreen to deploy. Bayer had even witnessed brainstorming sessions between the two that produced lists of excuses for Alaris to stay, but he could only aid Xayall for so long.

The stranger in gold perplexed Bayer most. The athletic meerkat was a Tremaine soldier, and despite being surrounded by the silent, white-clad swordsmen, he seemed more aware of his surroundings than them, and even kept an interest in Bayer, making eye contact with the ocelot and nodding affirmatively in greeting, where the other three had been tersely unresponsive to his presence. Despite his acknowledgement of Bayer, the meerkat had not said a single word. Tensions between Andarn and Tremaine had been tenuous for some time, so Bayer wondered if he was being tacitly silenced through being outnumbered.

Bayer set his eyes on the scroll in Kier's grasp. "So how long have you been Xayall's concierge?"

The fox turned the document over in his hand, inspecting the wax seal he'd broken to officially receive the request for the Andarn soldiers' entry. "Nothing wrong with being polite, especially when we're short-handed and Faria is in recovery. A pleasant reception can make all the difference in negotiation. But especially where our friend is concerned, I like to take point. I haven't trusted official communication channels since the siege and our Councillors, the ones who are still alive and here, are busy with repairs. We're lucky

Alaris is aware of our current situation and can command support for us."

"He won't be here forever," Bayer said, a hint of warning in his voice, mindful of the soldiers breathing down their necks.

"I know. He's managed to deflect most orders onto other regiments, but this is the first signed redeployment order we've received with an armed escort. Things are getting better here, but it's not enough. Xayall isn't strong enough to support itself without Andarn. I wish we didn't still need them, but… they're all we have."

They were heading to the reservoir and grain silos, set back towards the southern end of the city. Although many of the imposing stone cylinders had been left unharmed, the bombardment had ruptured enough to cause concerning deficits in their supply, and the fires in the city had damaged a portion of the stored grain. In itself, this wouldn't have left the city in too much trouble, had Dhraka not destroyed huge swaths of Xayall's farmland on their way to the forest. Patrols sent after the dragons had retreated were met by charred fields and devastated farms, with few survivors. Much of Xayall's food for the winter was being sought from other sovereigns. They were not being generous. Andarn was providing the most aid and protection; supply carts arrived like clockwork and their soldiers patrolled every street.

Bayer felt the bile in his throat at every glint of white armour. Seeing them in the city, taking and giving supplies as the governors of security, filled him with unquenchable ire. His expression became sour as they walked, and he refused to look about them for danger of losing control.

Kier felt his friend's tension burn beside him, and looked to him cautiously.

"What?"

"This is wrong," Bayer scowled. "We shouldn't be dependent on them for help. We'll be under their thumb soon. You can't just sell us out to Andarn like this – they'll never let go of the debt. Xayall needs to rebuild its strength from within."

Kier stepped towards him, trying to keep covert. "I am not selling out. Our debt is a fate we and Andarn shared on the battlefield. We're only alive because they defended us. At the very least Alaris recognises how close not just we, but *all* of Eeres, came to being destroyed. They're not doing this to usurp our land or control us, they're—"

"You don't know that," Bayer replied. "For being Aidan's attendant you haven't paid much attention to world history, have you? Andarn is one of the most invasive sovereigns there is – every city they get a foothold in gets bartered away from the inside. They're as bad as the Dhrakans."

"Bayer, control yourself!" Kier barked. "I expect better from you. Don't think for a second that I'm ignorant of world history *or* your personal misgivings of Andarn, but right now we have no choice." He tried to keep his voice low enough that the soldiers behind wouldn't catch their conversation, but he sensed they had heard all the same. "These soldiers allowed Xayall to survive. I ask that you at least be grateful for that and respect my position keeping the peace."

Bayer fixed him in a hard stare. "Fine. But I want you to remember which sovereign this is, and not take any more than we need. We can't afford to lose anything else."

The fox nodded, focussing on their destination – the yard in front of the granaries. "Trust me, I'm trying not to. I'm doing what I can for Faria, and to get us back on our feet quickly. We're on a dangerous precipice right now."

He caught distant sight of Alaris, and the soldiers behind had too, their armoured footsteps shifting in key to a harder, more forceful march. Kier would not let them break past him, however, and Bayer cast his eyes back often, resting his sword on his shoulder at just the wrong angle for them to get too close, or risk jabbing themselves in the face. He felt a long-absent glimmer of pride flicker within him for being able to protect his friend's dignity and passive-aggressively discipline Andarn soldiers at the same time.

"Well, if we are," Bayer murmured, "let's at least push someone else off first to cushion our fall."

Kier cracked a smile. "You are a cynical, suspicious, diplomatic nightmare, you know that?"

Bayer allowed himself a small smile at his expense. "I pride myself on it."

Chapter Three

"This will not stand, Tremaine! I tell you, it will not stand!"

The wine pitcher flew over the table, narrowly missing its target and hitting the floor with a piercing smash. Glass slid in all directions.

"Well, certainly not any longer…" Jed Othera, a stag of imposing proportions, muttered under his breath. He had been forced to preside over the untidy remnants of a former diplomatic meeting, as Andarn and Tremaine argued responsibility over the death of the Andarn Councillor Mattok a few nights ago.

The murder happened at the height of a conference with other Senate leaders that was, at its inception at least, regarding border disputes. Mattok had been Andarn's spokesperson and primary negotiator; his death had broken the meeting apart whilst investigations took place and security was increased around major officials, as first order of business moved to establish exactly what had happened to him. Unfortunately, everyone had their own opinion and the story changed so many times in its dissemination that no report, official or unofficial, could be taken without consideration of ten others. As the largest sovereign on the continent of Cadon, Andarn was not popular. There were few present at the meeting's start who believed anyone was being given fair treatment by the enormous city-state, and many well-documented Senate disagreements concurred. By far the loudest decrier of Andarn was Tremaine's Councillor, so Tremaine was accused of having the strongest motive against the city. The arguments between the two became so heated that Jed had asked the other envoys to leave until matters had settled.

They had been gone for a long time.

He repeatedly reminded the two Representatives that, until reasonable cause had been established to call it an assassination (as opposed to a coincidental occurrence of Andarn's already high crime rate), it was unhelpful to make unnecessary allegations. Neither side appeared to be listening, so most of the time he stood in place between the two diplomatic parties with his short-handled bardiches close at hand. When they became too animated he would throw out a powerful arm to whichever was the aggressing side, and generally they would calm down. His only other constructive presence seemed to be reciting rules and contracts of the Senate upon the eruption of disagreements far removed from the principle tragedy.

Jed had been told by Andarn senior military staff that 'good fortune' had placed him in the city when this happened, although he failed to see the benefit so far. Considering his representation of Sinédrion itself, he supposedly wielded certain administrative and diplomatic authorities over most Representatives of the same level. But that mattered little in battles of emotion and patriotism. From what he saw, the ascending hierarchy in these two bickering sovereigns tended to be populated by self-important brats, sycophants, schemers, or xenophobes. And since even politeness, much less sycophancy, was in drought in Andarn, he would have to make a bigger impression to calm the fiery, blue air in the meeting hall. Slowly, unnoticed by the squabbling parties, he slid one of his bardiches from its ring on his belt.

"How dare you be so condescending!" came the venomous response from Tremaine's Councillor, a slender, angular mongoose. "Your sickening fetish for violence and domination is finally about to bite you back, Andarn. You'll find no fault of ours in this – your bed is your own, and we have no part in your internal politics." The mongoose from Tremaine, Prince Haru Ekalibante, stood unperturbed by the glass that had almost shattered on his skull.

Enraged, the coati Representative from Andarn, Grand Councillor Vol, now lacking anything to throw, hurled his fists onto the table with bile in his voice. His grey robes of office rippled in his quaking temper. "How dare you! I'll see your sovereign eat your pompous words when we prove who's behind this outrageous crime! You dare to accuse us of murdering one of our own Councillors? Insolent whelp! Andarn is the pinnacle of civilisation!"

Haru's eyes narrowed. "Pinnacle? With every inch of your land crawling with vagrants and your main city surrounded by slums?" He let out a derisive, baleful snort. "Why wouldn't it be from within your own walls? A

31

disgusting city that fosters greed and opportunism. You seem blissfully content to have your soldiers raid our outlying settlements, by official order or not. Maybe if you controlled your borders more efficiently you wouldn't have such irregularities inside them. Cast your eyes inwards before taking arms against others."

"I *knew* you would bring a sack of lies to the table!" Vol roared, almost jumping onto the table. "Did you hear that, Sinédrion? Tremaine have been redefining our borders for years and claiming *we're* at fault! There's your motive! Councillor Mattok was going to read them the riot act over the disputes with our maps, and they—"

"You have no proof!" Haru spat. "If you weren't so gluttonously expansionist he wouldn't have had so many enemies to negotiate with in the first place!"

"*Us* expansionist!?" the coati fumed, pointing a quaking claw at the mongoose. "Your soldiers have been sighted within our borders for the last two years, and we have never seen any authorisation. If I didn't know better, I'd say you were planning an invasion—"

Something moved between them. A deafening crack tore the air, and the table that Vol had been leaning on buckled inwards, split down the centre. He scrambled backwards up the table's polished surface, shocked into silence by the blade that had cleft the wooden surface in two, a hair's breadth from his outstretched hand. Haru's eyes were wide in disbelief and fear, as Jed's powerful arm wrenched the axe from the splintered wooden rift and replaced it in his belt. His gold armour appeared ablaze in the light from the tall, arched window behind them, making his interjection even more impressive.

"This has gone too far," he warned, his deep voice authoritative in its composure. "I have stood here and listened to nothing but your endless, petty bickering. There is a serious case of a sovereign's inner security at risk, or an even greater threat to the peace of the nations. Andarn." He turned to Vol, who dared not look him in the eye. Jed was respected across Cadon for his ability to defuse and control difficult situations, not only because he was a skilled mediator, but also due to his immense and, at times, terrifying, strength.

"Yes, Representative?"

"What cause is there to believe Tremaine had any involvement in this?"

Vol scraped his claws against each other, a nervous habit made worse by a poor ability to control his frustrations. "Well, Representative, we are hosting a far larger contingent of Tremaine soldiers than we were anticipating, and it has caused some unrest in the city. We saw some fights between soldiers. During our investigation we received reports that several soldiers in Tremaine colours were seen out that night, and we *know* of their resentment of us…"

Jed's focus remained sternly on Vol. "Why Tremaine specifically, Andarn?"

"We… the… I just presumed that the motive was strongest with… The blade injury came from a curved weapon, much like the Tremaine officers' dress blades." He faltered, taking a chance every few seconds to cast his eyes around the room for cues; he came unseated rather quickly when put under interrogation. Unfortunately, for a sovereign the size of Andarn, positions were not always earned, but bought or bartered. *It's as well the military leaders are more competent*, Jed thought, *although not necessarily without the same bias*. Despite holding such a pivotal role in the Senate with a vast wealth of resources, Andarn's chain of domestic command was so strikingly weak that it was a miracle nobody had discovered it yet. Unless that had been the reason for Mattok's murder in the first place.

"Enough. Tremaine," he barked. Haru stood to attention immediately, although his face still held a distasteful expression.

"Yes, Representative?"

"Your response."

Haru took a deep, audibly trenchant, breath. "Our officers are all accounted for on our roster, and our soldiers were kept to a strict curfew according to the guidelines set forth by Andarn prior to our arrival. In fact, the commanders were holding safety briefings with their troops when we received news of what happened." He cast a steely eye over to Vol, who glared viciously back. "I do not wish to further aggravate matters, but I would like to politely ask where Councillor Mattok's guards were."

"What?" Vol choked.

"Mattok's guards. I gather the report read that they were absent."

Jed looked to Vol, who muttered something about 'not supposed to have read it'. The coati composed himself and stiffened his soldiers. "The guards were allegedly dismissed on Mattok's orders, and reported to their barracks."

A trace of a smile flicked across Haru's face. "And why was Mattok in that part of the city?"

Vol's face darkened, frustration rippling through him.

"We aren't sure," he grumbled. "After the guards were dismissed, he left his residence. We don't know where he was going, or why, or if he met with anyone."

Jed let out a gruff sigh. "So the evidence is all but negligible."

"Except," Vol said suddenly, wary of almost interrupting the imposing stag, "his murderer left a message: 'The shadow is coming'."

The room fell silent. The three exchanged concerned looks.

"Does this connect to anything else you've witnessed in Andarn?" Jed asked Vol gravely, whose nostrils flared and fingers twitched.

"No, nothing," he murmured. "We've searched the military, historical, prison, and judicial libraries and there's no reference to that phrase anywhere. We don't know what it means."

Haru stared blankly at the table. "It sounds like a threat to me. I mean, if it were just a crime of opportunity, there would be no need to leave a message."

"Indeed." Jed straightened, standing tall enough to almost completely block out the window. "Representative Andarn, I might offer some advice to secure your sovereign and capital city's control until you unearth the evidence, if you so wish."

Vol's demeanour shifted. He stiffened, and his whole body straightened to make himself as tall as possible. His face pinched in, showing off the slightest hint of a pair of long, white incisors. "With all due respect, Sinédrion, we are, as we have always been, perfectly capable of defending ourselves. If there is one thing Andarn can be proud of, it is our military strength. We will not be defeated, nor overthrown. Our troops' loyalty is intrinsic to their service." He gave Jed a stern look. "And not all of the power in the Senate can change that. We are proud and we are strong. We will survive."

Haru was unmoved, his yellow eyes brimming with unspoken derision. "How very noble," the mongoose sneered, looking towards the door, flicking his long robe sleeves from trailing in front of his feet. Eventually he looked back and locked gazes with Vol. "You have my admiration."

Vol's eyes flashed with suspicion. He gave Jed a quick glance, before deciding it a poor idea to make an inflammatory comment and gave a curt huff. "We thank you for your co-operation, and apologise for the inconvenience this…" He paused, with the look of an animal trying desperately not to bite off its own tongue. "…unfortunate event, and regret that we may not be able to resolve our disagreements until a replacement for Mattok can be found. We will try to fill his position as soon as possible. In the mean time, you are…"

He paused, his breathing laboured under the frustrating effort of extending diplomacy over argument. Jed took a small step back, watching them both, allowing the silence to linger.

"…welcome to stay, for as long as you wish."

Haru cracked a sardonic grin. "Thank you for your gracious invitation, Representative, but we will not impose," he purred, looking up and down at Vol's awkward shifting. "We shall stay until the scheduled departure, as you have already made plans for us to do so, and we shall not take unnecessary advantage of your... generosity."

Jed looked between them, satisfied with the courtesy, no matter how forced or oleaginous. "Thank you, Representatives. I will brief the other sovereigns on the proceedings."

The three bowed to each other, and Vol gestured for Haru to exit first. The mongoose sauntered through the doorway, saying nothing more, but giving the coati a sideways glance as he left. Vol's jaw tightened and the hackles on his neck stood on end.

"I hate him," he said once the wiry figure was out of earshot. "Wish we could be rid of their damned territory disputes. If I catch their troops within our borders one more time, there will be blood, I swear it."

Jed watched the mongoose gathering aides as he strode along the long, grand corridor. "Don't get complacent," the stag said sternly. "Andarn is far from guiltless, especially on your outskirts. If you don't increase the controls on your outlying settlements, the Senate might have to impose sanctions. You *are* aware of this, aren't you?"

Vol's jaw opened and closed a few times with inarticulate disbelief. "You have no idea what goes on in this sovereign!" he spluttered eventually.

"That, Councillor Vol," Jed fixed him with a damning stare, "is a significant part of the problem. Fix it before our next meeting." He marched out, not turning to see the indignation on the fuming Representative's face. "I would advise you brief Mattok's replacement well, *without* bias," he added with biting sharpness. "The whole Senate is watching your sovereign, and this will be a test of your mettle."

Vol stamped his foot and cast a furious claw at Jed's

back. "Perhaps our armies would be better placed than to protect a Senate that does not trust our honour!" he spat.

As soon as Jed halted mid-stride, the blood drained from Vol's face. The fire in Jed's eye as he glanced back over his shoulder shot a fear into the coati that wrenched his stomach from the inside. The diminutive creature made a faltering effort to correct himself, but no sound escaped his twitching mouth, and he simply stared.

Jed's sheer size and visibly demonstrated power, directed completely at Vol, gave him the same authority as if the stag was holding him by his neck from across the length of the corridor. "The protection of an army is worthless when it is so poorly ruled and so swiftly divided. Andarn's size will be its downfall without a strong leader. Farewell, Representative."

With the stag's resonant voice burning in his ears, Vol was left in the corridor, silent in its vast, unfriendly emptiness.

Chapter Four

For being an agricultural structure, Xayall's granary complex looked as grand as an arena. The huge cylindrical silos were built in looming groups of eight, set opposite each other in a giant x-shape. Each of the silo clusters had a large grain elevator attached, powered by complex water mechanisms running underground.

At least, that was how they were supposed to look.

Piles of rubble still lay strewn about the open spaces, pushed aside to make walkways for more urgent repairs. Miraculously, none of the subterranean grain elevators had needed reconstruction, despite the tremors that rocked the city while Faria was in Nazreal. The siege had been devastating aboveground, however. Several of the silos were scorched and cracked by the heat of the Dhrakan fires, and a number of the stout pillars that held the free-standing storage barns had been smashed to pieces, leaving their former burden either listing dangerously or collapsing in sections, bereft of their support.

At first, the work had been to strengthen the structures, but with the cold and damp setting in, the task had shifted to gathering unspoiled food and securing it inside buildings that were still solid. The rest could wait, as long as the city had food enough to last until next season. As it was, the city would be living hand-to-mouth for some time yet, given the devastation of the farmlands outside the walls. In some ways, given the allotted provisions, it was almost a blessing that many of the city's former populace had not yet returned.

Alaris caught sight of the approaching envoy from the other side of a rank of soldiers he was currently addressing. The affable pangolin looked distinctly more tired now than upon his arrival in Xayall five months ago. He hadn't slept, and it showed in his figure and movement: he stood slightly lower than normal, and moved with stiff joints that were in need of a decent rest. His armour, although washed in the white livery of the Andarn infantry, bore the captain's colours of red and gold in its adornments. It held its distinction on its own, but somehow appeared even more eminent with its scrapes and wounds, as yet unrepaired after the siege. Although worn out from constant reparation work and battling against diminishing troops and resources, he still conducted himself with politeness and sincerity. It was easy for many to see why he was one of the most respected mid-level commanders in Andarn's military.

Watching Kier advance and heeding the fox's warning glance, he swiftly finished his briefing and dismissed the soldiers with a salute. They dispersed, leaving the pangolin to rise to his full height (about a head taller than Kier) in anticipation of the meeting before him. He immediately noticed the Tremaine soldier and shot the meerkat a quizzical look. Bayer glanced round quickly enough to see the slim creature roll his eyes, fighting his impatience with as little noise but as many facial expressions as possible. Before Bayer could observe further, Alaris stepped to greet Kier with a formal handshake.

"Captain Alaris," the fox spoke with the air of one holding back a great deal of breath, in preparation for something important to break into the conversation.

"Representative Kier," Alaris replied, guarded in the presence of the new Andarn trio. "It's good to see you."

Kier nodded. "You too, Captain. Alaris, if you'll forgive my forwardness, Captain Camiyan is here from Andarn." He looked briefly over his shoulder. "I gather he has some urgent news for you from your sovereign, and I would hate to delay him any further." He stepped gingerly aside and gestured for the otter to approach. Camiyan strode forward, clicking claws against his armour. He was as tall as Alaris but not nearly as muscular. What he lacked in bulk, he seemed to make up for with dour countenance and a certain severity that no doubt helped keep his troops in line.

"Alaris," the otter grunted, reluctantly offering a salute. Alaris responded in like, giving him a short nod.

"I'm surprised to see you here, Camiyan. I didn't think you ventured this far South."

Camiyan let out a gruff, derisive breath. "This isn't by choice." He gave a sideways glance to Kier and Bayer, challenging their proximity. Neither moved. Kier had a right to stay and overhear military orders issued in his sovereign. Bayer was just being obstinate. Giving them another churlish look, the otter wrenched open the leather satchel at his side and pulled a scroll from it. "You're to return to Andarn immediately, by order of General Gallis." He jabbed the paper at Alaris, who took it with calm reluctance.

The pangolin whisked a claw under the seal and split it from its surface, unfurling the stiff parchment to read the dispatch. Bayer and Kier watched apprehensively as the pangolin's face darkened. Upon reaching the end, Alaris let out a long, sullen breath and shook his head before scanning it over again.

Camiyan cracked his knuckles, glancing around. "It's starting to get severe now, Alaris. We're at our highest state of guard."

"How bad is it?" Kier asked, his voice low, eliciting a piercing glare from Camiyan, vexed at the document's secrecy being broken. Alaris said nothing for a few seconds, still analysing the paper with cold regard. Without taking his eyes from it, he spoke with a distant voice.

"One of Andarn's Councillors has been murdered. And it would have been Mattok, wouldn't it..." he trailed off.

Camiyan sucked his teeth. "He wasn't in a great position. But we're facing some trouble, as you can tell," he growled, casting a glare over towards the meerkat from Tremaine. "I've been ordered to send you and your personal troops home."

Alaris folded the scroll and tucked it into his belt. "He can have two companies. The rest must remain here over winter. Our agreement with Xayall has to come first, short of a declaration of war. Gallis knows that; our protection charters haven't changed in years."

"Sure. You can tell him that yourself," the otter scoffed. "And I'll grab a front row seat."

"Gladly," Alaris snapped, his harsh stare halting the otter's trailing sneer. "In the mean time, I'll pass you executive control of Andarn's remaining troops and have you send them back after me once their duties are completed."

"They're leaving now. We *all* are," Camiyan snarled.

Alaris remained defiant. "Gallis' order specified for me and my command to return. I will abide by his request and return, and the troops will follow once their orders are complete. We are not in a position to leave without sacrificing rations that both we *and* Xayall are in desperate need of. Under Senate provisions, our duties as a vital support unit are locked in Xayall's protective schedule."

"You are not a Brigadier, Alaris," Camiyan gnarled, clenching his fist. His words, although quiet, pierced the air with poisonous malice. "You shouldn't even be in control of *one* battalion, let alone two."

Bayer watched the meerkat from Tremaine with cautious regard. He hadn't moved, staying completely silent between the two other guards, both of whom were stone martens. They looked oddly out of place in uniform, but he couldn't tell why. Perhaps they were just new recruits, standing with an over-rehearsed rigidity as a result of Camiyan's severity. Maybe their armour was too cold.

"Given the absence of higher authority at the defence of Xayall, I was assigned command of these companies under Major-General Dion, who is happy to enforce my authority as superior commander of our temporary outpost here until every last soldier is out. My brevet with his signature is in the command centre in the Tor. Even though Gallis is a higher rank, the agreement has been counter-signed by the

43

Councillors of Xayall and could constitute a fine against Andarn if the contract is broken. Unless you want to face a disciplinary term in the cells and pay for the troop redeployment yourself, I'd suggest you play nicely."

Camiyan said nothing more, but judging by his expression his next words would rather have been spoken with his fists than his mouth.

"It pays to know the rules, *Captain*," Alaris continued. "Thank you for the communication. I'll brief you in the library shortly. Dismissed."

Camiyan gave the shortest, most spiteful salute he could, and promptly vanished, his martens at his heel. The meerkat, who wore an expression of open amusement, remained in place.

"We're being very officious today," he hummed, tucking his thumbs into his belt and tapping his tassets rhythmically with his fingers. His smug grin was so big you could probably see it through the back of his head.

Incredibly large for his species, the meerkat stood at least as tall as Alaris, with a high-but-controlled energy that seemed to drift from one end of him to the other. When listening intently to the conversation in front, he kept his head straight and his glistening dark eyes forward, but his ears tilted and twitched intermittently, like a tic.

Alaris looked at the meerkat for a second with penetrating incredulity, as if the gold-clad visitor had just performed some ludicrous juggling display. "*Why* are you here, Rowan?"

"Well," the meerkat said jovially, "I had been hoping to deliver the news of Mattok personally, as I was stationed in Andarn at the time. Not that I enjoy the horrific tragedy itself, of course, but any excuse for a jolly to see you is a good one. Anyway, your military insisted that, as one of several hundred suspects, I couldn't be trusted and decided to send their own messengers."

The pangolin looked at him blankly. "Imagine that. Yet you're still here."

Rowan laughed and clapped an arm around Alaris' shoulder. "Oh, I've missed you, Alaris." He turned to Bayer and Kier and gave a quick, precise bow. "Pardon my rudeness, by the way. I'm Rowan Ibarruri, Captain of Tremaine's Seventeenth Company." He swivelled back to Alaris just as quickly, leaving Kier and Bayer no better equipped for conversation. "But yes, to respond to your question-in-a-statement, I volunteered myself as an emissary to ensure the news got delivered without bias or miscommunication. *My* superiors were very keen on the idea, given the situation, so here I am."

Alaris shook his head. "You're just asking to be killed, you know that? Such a nuisance."

Although conscious of interrupting the two friends on their unorthodox reunion, especially as it acted like a mirror to his own friendship with Bayer, Kier stepped forwards.

"How serious is the situation surrounding Mattok's death if they're calling you back?"

Alaris pried himself from Rowan's grip and paced a short distance, flicking his claws with increasing rapidity. Not for the first time in recent weeks, frustration began to show through his fraying composition.

"Well, he's dead – that's serious enough. But I don't know," he muttered. "Something like this has been a long time coming. If I were optimistic, I'd say command is just getting nervous and wants to step up security in the city."

"*We've* not been optimistic for a while," Rowan cautioned, far too brightly for the nature of the conversation. "The tension between Andarn and Tremaine has been close to breaking point for as long as I can remember. They're always looking for excuses to bring up arguments and try winning back land that the other has allegedly 'stolen'. It's been getting... worse, to say the least."

"I thought Andarn and Tremaine were sister sovereigns? Aren't you both duty-bound to protect Sinédrion?" Kier asked.

Alaris nodded. "That makes this all the more volatile if something happens, because the Senate gets caught in the middle whether they want to or not." He massaged a claw into the bridge of his nose. "We're as argumentative as any pair of siblings, I'd wager. Really, we're too close to each other, and so pressed for resources that we're constantly vying for space along our borders."

"Deploying more troops isn't going to help matters any," Bayer said irritably.

Kier watched his friend with caution; he knew that any extra doubts in Bayer's mind might force his continued distance from the world. As he struggled to find something reassuring (or at least dismissive) that might have dissipated some of the feline's anger, Rowan answered in his place.

"No, you're right. It rarely does."

Bayer's ears pricked.

"The problem is," the meerkat recounted, "that neither side wants to concede what they already have in order to make peace, even if they don't need it. Because giving up would be weak and set a standard for further appeasement."

Dusty white snowflakes began to drift from the sky. Kier shook his head, brushing a large frosty clump from his muzzle. "Do they actually talk to each other?" he said, scrunching his nose at the cold.

"They do enough talking for the whole Senate," Alaris retorted. "Problem is, it's all insults, and at a high enough volume that everyone overhears and starts offering their own opinions or taking sides." He sighed, a breath that rose from a whisper to a grunt, irritation swirling in the fog from his mouth. "Either way, I can't ignore this," he continued. "Things will get worse unless someone can convince the hierarchy to back down." He folded the dispatch and slid it into his belt, and his face dropped with the silent acceptance of his duty. "If there's one place where opportunity and honesty can live freely, it should be this place – Xayall. Andarn will never be like that. Kindness is too rare among politicians."

As he turned to go, Kier took his shoulder to halt him. "Is there anything we can do or send with you? Will you be safe?"

The pangolin opened his mouth but Bayer stepped forwards, stealing his opportunity to speak. "I'll be an escort."

Kier watched his friend with a furrowed brow and wide eyes. While the ocelot had been diplomatic for Faria's sake when Aidan was alive, to preserve her informed opinion of other sovereigns' governance, his distaste for Andarn or any hierarchy had recently become more prevalent. The shadow over his behaviour unnerved Kier, and threatened to betray the trust he held in his friend.

"Do you understand what you're asking, where you're

going?" he asked, not taking his eyes from Bayer's.

Bayer gave a firm nod. "It would be an honour to return some of the favour that you've granted us, Alaris."

Alaris bowed his head appreciatively. "Thank you. I've heard nothing but praise from Faria about you."

Bayer looked to the sky, tracking a shape sweeping through the snow above. "So I gather. I hope to do her compliments justice one day."

The others looked to where Bayer was watching, and immediately recognised the figure of Osiris swooping towards them. He passed them in a narrow arc that awakened the breeze at their side, scattering the snowfall, then righted himself and spread his wings wide to land abruptly nearest Kier, staring directly at the fox.

Alaris quickly turned to Bayer, sensing that the cantankerous look on the gryphon's face spelt a dressing-down for the Junior Representative. "Well, we'd best get ready," he said swiftly, nudging Bayer to follow. Rowan made no effort to hide his wide eyes at this enormous gryphon that landed before them, but seeing the severity on the creature's face, he shot Kier a worried grimace before turning away as Osiris advanced on him. As Bayer left, he gave the fox a casual wave, partnered with a slow shake of his head. Kier, watching his moral support leaving footprints in the thin snow before him, faced Osiris with a sinking pit in his stomach.

"I need a word with you," the gryphon rumbled.

Dust lay everywhere. Although the room had not been used

in a while, this wasn't the dust of inactivity, but dust of battle. It hardly made the place less depressing, though, and it had never been particularly cheerful. Wiping the patina of stone from his plain, wooden shelves, Bayer wondered why it had been so important to almost ignore that he even had a room in the Tor. The barracks had always appealed more to him. It was further removed from the autocratic powers he resented, and closer to the soldiers who believed in the city they gave their lives for.

He disliked introspection. It had felt easier for a long time to blend with his surroundings rather than try to find a shape that fit him. It had been simpler when there was nothing to question – his duty was his persona, and for a long time, his duty was resolute. Aidan's revelations, however, and failure to adequately defend Xayall, destroyed everything he had been so prepared to face, and now there was no place for him. He could not even be upset without feeling insignificant or selfish, compared to how badly Faria should have been reeling from her experiences. And yet there she was, still willing to continue despite it all.

Because she had no choice, perhaps.

A pile of old clothes, formerly in a wicker box on the shelf, had been knocked to the floor. The box itself lay flattened across the room, with a trail of dry wicker flakes in its wake, and a mound of dust-painted cloth sitting quietly underneath. He picked up a black shirt, one of his oldest garments, and rubbed the fabric gently. It had lasted well, probably because he hadn't worn it since being assigned as Faria's bodyguard. It pleased him to see it undamaged, however, and after giving it a perfunctory shake, he slipped into it with ease. Almost instantly he felt more relaxed, and allowed himself a moment to enjoy the change. The thoughts still pulsed, but for now he could start to think more about himself as just himself, and not as a sum of his doubts and duties.

His armour lay in one corner of the room, opposite his bed. The metal still wore its scars, dents, and holes like badges of service. He regarded it with a certain degree of reluctance, crumpled in the shade like a dismantled skeleton: a reminder of what had failed to protect him, and in turn what he had failed to protect.

He balled his fist thinking about how easily he'd been attacked in the Tor and the severity of his wounds. Attacked and saved by resonators in the same battle, against a legacy of death that tore back across millennia. Slowly, he walked towards the metal suit, and took the battered green and grey torso plate in his hands.

A sharp knock rattled the door.

"Enter," he called, without turning. He knew who it was.

Kier strode in, looking harried. As much as Bayer respected his friend, it always amused him to see the fox in quiet disarray. It suited him rather well.

"Everything all right?" he asked, knowing full well that the fox had just received a fairly brutal dressing-down, as was Osiris' habit.

Kier looked unimpressed. "Yes, excellent," he said curtly. "At least until Osiris tore my head off for not reporting to Faria. He has some serious anger issues, that bird."

Bayer raised an eyebrow, casting the armour onto his bed. "*He* has issues? That's your excuse for avoiding Faria?"

Kier avoided the response for a few seconds, trying to find something in the room to distract himself with. Facing only dust, mostly-empty shelves, and some old, plain chests, he leant back against the wall by the door and folded his arms. "You're not exactly being honest with her either. When was the last time you saw her? And now you're just leaving? Why are you even going?"

Bayer paused for a moment, and then threw the remaining pieces of his armour roughly on the bed. "I was planning to meet her before I left. And you?" he continued, straightening out his arming doublet.

"I, er, have to give her an update tonight, if she's awake," Kier replied hesitantly.

The two stood in silence for a while as Bayer assembled his armour, checking the straps for damage. Kier rolled his shoulders under his own breastplate, feeling uncomfortable at his friend's distance. They argued like a married couple at times, and while Aidan and Faria had found it humorous at least on a superficial level, it made Kier anxious. It was no secret that he relied on Bayer's stoic attentiveness to duty as a means to guide himself, and the cat's emotional outbursts were unsettling him.

"Will you finally tell her your secret now that Aidan's gone?" Bayer asked suddenly. Kier jumped, almost losing his balance.

"No... Not yet," he said quietly, after steadying himself. "And don't ignore me, why are—?"

Bayer cracked a smile. "I have to admit, you've kept if far better than I thought you would. But you won't hide it from her forever. She might already suspect something about you."

The fox leant his head against the wall and let out a defeated grunt. "Maybe. But I don't want to risk that yet. She's lost her father, and... I don't want to present myself with the wrong intentions. I have to remember my place; I'm not trying to be a suitor."

Bayer turned round, armed with a chiding look, which he threw straight at Kier. "Liar. You've been avoiding this girl your whole life for that very reason."

Kier took a step forwards. "That's not true, I—"

"Fine, you've been avoiding and/or *stalking* this girl since you got here in the hope that she would notice you through some bizarre, invisible means whereby you wouldn't have to put yourself forward or have her pursue you, neither of which make sense to any rational being." Kier made to interrupt; Bayer counter-interrupted instead, rounding on the fox. "And even though you're in the perfect position to step in and help her and be that supportive influence I know you've always wanted to be for her, you're standing here trying to think of excuses to tell me about how reasonable it is to avoid her." He shot him a sharp look. "Am I right?"

Kier licked his teeth. "Yeah, pretty astute. You know, for a serial escapist of his own emotions. I understand why you're going to Andarn now," he said, his voice steady, almost menacing. "You've always been afraid that everyone is looking for an excuse to get rid of you. So you attach yourself to the fewest you can afford and pretend not to have any personal loyalty to them. And if things go wrong, you can throw them to the wind and tell yourself you were right all along – that nobody is worth trusting or defending, not even yourself." He paused, watching for Bayer's reaction. The cat said nothing, but stiffened angrily. "And

these outbursts, they're not because you're angry at Aidan –
you're upset because your expectations of yourself were too
high, so despite the fact that you were the best protector
anyone could have been in that situation, you're angry with
yourself for not doing better. Going to Andarn is a perfect
way to punish yourself with your nightmares for a crime you
never even committed!"

Bayer lunged forwards, grabbing the fox's collar. "Do
you see everything with those eyes, Kier, do you? Were you
there? Don't tell me about what you don't know!"

Kier brushed Bayer's arm away. "I *do* know, Bayer! I
took you from that siege! I was *late*! How stupid do you
think *I* feel, not even being with Aidan or Faria when this all
started, and allowing him to get captured in the first place?
Do you think I don't see Faria's devastation or the damage
in the city and think that I might have prevented half of that
if I had been there to protect either of them when he left?
Don't be such a martyr."

The two warriors locked each other in a tense stare.

"You're angry because you're hurt and confused," Kier
rasped. "We all are. But we are still alive, and we're the ones
that have to move forward. Stop indulging your self-abuse,
Bayer. You'd be no help to anyone if I'd let you die at
Vionaika's hand. Am I not right?"

The ocelot watched him for a few seconds, ears flicking
with impatience. Kier may be correct to a degree, but
Bayer's past was slowly catching up with him: that deep,
terrifying pit that he had ignored and never challenged. If he
didn't do something to find closure, he'd leave anyway.
Kier's return midway through the siege was well-timed,
certainly, but Bayer had been prepared to die then and there.

At least he could have been spared some awkward and painful emotions.

Eventually, he turned back to his bed and his meagre belongings. "Somewhat," he grunted. "But I also want to get out of the city for a few days, clear my head. I never said I was leaving permanently." He looked over his shoulder at the fox. "I knew you were angry that I'm leaving for Andarn. But staying here right now is too frustrating, and this gives me purpose, even though… even though it *is* Andarn. I'm not going to wander aimlessly or sit on my haunches, I can't do that. I'm touched that you still care about me so much, though. So I guess win this round."

Kier smacked his gauntlet against Bayer's good shoulder with a hard, playful jab. "Fine, take it, you need it more than I do. Just look after yourself."

Bayer shook his head as he rocked back from Kier's jostling. "All right. Call it recuperation on my part. I'll come back once I'm sure Alaris is safe." He turned back to the armour on the bed, letting out a small laugh. "We've been around each other too long."

Kier rolled his eyes in reply. "You could bring yourself back a *real* wife if you're that tired of me. I'm fed up with mothering you."

Bayer whirled round. "Deal! I will bring back some beautiful feline companion, and you can finally introduce yourself to Faria. That should take you about as long as I have to return. I think that's fair."

Kier clenched his jaw and punched his right fist into his left palm. "She knows my name, you git. But fine, whatever, I'll work something out and defy your rude expectations of me. Take care, Bayer." He spun on his heel and left, ignoring the ocelot's satisfied chuckle.

Chapter Five

The snow still fell within Andarn's forests. Although a more temperate region than Xayall, especially at this time of year, the wind pressed the cold right against them, as if a reminder of how oppressive the sovereign was by stealing other nation's weather and beating anyone inside the borders with it. Bayer had been deeply unsettled by the sovereign, and the nearer they rode to it, the more uncomfortable he felt. His steed, a tall, slim, dinosaur creature not unlike an ostrich, called an Anserisaur, reacted to his tension and would uneasily flick its head as they walked.

He, Alaris, and Rowan had talked little on the journey, each dealing with their own deep preoccupations, but Bayer's increasing sullenness and withdrawal became further barrier for communication. Rowan could find conversation in most things, however, but would mostly direct this towards Alaris after Bayer's noncommittal responses. Bayer, while refreshed at being effectively left alone on the journey and away from the multitudinous pressures of Xayall, still found himself on alert. The traffic increased steadily once they entered the borders, and Bayer read dejection in most travellers they passed, even then he would doubt whether it was a product of the season or a projection of his own feelings onto them. He watched the trees change along their route; they grew taller and withdrew their branches to a higher canopy, and the forest floor turned from soft winter greens to dull brown and grey.

"A mire is no place to build a house," he murmured, casting a wary eye over the short, coarse grass dotted along the stony road.

"I'm sorry?" Alaris called, surprised to hear him speak.

"Nothing, just thinking. I apologise."

Alaris shrugged. "It's all right. I'm sorry this isn't more exciting. I'm not as high priority a target as you're used to."

Bayer's snort puffed condensation into the air. "I don't mind that. My usefulness as a guard is under question anyway, so a quiet adventure is a welcome one. It's not you I have an objection to."

"It's not me, is it?" Rowan chimed, cheerily.

Alaris waved dismissively at the meerkat's interjection. "Rowan, stop it. Bayer, I understand. I'm grateful for your company, though. The world's confused and scared right now, more than it ever was. It's good to know where friends are."

Bayer wondered if Alaris was being genuine or just polite. The feline nodded once, content to say nothing more until they were within the city – perhaps even after that. While distance was welcome, the act of leaving Xayall had not helped ease him much, and with past memories crawling under his skin, his recent departure repeated too insistently in his mind.

Faria hadn't accused him of anything. Nor was it a question, nor a demand. It damned him for selfishness in her distant response, and she barely said a word.

"Oh, you're leaving. I… I see."

"Do you know much about Andarn?"

Bayer looked sharply round; he hadn't quite heard Alaris, and it startled him from his thoughts. The pangolin looked at the sky ahead, searching for a sign of the city's approach. Something in his eyes suggested it was more to see if it was still there. As if he expected trouble.

"I'm sorry?"

"What do you know of our sovereign, Bayer?" Alaris repeated. Kindly, but not without purpose.

Bayer wanted to retreat into his mind again, but for politeness' sake he continued. "Nothing good or useful," he sighed, keeping his cards as close to his chest as he could. He didn't want to be played for idle conversation that motivated politically-charged arguments.

"Good. That's the best way to enter Andarn," Alaris said pointedly. "It's a virtue to keep your trust frugal here."

Despite his intentions, the pangolin's words piqued Bayer's interest. He briefly caught a look from Rowan, who seemed in agreement. The feline's ears flicked with curiosity as Alaris spoke. "I'm surprised to hear you talk about it so sceptically. I thought you were loyal."

Alaris sucked his teeth. "You can be loyal through your actions and be doubtful in mind. I will gladly protect those who need help, but the sovereign itself is a corrupt mess." He leant over the two quietly: "It's terrible to have escalated this far, but a murder was all but inevitable with the way both sides have been fighting. There've been blatant power struggles under the surface for a long time, now."

"From within Andarn, you mean?" Rowan asked.

Alaris made a wide gesture with his claw. "From everywhere. Andarn doesn't make friends – it's too self-obsessed for anything other than the Senate, and even when our troops are needed we protect Sinédrion to the bare minimum to avoid drawing troops from our other commitments. Most of our Council think we should control Sinédrion because of our size, but… I don't think any of the Generals or Representatives have the capacity. Or integrity. We can't govern our own city, let alone a whole continent's worth of pushing and shoving."

"There aren't many that can," Rowan mused. "Andarn is a particularly big mess, though. What's your take on it, Bayer?" He looked pointedly to the ocelot.

Bayer cast him a dubious glance, sensing a baited question. "I have no interest in Andarn. Why don't you go somewhere that better serves its people, Alaris, if it's so corrupt?"

Alaris sat back on his saddle and straightened himself. "It's my home, for one. I want to see it overcome its problems. You only need to see the damage done to somewhere like Kyrryk to know what corruption can do. If all those with good intentions left out of exasperation, all you'd have left is the power hungry. Again, like Kyrryk."

Bayer tensed at the mention of the other sovereign. "That's easy for you to say as a commander. Most never even have the option to leave."

"True. Citizens should never feel as if decisions are out

of their own hands. Kyrryk's struggle was borne of warlords with too much ambition and no conscience, and now you have dozens of factions, including the Senate peacekeepers, all vying for survival and revenge, and no unity. It can take just one person to prevent that damage from happening, if they're the right person."

Bayer fell quiet. Lectures on the damages of war were tedious to him, having experienced much of it firsthand in his youth. Even so, Alaris' words stung his mind with damning poignancy, and he couldn't shake them. He knew the pangolin spoke in general terms, but he felt the cold burn of blame pressing into his shoulders for leaving Xayall.

"So you would stay to be that one person to save the entire sovereign if the task were handed to you?"

The pangolin shrugged. "If I had to, yes. I don't think I'll ever have that kind of position, though. I've always valued life and tried to defend the right for anyone to survive and live as they want to. I don't have ambition for supreme command or riches. I want to see the world becoming more than it is, and for people to realise they don't need to slit each other's throats to be a part of it."

"There's a whole army and far too many politicians who could stop you with a simple order." The cat could not hide his bitterness. "No idealism in power other than fanatics."

Alaris frowned, giving him a disapproving look. "That's where honour comes in. If I were killed for following my ethical code, my actions live on in the people I've helped. There's nothing wrong with a benevolent ideal, even if it's impractical or uncommon. I don't believe I'll be the one to save the world – I haven't done enough. But someone I save could be."

"Is that why you saved Faria?"

He shrugged. "I didn't know her well enough to know at first – I acted on instinct. But... there is something unique about her, don't you think? From what I've seen so far, she *could* be the kind of person to save the world, although I hope it wouldn't fall to her alone."

None of the three spoke for a while, the steady beating of the Anserisaurs' heavy feet on the rough stone pathway the only sound in the cold air around them. Bayer's silence sunk into more than the physically soundless from that point; the boundaries of his conscious mind seemed to retract and all he was left with was the memory of leaving Xayall again, playing over and over in his mind.

"I hope you find what you're looking for."

She had been so blank, saddened, like she had already lost him. He wanted to just dismiss it as his paranoia, but she had been through so much he couldn't tell if her feelings were genuine or shaded by fatigue. He had always kept her opinion of him as a standard to live by, and lately he had ignored his commitment to it. But for saying so little himself, telling her flatly, with no discussion, that he had to leave, the few words he released somehow made him feel smaller. And guiltily, he resented her for looking so hurt. His wounds were nothing, and yet he couldn't bear to be near her, knowing how little he'd been able to protect her or the city that had sheltered him from such a young age.

"What do you believe?"

Alaris reignited the disjointed conversation he didn't really want to be part of. Bayer kept his objection in check, however, and tried to appear interested.

"About Faria? I don't know. She's young, and for the

most part knows very little about the world. I would say she's not cynical enough to see it work, but…" He chewed his thoughts for a second. "There is something to be said for innocence and idealism. The gift of the young is being able to ask the questions that the old are too hurt to. I hope her experiences haven't damaged her. That would be the greatest detriment to her prospects. But if she continued as she was, then…"

"You'll always be welcome here. Please remember that."

He sighed. "It's impossible to tell what will be asked of a single person. She's too kind for her own good, sometimes. She needs time, but if she is asked or able to save the world, then I'm sure she will."

"That's a great hope for us," Alaris replied. "There are few who, if given her ability, would not be tempted to just take the world for their own."

Bayer surrendered to the flow of conversation and felt a grudging acceptance of Alaris and Rowan's company. Somehow, against his wishes, they had alleviated some of his ill feelings, even if his self-confidence was still in the doldrums. "That's one of the reasons I have no interest in Andarn," Bayer said. "The corruption, the self-obsession, is vile to me. There seems to be no respect for citizens except when it comes to favouring agendas or settling unrest, and it's always with selfish intentions."

He noticed the pangolin giving him a strange look, studious and discerning. "What?"

"You're not from Tremaine, are you?"

Bayer shook his head. "Why do you ask?"

He shrugged. "Oh, that's how most of Tremaine sees us, even the nicer soldiers."

"Yup!" Rowan cheered, having been very restrained in not jumping all over Bayer's conversation previously. "But you're not supposed to know that." After a second he shrugged. "It is true, though. Most of us think Andarn's filled with power-hungry scumbags, trolls, and thieves. And Alaris."

The pangolin ran a claw over the scales on his head, trying to dilute Rowan's pervasive enthusiasm for jokes in continuing the conversation at hand. "I was just wondering where you were from, Bayer, in any case. Not that it would change anything."

"I'm from Kyrryk."

Alaris froze for a moment, then seemed, oddly, to relax. "Ah, that makes sense." He laughed, embarrassed, and scratched the back of his head. "I'm sorry; then I completely understand your mistrust, and it's not unfounded. When I hear about the mess over there I just… wince. You don't have to enter Andarn's walls if you don't want to. But if you do… I'd keep that part of your history quiet."

Bayer nodded, looking ahead. A wide, white tower, barely visible against the blanket sky, rose in the distance. "I'm used to it. I'll follow you inside, though. I want to see you safely to the barracks. It'll be an interesting experience, I'm sure. If nothing else, I might find out where I don't want to be for the rest of my life."

"As good a reason as any, I suppose."

Even before they were near the gates, the roads were so cramped with carts and travellers on foot that they were

62

barely able to move. Generally, people made way for the Anserisaurs, their presence imposing even next to bulky Theriasaurs (cattle-lizards), but most travellers were so focused on the looming city before them and the tiny steps with which they paced that anything behind them was completely out of sensory range, short of when something actually touched them. It was stifling, claustrophobic mindlessness.

The sheer number of people spilling through the murky white walls was beyond belief. Carts laden with wares or produce, carriages with silken drapes drawn tightly closed, wandering traders with their stalls attached to their backs, and any number of pedestrians shambled at an infinitesimal pace towards the huge archway. That was even before oncoming traffic could be taken into account. The southern gate in particular appeared to have problems with lane control as a yet-unseen obstacle blocked the majority of the walkway. Impatient opportunists jumped the tiny gap in whichever direction served their purpose, only adding to the frustration of the guards trying to control the unravelling chaos. In Bayer's mind, it was a conflict waiting to happen, and even Alaris noticed his distress at watching the line ahead.

"Don't worry, they'll handle it. They're used to it, I'm sad to say. We'll take the secondary gate."

He pulled his Anserisaur to the right, circling along the wall a short distance to where a smaller, auxiliary gate stood, flanked by guards with heavy shields and barbed spears. They saluted Alaris on his approach, and he responded in kind.

Without any further command, they signalled to the

guardsmen on the short turret above, and within seconds the doors were winched open. Bayer could sense satisfaction in the power his rank wielded. Knowing better of Alaris than for him to be prideful, Bayer saw it as dedication to duty, which the pangolin took to with an enthusiasm that Bayer had not seen in himself for a long time.

"It's all right to be jealous," Rowan called to the ocelot. "Most troops in Tremaine won't even give me the time of day if I knock on the portcullis. I'm lucky to get inside some days."

The boom of the closing doors punched through Bayer, and a coldness rose from his legs up his body. He gripped the reins tightly, trying to rid his mind of things he did not want to remember, that this city wore in its every stone.

Chapter Six

The ringing of chains thrust him back to the present.

Passing a portcullis, Bayer followed Alaris through the tall, torchlit archway, watching the walls and floor pass in detail that he was helpless to ignore, his heightened senses almost sending him into a panic. He had created such a monster of his memories that being here was like the most vivid dream, paired with shadowy uneasiness that threatened to make him violently sick. He held himself in, though, and in seconds the Anserisaur burst into the city, throwing him into a web of high stone and wood buildings, the grey sky's sun casting everything before him in a white bloom. It hurt his eyes to look, so he fixed his gaze on Alaris, his Anserisaur's pace now slowing to a polite but purposeful march through the streets. The rising noise of the city echoed all around him; rumbles of carts, the drone of voices close and distant, and a million other sounds too layered and numerous to discern, each one adding an increment to his rising tension. He did not want to be seen, nor heard. He couldn't even focus on their destination as he had no idea where they were going, and Alaris kept making turns down one corner or the next, throwing him into disorientation. He tried to keep his eyes straight, and calmed his rapid breathing. He was stronger than this to lose his head.

Alaris looked back over his shoulder to him. "Big, isn't it? Sorry I can't give you a guided tour right now. I'm sure you'll want to find a place to rest first."

Bayer nodded, not really taking in what the pangolin had said. He could hear shouting in the distance, and wondered vaguely what was happening. It rose above the steady clamour of the rest of the city to a higher, almost frantic register. Whatever the commotion, it was over to their left somewhere. The pangolin hadn't appeared to notice, heading still towards a large, domed building in the middle-distance. Bayer tried to put it out of his mind with the augury that had been the overcrowding of the city gates, willing himself to think better despite the growing sense of dread creeping over his shoulders. It felt like claws, waiting to pick beneath the surface of his skin.

A barking cry to arms rang across the streets; civilians scattered to the sides of the road as a company of white-clad troops sprinted through, their armour clattering with urgent authority.

Alaris pulled his Anserisaur to an abrupt stop as the pike-wielders rushed past, almost crashing into the steed's thick neck. One soldier, a polecat, caught sight of him in his dash and broke from the formation.

"Captain Alaris!" he called, his polearm shaking uneasily in his hand. "There's a riot in the Southern Plaza! It's us against Tremaine!"

Alaris hauled back on his mount's reins as it twisted its head in irritation, resistant to standing calmly. "A riot? What happened?"

"We don't know – we just need to get it under control. Please help, sir!"

The soldier sprinted away at top speed, following his disappearing company. Muttering something dark and threatening, Alaris kicked his steed into motion and flew down the unfurling street. Bayer followed suit. Battle would be a welcome distraction at this point; it sharpened his focus, and now, with the Anserisaur's heavy legs pounding underneath him, he could feel his ideas being proved right about the state of the world, and the chaos which lay, thinly veiled, beneath its surface.

The buildings blurred and the shouts grew louder as they rode and, closing in on the uproar, came the ringing of metal and splintering impacts of riotous destruction. Two more buildings whizzed past, and the street opened out to a huge, circular plaza, with a sprawling, thrashing melee at its centre. Citizens had retreated to the courtyard's five entrances or huddled within buildings as the armoured groups clashed in the middle. The main battlefront surged between sizeable detachments of Andarn and Tremaine troops bisecting the space in an undulating, uneven line that swayed and shoved back and forth. Immediately, though, Alaris could see smaller confrontations overlapping and entwining the whole circle. Further groups of Andarn and Tremaine soldiers were trying to hold each other back on either side of the fight. Terrified onlookers hung behind windows; guards flanked every door, bolstering their spears against the wood to keep those inside safe. Some civilians, blind with rage or panic, railed against the Andarn troops while screaming death threats and murderous intent at the Tremaine regiment. More guards surged in from every street, desperately seeking a place to aim their weapons. Among the troops, it was an even split between those who leapt carelessly into the battle and those who hauled combatants away from the fringes, trying to elicit control.

Rowan pulled up beside Alaris and took in the fray. The meerkat's face gnarled.

"So it's a war already," he cursed, scanning the battlefield. "Some people need no excuse to-"

Something caught his eye on the far left – a ring of Tremaine soldiers, surrounded by Andarn troops all pressing in on them. Instantly he kicked his Anserisaur into action; the dinosaur reared up and charged forwards, barrelling over combatants from both sides and casting a swath of collapsed bodies across the plaza.

"Damn it, Rowan!" Alaris cursed, looking about. "Bayer, follow him! I'm putting an end to this."

Bayer nodded and thrust his mount into Rowan's wake, re-trampling those who had fallen before. As he rode, gauntlets rose from the crowd to pull him from his steed; he could see Rowan had unsheathed his gilded spear to thrash against Andarn aggressors trying to wrench him to the ground. Bayer left his sword in its scabbard for now, but pressed quickly ahead.

In the main crush of soldiers, moving even a few feet was impossible. Rowan had used his Anserisaur to either knock or intimidate combatants out of the way, but within the centre, the disruption, violence, and immovability of the fighters rendered the battle impenetrable. They were less than twenty feet from Rowan's target when the reptilian steed stopped, the density of clashing soldiers too great to allow him to pass. A team of Andarn troops standing outside of Tremaine's struggling circle turned to him with eyes hungry for violence.

"Get clear!" Rowan bellowed, the blunt end of his spear at the head of the nearest soldier. "Disperse immediately and let me pass!"

"Screw you!" the civet spat, reaching for the spear. In a split second, Rowan flicked his weapon and struck him square in the side of his head. A mass of roars erupted from the group ahead and Rowan's Anserisaur was overrun by soldiers. The meerkat jumped to stand on the saddle, and before he could lose his balance, planted his spear on the ground and swung himself over the flailing punches to land somewhere near the Tremaine line – Bayer lost sight of him as soon as the meerkat dropped the spear.

Too far back to assist, embroiled in the crushing movements of each front, Bayer's Anserisaur began to groan and thrash with each push, becoming more agitated. An upward thrust of a shield near the lizard's eye sent it reeling back; Bayer twisted from the saddle and leapt onto someone's armoured shoulders, lingering long enough to spot Rowan in the centre of the protective ring ahead, before jumping again to another set of shoulders, and then into the circle beside Rowan. Here, the cause for Rowan's dash was immediately clear; the soldiers were protecting a fallen General from being torn to pieces. They were holding well with more Tremaine guards engaging their attackers from behind, but blood seeped from the officer's breastplate, staining its worn, golden surface and making his critical situation clear.

Rowan knelt by the officer's side, placing a hand on his shoulder.

"Commander Siegl: what happened?"

Siegl, a ring-tailed mongoose, gave him the only acknowledgement he could manage: a simple glance, the rest of his energy focused on breathing over the injury to his lower abdomen.

"Rowan," he croaked, blood trickling from his mouth. "It was… They tried to… Stop them…"

His breath grew shallow. The words formed in his mouth were swallowed by rising blood from his throat. He closed his eyes, pressing a bloodied claw into his wound to try and stem the injury's flow. Bayer feared they were already out of time.

Rowan cast a desperate glance to the space where Alaris had been. "Alaris, hurry up!"

The pangolin's Anserisaur charged around the plaza's periphery, heading for a tall, fortified building that rose above the city's canopy of slate and timber – one of Andarn's many watchtowers. Throwing himself from the saddle when he reached the turret, Alaris skidded to the door and wrenched the handle. It stuck, locked from within. A growl rising in his throat, he whirled round, drew the double-handed sword mounted at his Anserisaur's side and, with his full strength behind it, slammed the pommel into the wood by the latch. The metal bar within buckled both above and below the door, scraping the brickwork as it flew open. A pair of terrified, dumbstruck guards fumbled for their weapons as he sprinted inside; by the time their spears were in their grasp he had already ascended the first flight of stairs.

He broke onto the second floor, met by a large room with wooden shutters on every wall. Before him stood the weapon he sought to end the melee below – a bombard.

The two guards tumbled up the stairs behind him.

"Where the hell is the gun crew?" he roared.

They gave no answer, struggling to find any words at all in their panic. They looked young – junior soldiers on their first posting.

"Never mind," he seethed. "Double-load this with powder, immediately, no shot! I'll open the gun ports."

Bayer lent his weight to the Tremaine soldiers as they repelled the Andarn oppressors. The fight seemed to surge periodically; every time he thought it was beginning to calm, another wave of uncommanded soldiers leapt into the fray, adding to the confusion. The ocelot batted away knifepoints and spearheads aimed at the defending guards as animosity and violence shot back and forth. They had already moved their battle line as a huge push threatened to send half of the circle trampling over the critically injured Siegl. Rowan took command, trying to manoeuvre them into the safety of a building or archway, but they were completely surrounded.

Bayer could not believe the chaos. Even in the heat of battle, vengeful contempt boiled in his stomach for the brutality of these soldiers.

Suddenly, a muskrat in Andarn colours pushed upwards from the soldiers behind, landing himself on the shoulders of two Tremaine guards, now pinned. He aimed a flailing swipe of his curved sword at Rowan's head. With inches to spare Bayer deflected the blow with the back of his gauntlet, and landed a clawed uppercut to the rodent's neck. It landed with a satisfying crunch – not a kill, but enough to knock him out cold and send a dead weight back onto Andarn's pressing advance. As he watched other soldiers drag him back, he noticed an ornate marking on the creature's loose pauldron, one of its buckles torn by the untidy collapse. Before he could study it further, Rowan's voice pierced the melee.

"Cover your ears!"

The wooden shutters of the bombard tower were fully open, and Alaris stood by the formidable cannon with a lit fuse, the barrel aimed to overshoot the plaza. Bayer had enough time to see Alaris lower the match before he ducked, throwing his hands to his head.

The explosion tore through the air above them, a huge plume of smoke erupting over the fray. The boom of the cannon's fire shook the ground, and all around them a shower of glass spilled from the buildings' former windows. Bayer felt the impact in his chest and his eyes. The shockwave hit the crowd, an upheaval from below and an impact from above. Many soldiers fell to the ground, dazed, clutching their ears, while others scattered in fright or away from the cascading debris above.

As the whine in his ears subsided, Bayer heard a new sound. The fighting had diminished, shocked to silence, but the military march and rhythmic clashing of swords against shields rose in the streets around them. He stood up to see, and at each of the plaza's exits stood rows of Sinédrion guards, striking their tall, curved shields with short swords in perfect unison. An enormous stag stepped forwards at the northern entrance, nearest the centre of the city, and glanced around.

"Sovereigns," Jed bellowed, his voice every bit as penetrating as the bombard preceding him, "Stand down, immediately! This is a command from the Senate High Guard! Resistance will not be tolerated!"

Never had Bayer seen such a sudden and widespread loss of intent. Struck with bewilderment, soldiers started filing into ranks of their respective sovereigns, and the injured were exposed, seen to by their comrades. Fortune had been kind to many of the combatants despite the ferocity of the battle, and only a few had been seriously hurt. Siegl was the most desperate. Physicians who had been kept from the main field burst through Sinédrion's ranks and took to him straight away. Satisfied that his protective role had been completed, Rowan steeled himself to patrol the line of Tremaine soldiers, battered, but predominately standing tall.

Jed surveyed the scene. "Where are Andarn's officers?"

Several soldiers marched hurriedly from the streets and lined up before Jed, looking nervous. "Apologies, Your Excellency," a coyote called. "The Generals called a briefing in the barracks for all ranked Captain and above."

The stag looked up to his right, at the opening in the bombard tower, where Alaris stood to attention.

"And you fired the bombard?"

Alaris nodded and called back, "Yes, Your Excellency."

"What is your name and rank, soldier?"

"Captain Alaris Hiryu, Your Excellency."

Jed gave an approving nod. "Congratulations, Captain. You have excellent judgement. There may be hope for your sovereign yet."

Rowan shook his head at the pangolin, a wry smile peeling his face. "Always in the right place at the right time. Fortuitous git."

Bayer watched as the stag patrolled the line of troops, the Sinédrion soldiers still standing perfectly still, weapons brandished, at the plaza's gates. It was amazing the respect Jed wielded, and terrifying to consider there could be even more authority hidden within, which he currently controlled himself and suffered no opposition. Despite his intimidating stance and honed fury there was majesty in everything he didn't say; the restriction of impulsive action or incensed criticism spoke of a much more respectable power than brute force alone. Bayer had never witnessed such a thing before. Even though Aidan had experiences more painful than his living years, he hid them poorly. Jed seemed more like Osiris, but with a more open sense of duty, and a cynicism more tactfully displayed than the gryphon's.

Alaris descended the tower and followed next to Jed, sending soldiers to the physicians if they were standing wounded. Within only minutes of Jed arriving, a cluster of officers broke through Sinédrion's protective line, and immediately began taking charge of their own troops, dividing them by company. The higher-ranking officers formed before Jed and gave a salute in perfect, rehearsed unison. Bayer saw yet more powerful creatures, although this time their display was merely of physical size. Two bears, a maned wolf, a leopard, and a giant otter were the largest and the highest-ranked.

It appeared that Andarn reserved its highest military

privileges for the greatest amount of muscle one could display, and while only a superficial observation, the fact that each one was late served as adequate confirmation bias for Bayer. He did not doubt their efficiency in battle, however, as physical strength and resistance to fear was a big part of any combat. And, to an undisciplined army, image was a great part of intimidation. Andarn particularly had a great number of adversaries and subordinates to intimidate, and the most to lose of any sovereign should war ever break out.

"You already understand the severity of this," Jed rumbled to the assembled ranks before him. "It is not my position to dictate investigation or punishment amongst your military, but you *are* under scrutiny. As powerful as Andarn is, the execution of that power is in the hands of the soldiers. Where there are warriors, there will be war. Do not become complacent. None of you are above reproach."

He whirled round, giving a nod to one of his commanding officers. Within seconds, the troops of the Sinédrion machine dissolved their protective shield wall and formed a line, steadily marching back through the city. As Jed followed, he broke away to catch Alaris, now standing with Rowan and Bayer by the base of the tower.

"Captain Hiryu, are you currently on assignment?" The stag stood taller than all of them, casting a great shadow across their party.

Alaris bowed his head in respect. "No, Your Excellency. I've just returned from duty."

Bayer smirked.

"Good," Jed grunted. "I would like to congratulate you on your pacification of the storm. And, if I may, I wish to discuss something with you."

Chapter Seven

There were few places to be inconspicuous where Jed was part of the picture; he was anything but subtle. Thanks to the earlier battle and its dramatic finish, he was also very identifiable. Even Alaris, not nearly as imposing as Jed, was an issue: for one, pangolins were rare enough creatures to see, and for another, as a higher-ranking officer with a decent reputation, civilians often noticed him. Jed had made it very clear as they walked that he did not want to arouse any suspicion, nor be disturbed.

So Alaris, Rowan, and Bayer found themselves marching in formation with the Sinédrion troops to their temporary accommodation in a smaller section of the city barracks. Bayer had been deeply uncomfortable at the apparent solution to their problem of avoiding Gallis, a feeling not eased in the slightest by Rowan's chatter.

"You look like you've been in the military before," he mused, glancing over the ocelot.

"An army doesn't make a soldier," he retorted. "I know

discipline when it's needed, but ranks diminish the responsibilities of the individual, and limits their judgement and freedom."

Rowan shrugged. "They've always been about merit and strategy to me – those with experience and strong enough intellect to win battles get more responsibilities. Not everyone is a brave and effective warrior alone, but there are opportunities for each of us in time to show what we're made of."

"Lucky you," Bayer retorted, to which he received only a shrug.

Bayer fell silent, too frustrated to press the issue further. The scarred and battered soldiers who had risen through the ranks on the battlefield did not worry him. He identified with them far more than any other part of the military, and respected their ascension through valour. To that end, Rowan was right, but only insofar as the lowest ranks are the ones to make life-or-death judgement calls on the battlefield. They protected the ones standing at their shoulders, broke their blades for both country and civilian. An infantry soldier knows he has to fight because he may have no alternative, and knows only as much as he is told about what or whom he is fighting for. The one who put him in his place, however, would understand exactly what is at stake and the motivation behind their tactical gambles. Bayer found something deeply sinister about plans made behind the battlefronts, and the deadly indifference of those in control who talked only in numbers and possibilities. Power was too easily abused, and life too easily lost.

His silence carried him until they reached Sinédrion's quarters. Two soldiers had been left guarding a large amount of supplies, an indication that Sinédrion had been on its way out of Andarn, but had been delayed by news of the riot. As the troops around them stood to attention and were addressed by their commanders, Jed beckoned for Alaris to accompany him inside. Rowan and Bayer took a tentative step forwards to follow, then stopped.

Jed looked to Alaris. "Do you trust them?"

"With my life, Your Excellency."

Jed signalled them to approach too. He gave a quick scan of the surrounding area, watchful for prying eyes, and entered. The barracks were one of the few buildings, other than the royal, judicial, and governmental buildings, that Jed could walk into with ease, the doors being large enough to accommodate his impressive, sharpened antlers. They followed him through the door, which the Sinédrion guard closed firmly behind them.

Jed wasted no time on getting comfortable, instead pivoting around to address them directly the moment they had reached the centre of the mess hall.

"Forgive my lack of introduction. I am Representative Jed Othera of Sinédrion. As you can tell, the political situation is not stable." Even in a muted whisper, his voice carried, loud and imposing. "I believe it is about to get worse, perhaps turn into all-out war, and none of us can afford that to happen." He turned to Alaris. "Having witnessed the dire conflicts both inside and outside this city, you were the first instance of practical thinking and willingness to undertake any means by which to end it. You have my greatest respect, and I wish to ask your assistance. I need someone within this city whom I can trust."

Alaris' scales flared on his neck. "Of course, Your

Excellency. It would be an honour."

Jed nodded. "Let me explain before you decide on the level of my integrity. What I am about to ask of you breaks most of the protocols set by Senate guidelines, but right now I'm willing to undertake whatever tactic I have to in order to secure peace." He leant in closely, addressing each of the three with a softer, but still highly authoritative tone. "You understand that you have the right to refuse any duty that I offer you, as you are not part of my command, and that if you accept, you risk being accused of treason by your own sovereign?"

It was a heck of an opener. Alaris and Rowan exchanged quick glances. The meerkat shook his head, almost invisibly, as a warning.

Alaris spoke first, choosing to ignore his companion's doubtful countenance. "I'm not generally one to refuse an order that serves the greater good of the continent, Your Excellency, especially where my own sovereign is concerned. However, I would prefer to know that my protection is assured before accepting any assignment."

Jed raised his head slightly, watching the pangolin as if to discern his intentions. "Unfortunately I cannot promise that. I shall attempt, of course, to grant you amnesty should this matter arise, but given the current climate my assistance may be severely limited. I have real concerns that a war is about to occur, and taking into account the disorder already created by the Southern invasion and defeat of Dhraka some months ago, I believe this battle may damage the continent irreparably. I have overseen the diplomacy between Tremaine and Andarn weaken for the last three years, but nothing has prepared me for the hostile escalation I've witnessed in the last eight months. Something has to be done, and Sinédrion is not powerful enough to mediate alone."

Bayer watched Alaris and Jed talk. Alaris' focus on the stag was absolute – he knew with total conviction that greater fights than a petty squabble with Tremaine were on the horizon, and this could be the key to ending it.

"Are you suggesting it's a war between Andarn and Tremaine?" the pangolin asked, checking Rowan's grimace.

"Most likely, but the real concern is deeper than that. Since I came to arbitrate, the number of changes in high-ranking political and military positions has increased dramatically, and they all appear to be supporting a front for aggression. As such, the intensity of the fighting between your two nations has caused splinter conflicts and divisions between other sovereigns, and the dissent within the Senate is palpable. Battle lines are being drawn. The Representatives are heading towards a violent upheaval." The stag began pacing; with his long legs he covered most of the distance of the wide room with only a few steps. "However, even excluding the effects a continental war would have on our citizens and sovereigns, I believe the governance of the Senate itself is at risk also."

The three looked to one another. Bayer's eyes narrowed.

"That's… quite a claim, Your Excellency," Rowan said cautiously.

Jed frowned. "It is. I do not come to these conclusions lightly. My informants in the Senate archives have been monitoring communications since Dhraka forged that quarantine order against Xayall, and they have uncovered some unsettling patterns."

Rowan tapped his foot with increasing rapidity, a frown darkening his face. "Patterns showing… what, exactly?"

He was met with a stern glower. "It is hard to discern. They are more holes, voids of information, than direct patterns. Dhraka upset Cadon's communication network and raided a number of the Senate's embassies shortly after Xayall's invasion, so we haven't a detailed record of what has changed or where discrepancies lie. But updated reports confirm that several sovereigns are amassing troops and ordering armaments."

"Isn't that a precautionary measure, Your Excellency, given recent history?" the pangolin asked, trying not to sound too doubtful. "Or retrospective reports following bolstering of forces prior to when the records went missing?"

Jed pulled his ear, removing a splinter of wood from behind it. "Were it so simple. These troops have appeared from nowhere. We receive frequent reports of new recruitment from each sovereign, but they do not correlate with the population indices we have on record. Nobody can confirm where these troops are. In short, it seems as if someone is building an army and using Senate records to hide it. If this is true, we have no proof of where it is."

"Do you believe it's in Andarn?" Bayer asked quickly.

"I think there may be some involvement," Jed rumbled. "It would be remiss to make a blind accusation, but Andarn's current foreign policy is not exactly in accordance with Senate peacekeeping guidelines. It has become too big for its land, and is beginning to push outwards. It is not to be trusted, even if the orchestration of this conflict is coming from elsewhere."

"What do you want us to do?" Alaris asked. "We're not formidable enough by ourselves to significantly damage a battle plan."

"Perhaps not," Jed answered, "but at the very least you can gather some information for me. I am limited to the investigations I can lead myself. Simply by submitting a request to any given sovereign I make myself known, and give any suspicious parties time to hide. Even if I wasn't noticed, it would take months to organise, and we do not have that time." He took a deep breath. "A mustering of troops on such a large scale would be too obvious to hide within the walls of any major sovereign without word escaping, so I believe an army is being raised in another. Probably one which is currently not directly tied to the Senate, to make trails easier to conceal."

"Kyrryk," Bayer growled, eyes alight with fury. He felt a swell of dread anticipation at the thought of returning to his sovereign. At the least he had updated himself on Kyrryk whenever he had the chance, including battle counts and troop requisition records from the Senate. His hackles stood on end. As fearful as he might be, and as resurgent the memories of his childhood currently were, he knew could not back down.

A new duty for an old life.

"That is the most obvious assumption, Hadris notwithstanding. There have been reports of unusual military activities around Kyrryk, beyond the observed conflicts. At this point, communications from inside are so poor that most official messages are relayed third-hand through the Andarn chain of command, and end up vague, incomplete, or completely detached from the initial declarations. Furthermore, my scholars found that many of the newly-appointed positions in Andarn, military and government, appear to have served or administrated solely in the Kyrryk dispute. Many have no other recorded background on the current Andarn censuses. I want you to investigate and find out how much of this is true, or if I am simply paranoid. Either way, I will require a direct and honest report."

Rowan folded his arms. "Why not use a Sinédrion unit for this?" He fretted, clearly uncomfortable with being put in this position, and not unfairly so.

"They aren't aware of Andarn or Tremaine military structure, history and protocols, and I do not have the time or resources to educate them. Their lack of knowledge on these subjects would make them all too obvious during a covert operation."

"You think the situation is that serious?" Bayer asked, his expression darkening.

Jed nodded. "The new Senate members are exploiting loopholes and handing each other shortcuts in ways that undermine the ultimate authority of the Senate, and may threaten our stability. I do not trust it any longer."

Bayer watched the stag carefully. He had seen others taken in by the eminence of military figures before, and wanted to ensure that they weren't being misled.

"This could be seen as an attempt at a power grab, Your Excellency. Do you have any safeguards against that?"

"Very shrewd, Sir," Jed replied bluntly, but not as if offended. "I simply stand to uphold the laws of the Senate and reinforce discipline. As I am not the Chief Senator, but just Sinédrion's Representative, I do need to exercise caution. Let me see…" The stag looked to the ceiling and held his forehead, trying to recite a passage from memory. "The Fifth Protective Decree reads that 'If reasonable cause can be given, a sovereign can undertake espionage activity within another sovereign's borders providing either: that evidence of danger to any other sovereign can be found and presented to a Senate panel, or, if no clear danger is found, that any secrets discovered and agents of the espionage are surrendered to the aggrieved sovereign under witness of a Senate committee and that adequate reparations are made for the intrusion'." He looked back to Bayer. "Does that satisfy?"

Bayer smirked. "There must be a lot of reparations due."

"I've no doubt," Jed said flatly.

Rowan held up his hand tentatively, giving Jed as firm a stare as he could manage. "Your Excellency, while I am fully prepared to try and curtail war efforts in my own sovereign, with all due respect I decline your assignment – I already have scheduled orders that will result in my court-martial if I refuse them. However, if I discover any information within Tremaine that corresponds to your fears then I will notify you immediately." He looked straight to Alaris, expecting and silently urging him to follow suit.

Alaris considered the meerkat's unspoken request for a few seconds, then looked slowly back to Jed. "I'll help, Your Excellency."

Rowan gave him a cautioning nudge. "Are you serious? If he's wrong, or even if he's *right*, you could be locked up. That, or Gallis will murder you before you even leave the city. You're on orders from him to return as it is."

Alaris gently patted the meerkat in reply and brushed off his arm. "As if you ever objected to rule breaking before. I've fulfilled the General's request: I've returned to Andarn and my troops will be back soon." He pulled the crumpled scroll from his satchel and pushed it into Rowan's face. "For such a high-ranking commander, he didn't drill his page to write specifically who to report to, and I'm not naive enough to find him just because the order has his name on it."

Bayer's image of Alaris' dedication to duty tore like old paper. "That's incredibly defiant of you, Alaris. I'm shocked."

Alaris waved his claw dismissively. "It's complicated. Gallis is powerful and influential, but I want nothing to do with him. As if his ambition wasn't dangerous enough, he was the one Aeryn found smuggling weapons." He balled his fist. "The proof disappeared, but he weaselled and bullied his way out of that one, I'm sure. Even though he's apparently dedicated himself to his position with 'great passion' now, I won't ever trust him. He's corrupt and dangerous as hell, and I have no desire to be drafted into any of his orders."

He looked at the others and realised his rambling had become a little too embittered. He cleared his throat. "In any case, my view of what's important has changed. I believe there's a greater cause than Andarn's security alone. Breaking the rules saved Faria, and I would not risk seeing the world that might have happened if she weren't alive right now. That's a chance we take with every life we don't save. If my career is on the line as a result, then so be it. Preventing a war and protecting people from chaos is far more worth my time. And besides, I think I know a few people who can help me out if things turn for the worst." He gave Bayer a knowing look, and shot him a quick smile.

The feline stood dumbfounded for a time as he tried to take everything in. This was turning into a much greater endeavour than he anticipated.

It had been a long, long time since he felt under such enormous pressure. He wanted to sit down with a stiff drink (or at least be alone in a quiet room) and take it in before making a decision, but ultimately he already knew the answer he should give. Determined not to be robbed of the chance to volunteer, he stepped forwards before Jed could address him.

"Your Excellency, I offer my services to your command. Kyrryk is my homeland, and while I haven't been there in many years, I know the old civil war well, and hope to be of some use to Alaris as a guide. I…" he paused for a second, thinking of his former duties to Xayall and the purpose he once had, and still wished to conjure within himself. "I have been assigned to protect Alaris, and I intend to see him safely guarded until the completion of his mission."

Jed nodded approvingly. "Excellent. You have my thanks. May I know your name?"

"Bayer Kanjita, Your Excellency."

Jed bowed his head respectfully to his agents. "I am greatly aware of the dangerous position into which I have placed you two, and I will be in your debt for a long time, regardless of the outcome. I hope you will be able to discover something that will place a tourniquet on this bleeding conflict." He strode around them to the door, and turned back to them as he opened it. "If you need help getting free of this city, I can conceal you among my troops."

Alaris couldn't stop a small laugh from escaping. "No, Your Excellency, that won't be necessary. We've both had experience enough sneaking around and breaking out of places, and I know Andarn well. We won't have any issue. Good luck, sir."

"To you as well. I have investigations of my own to conduct. Farewell." He pulled the door shut with a slam, leaving them in overwhelming, stunned silence.

"All right," Rowan said, very slowly and deliberately. "You understand what you've just done, correct?"

"Yes. We just agreed to treason," Alaris said quietly.

"I thought so."

"Well, Rowan didn't, and I didn't," Bayer replied, smiling despite his growing apprehensions. "I'm a free agent right now."

Rowan slapped Alaris on the back, wearing a completely unsympathetic grin. "Looks like you're the only treasonous one, my old friend."

"Damn you both."

The meerkat gave a light, airy sigh and stepped away. "I need to report back. We're supposed to leave today, and – no offense – I'd rather not be stuck here by myself. The sooner our troops get out of here, the better for all of us." He locked Alaris in a firm stare. "Are you sure you know what you're doing?"

"No," the pangolin replied bluntly. "But we do not need another war. I almost lost one friend to corruption in this military; I will not risk losing our whole sovereign, or worse."

"Fine." Rowan waved a threatening claw towards him. "But you had better come back alive." He walked a short way towards the door but spun round, again brandishing his claw. "And with no scars that make you more attractive than me, so we can still go out together."

"I think that illusion is broken as soon as you start talking, Rowan," Alaris said with a lilt that made Bayer look to the floor awkwardly. He hoped he and Kier didn't look like that when they argued.

Thankfully, Rowan laughed, giving Alaris a boisterous slap on the shoulder. "See you soon, Alaris. I'll bring some nice blankets if you're incarcerated by my next visit. Maybe a nice wall hanging that reads 'One was warned-eth so…'"

The door clicked shut as he left. For a while the remaining two stood in silence, taking in their new assignment. For his part, Bayer's mind swept between the dread of seeing his old homeland again and concern for Alaris' security. They were stepping into a huge unknown; his knowledge may now be completely redundant, and if the corruption of the troops was as widespread as both Alaris and Jed feared, there may be little they could do to unseat them, even if they managed to secure a piece of evidence strong enough to force the Senate's hand.

There had not been another Senate meeting since Xayall's siege. From what Kier had said, a general state of emergency had been declared amongst the storm of confusing reports, the Dhrakan invasion of Andarn's bay, fear of false contagions, and further declarations trying to deny all of these. Apparently the warring dragons had a further-reaching plan that they were unable to execute, for reasons not yet known.

Faria, Osiris, and Kier in particular seemed to suffer the burdens of trying to wage diplomacy against other sovereigns. Bayer had always been sceptical of other nations, preferring to invest his protection in individuals and families, removed from the greater pictures of corruption and destruction. Faria had an innocent idealism to her view of the world that made her kind and honourable, and Aidan, with his infallible temperament, had inadvertently reassured Bayer in his conviction against the dangers and responsibility of power. The Phiraco family had been worth defending, and Bayer would have given his life for them.

He had nearly done so once already.

His claw tightened around the hilt of his sword. This two-man espionage would never be enough to stop even a skirmish. *He* hadn't been strong enough to stop the Dhrakans who besieged the Tor, and now he was jumping headfirst into the boiling tensions of a war with the intent of stopping it? It was madness.

He looked to Alaris, words of resignation burning in his mouth. He stopped them short of being spoken, however. The honourable soldier had put faith in Faria to find the truth when she was lost, and thus played a crucial part in saving the world from Raikali by protecting Faria's journey. Without him, the continent would already be at war, or worse: would have lost one. A single person could hold far greater significance than they realised. *Maybe that's what Alaris meant when he was talking about saving the world*, he thought. Bayer had done the same by protecting Faria at the very beginning and allowing her to escape the Tor. Did he really fail her, or was it damaged pride that drove him to frustration for not continuing his journey as her bodyguard?

"A duty may change in its scope, but it will always be a duty," he said finally.

Alaris raised an eyebrow. "I'm sorry?"

"I was just thinking that duty isn't necessarily bound solely to the task in front of you. It extends beyond that, into ways we only discover when we meet them."

Alaris smiled, straightening himself and flexing his shoulders, gearing himself for the journey ahead. "I couldn't agree more. We'd better get moving, though."

Chapter Eight

The back alleys of Andarn were dark even in the middle of the day. The streets pressed together with tall, overbuilt houses all crammed alongside each other, with roofs that leant inwards ominously, like guards watching with unrelenting suspicion.

The atmosphere didn't bother the hooded figure prowling its channels, however – he was well used to places like this. He actually enjoyed it. It fit his personality more than the pomp and promenade of the Tremaine assembly he often had to contend with. The attention stifled when it wasn't directed solely at him, and the ceremony was far too jovial. His older brothers were the sponges of spotlight and always first to be addressed. It was sickening.

He, on the other hand, enjoyed the reverence of the fearful. The atmosphere of oppression made him stand much taller, and the soothing chill from the shadows of conflict darkening his city filled his blood with fresh vigour. Celebrations and parades could be damned. Equality was a lie – it was all about heredity. By simple dumb value of being there first, his brothers were the ones with all the command and took all the credit for the prosperity of his sovereign, while *he* had to fight and negotiate with idiots and greedmongers, and be chastised for coming back with blank treaties and empty pockets. None of them, neither the First- or Second-seat princes, nor the citizens, could ever understand what it *meant* to be him, what he had done, or what he was now capable of. If they did, they'd clear the way for him out of equal parts intense fear and immense respect. Peasants, all of them. Ungrateful, useless, insignificant. Someday they would see his worth, and they would fear it.

He swept through a narrowing in the slender alleyway and caught a movement behind him. A tall, emaciated badger rounded on him from behind.

"Hold it, pal! You're not-"

The hooded figure whirled round and plunged his curved blade deep into the animal's thorax, twisting it upwards. He held it there for a second, locking him with his fiery yellow eyes.

"No-one will remember you. Think on that as you die."

Haru slipped his blade free and pushed the badger to the ground. Turning, he flicked the dagger, spattering the rough, uneven ground with spots of blood. The badger's final, desperate gasps buzzed in his ears, while the thrill of his punishment taking its inescapable hold sent a whirlwind through him. This was his order, *his* command. Soon everyone would be bound to his judgement, and the idea of it made him salivate with anticipation.

He continued forwards, holding the blade just underneath the folds of his cloak in case of another bothersome interruption. Almost to his disappointment, within another minute he had reached his destination, and received no further chance to rid the world of a parasitic hindrance.

The door was already open when he arrived at the shabby, greying building. He walked straight through the lobby, coated with shadow, ignoring the dead bodies that lay around the edges of the wall, and ascended the old, wooden stairs. Although wizened and splintering, they barely creaked at his light touch. The stairway hugged the outer wall of the tall, narrow dwelling. It had been a sentry tower when the city was smaller and the borders were more constrained. Too fat the city had grown, an obesity of corruption and avarice. He looked up to where the staircase ended, at the top of the tower's hollow shell high above him. Dusty sunlight pushed through the pinched, slatted windows, illuminating the wooden beams long bereft of care.

Haru hesitated for a moment as he reached the door; despite being familiar with the thing inside, the sheer strength of it still drove a cold nail of fear through his chest. The time drew closer when they would need to divide their rule, and he was uncertain of how well it – he – would cooperate. As long as Haru had his own assets in order, he could prove himself powerful enough not to tangle with. But an air of cold calculation in the eyes of his assignation told fantasies of an awe-inspiring and terrifying capability to eliminate anything seen as a threat. Haru had to be seen as an equal, or he would be killed. Surpassing him would come later.

He took a breath and reached for the door, slowly.

"If I had wanted to kill you I would have done so

already. Get inside." The deep, growling voice sent an electric chill up his spine. Haru cursed for giving himself away and pushed open the door.

Three candles illuminated the dark room from a table in the centre of the room, and a little natural light crept in through a crack of light from an unclosed window shutter. Deep shadows pulsed with the flames' uneven, timid twitching, making it difficult to focus. In the dimness the room had its own heartbeat: a palpitating, nervous rhythm, anxious of the dangers held within.

"Suffering from a crisis of confidence, are we?" the voice spoke again. "It is a little late to be cautious."

Haru pushed the door closed. "Hardly!" he snarled. "Nothing will keep me from this plan. I had to take care of a witness on the way in, that was all."

The voice gave a rumbling snort. "I could smell your bloodlust before you even touched the stairs. You should be careful not to give yourself away."

"That's rich, coming from a murderer like yourself."

The hulking figure moved in the shadows. Haru could feel him turning. "I do not murder," the figure boomed. "I execute. As a machine of the battlefield I meet my enemies head on, using strategy to back them into a corner until there is nothing left of them. You, on the other hand, have a habit of taking the ground right from underneath them. It has served you well, but without a plan to fall back on, one day you will become undone."

Haru grimaced, scowling into the darkness. "I refuse to give my enemies a chance to back down. The quickest blade wins, and mine will always be quicker."

"You hope."

Haru gnarled his claws in ire. "I didn't come here to be lectured. We're equals in this, Kura."

The shape in the darkness slowly leant forwards, his hulking size somehow even larger than the shadows he cast on every wall. An enormous bear stood before Haru, his shoulder muscles huge, almost distended with their rope-like tension, winding down to wide, gauntleted, ebony black claws. He wore only a half-breastplate, covering from his right shoulder down to his abdomen, but had large, oval pauldrons that made his imposing frame look even greater. Where the absence of armour only demonstrated the confidence in his strength and capability in battle, the light rippled over his coarse fur as if it were alight with dark flames. This, with his brick red eyes flaring in the candles' same orange glow, gave him the appearance of a monster.

"Tell me exactly how we are equals."

Haru stiffened, his body betraying the fury he held for the bear's sheer size and power. While Jed had been imposing, Kura's cold rancour and calculating, deliberate manner burned with sinister intent. Haru was glad to be on his side... for now, at least.

The mongoose bristled. "The plan would never have come this far without me. Tremaine's spies are far more effective than Andarn's, and I have a great many resources at my disposal. Resources that would have been wasted or discovered if it hadn't been for my talents, intent, and diplomacy."

Kura didn't move, but kept his unblinking eyes on Haru. "And are these 'resources' in place?"

"Principally, yes. It hasn't been easy trying to coordinate these troops by myself without the Dhrakan networks for

97

support. I've almost been discovered several times."

"It only becomes relevant if you *were* discovered. And if you were, you would not be here and I would have someone else in your place. Do not inform me of your near-misses or I shall be tempted to look elsewhere."

Haru balled his fist. "Nobody else can command these troops!" he hissed defensively. "Your plan would fail without me here now, and don't pretend that you've never had to cover your tracks in haste. Besides, only *I* know where the device is."

The bear's expression tightened: the tiniest of fractions, but enough to convey deep dissatisfaction. "Do you have it?"

Spiked with a sense of confidence, Haru straightened slightly in an effort to display a hold over the bear. "It is being transferred to our stronghold as we speak. It was not easy to obtain, but everything is in place."

Kura's voice rose, sending creaks through the old wooden structure around them. "If you do not hold it in your hands, then it is not in place. Do not deceive me, fool!"

"I am not a fool!" Haru protested, shrinking back. "After the Dhrakans dissolved I was damn lucky to even *hear* of that cursed object again! My contact procured it *and* the mechanic who knows how to operate it. You might intimidate others with your strength, but I have enough political power to have you vanish from the face of Eeres, and nobody would dare ask why!"

"And if you did," Kura said quietly, pulling his huge, gnarling face over the flame on the table, "there would be a thousand creatures who would stop at nothing until every last drop of your blood stained the earth."

The two glared at each other in the flame light; eventually the bear rose to stand, once again disappearing into the darkness, save for the red flare of his eyes and their penetrating focus.

"Assemble yourself," Kura growled. "We begin our final assault as soon as the device is delivered."

"I already have several thousand troops assigned to the main battlefront, awaiting my orders," Haru boasted. "Even the ones you sent me are behaving themselves, despite their commander's arrogance."

The bear ignored his remark. "I have arranged for several disruptions to occur in the city. Have you made plans on your home front?"

Haru cracked a grin, displaying his needle-like teeth. "There is nothing I will do that cannot be hated. There will be no question of war when my campaign is finished."

The bear turned to the window, the narrow slit of light illuminating his face like a scar. "Good. There is one more matter that needs to be taken care of, however." He cast a piercing look at the mongoose, who eyed him suspiciously.

"What is that?"

The red eyes fixed on the shaft of cityscape visible through the window. "There exists something, or someone, strong enough in Xayall to kill the Dhrakan leader, destroy their war machine, and unseat their hierarchy. That cannot happen again. Our plan cannot be discovered, or else we may face the same battle that they did. Dhraka was poorly conditioned despite its violent history, and dismally unprepared to lose its greatest war assets and strategist. We had been working at infiltrating Xayall for some time but were unsuccessful until they were attacked. Now, with their defences unstable, it will be much easier. I will be sending a disruption their way that should gain access to their secret weapons. Apparently they are deep into reparations. If we strike at the right place, we should strip them of power and motivation, and gain complete control."

Haru eyed him suspiciously. "You're keeping things from me, Kura. The Dhrakans said nothing about their purpose in Xayall after we gave them the Emperor and the quarantine order. What are you striking at, exactly? We can't afford another theatre to fight."

The bear cast him a sideways glare. "Do not accuse me. I do not know what they were after, which is why the anomaly of their defeat must be investigated and any threat removed. I am not naive enough to send a whole army; it would draw too much attention. My sabotage has already begun, in fact, and soon I will have a scapegoat within my grasp to free me from suspicion. With luck, we will take hold of whatever the Dhrakans were hunting before they dissolved into civil war."

Haru nodded. "If this device I retrieved is anything to go by, they could hold some incredible weaponry. It seemed like a pithy little wand until my engineer showed me its true potential. Should the Dhrakans have been hit by this kind of power unsuspectingly, it could have caused their downfall."

"Hmm." Kura said little, pulsing his claws into the pad of his hand in thought. "They were always an unsteady element. Had Crawn been willing to reveal his hand, we may have been in a better position to help. But now we may be safer," he raked a claw through his neck fur, still watching the city below. "I have everything under control; the only exception is Xayall. They have proven more dangerous than

I anticipated, and that is an unacceptable instability." He aimed a pointed stare at Haru. "We cannot afford any mistakes."

Sensing that the word 'mistake' was directed at him, the mongoose felt an angry rush, electric bile rising in his throat. The insolence of this monster was disgusting. He could think of at least three ways to kill him right where he stood; even for his size, he was still just a creature. Killable like any other. Haru would be second to nobody, and would not be talked down to so impetuously.

He stepped forwards, gnarling. "If you dare—"

The walls rocked; a rumble cascaded around them for a brief second. Haru faltered, fearing the tower was falling to the ground. As he grabbed the wall, he saw the bear's eyes glowing a deep, bloody red.

"Leave."

The voice tore a hole in Haru's chest, a deep, infinite void of sheer terror. Saying nothing, his hands quivering, he grasped at the door handle and slipped away.

Kura silently cast his gaze back over the city.

Chapter Nine

"**D**o I really have to be your excuse?"

"Yes. Now stop pouting. This is difficult enough already."

"So we're adding theft and impersonating a soldier to your charges as well, now?"

"If I'm committing treason, the rest is immaterial. Besides, *you're* impersonating the soldier, not me."

Bayer groaned as Alaris led him through the Andarn barracks like an unwilling child to a physician's appointment. To prepare for their tiny infiltration of Kyrryk, they needed supplies, and Alaris knew of no better place than the barracks' armoury. Surrounded by guards. Armed guards. Armed guards who were currently ablaze with the retelling of tales from the riots, or discussing fervently the repercussions that the battle would have on politics, their shifts, and the further-deepening judgements of Andarn's future. Opinions ranged from apathy to sympathy to outright hatred of Tremaine. Bayer cast the soldiers only furtive glances, hoping that they would be too involved in their own conversation to consider his un-uniformed presence through the wide, echoing corridors.

They ascended wide stairs, whose centres dipped from years of armoured footfall.

"I guess these steps train you to never let your guard down," he muttered.

"Why do you think we're always fighting everyone else?" Alaris replied brightly. "Can't wage war against a staircase."

The passageway ahead was almost a wall of white armour. These were the upper sleeping quarters, but it seemed the riots had everyone up and talking. Soldiers stood *everywhere*, and Bayer's stomach rose to his gullet. Alaris gave a quiet whistle.

"So much for that reprimand. It's as if nothing even happened."

Bayer's eyes darted from one officer to the next, his head lowered. His tail flicked tensely back and forth. He might as well have been waving a flag for how conspicuous he felt. Thankfully, Alaris appeared to be deflecting most of their attention with casual waves and salutes as he marched, looking purposefully towards their destination, or at least the unwinding path that led to it. A few tried to engage in conversation with the well-respected Captain, but he countered them with friendly dismissal.

About halfway along the hallway he turned to a door, which he barged open and slipped through, Bayer at his heels.

Despite the size of the conversing mass outside, the pangolin's quarters muted the rabble. Bayer leant his head back and blinked his eyes open a few times, and only then noticed the carvings on the wall. Wooden plates hung around the brickwork; into each was engraved an image or sigil. Between them were weapons, scraps of fabric, and odd tools or statues, looking to be from all over Cadon.

"Did you find all of these on assignment?"

Alaris looked over his shoulder. "Most of them. The carvings are mine, though. I get bored when I'm off duty."

Bayer took in the scenes in the carvings – a few landscapes, some portraits – one of Rowan. There was one that had been lightly painted, hung over Alaris' large, circular bed. Adorning it was a set of stylised, caricature-like soldiers on it. He studied it, until he came to a familiar-looking wolf wearing a cheeky grin. "Is that Aeryn?"

"Ha, yes! That was our company before she left."

"These are really nice," Bayer said softly. "It's very different to the life I expected to see."

"I've had the good fortune to experience a better service than most, but it's not been without its conflict," Alaris replied, speaking into the clothes he was turning over. "I hope to carve more sometime, when I can afford a break. I'll make one of you if you like."

Bayer let out an apprehensive laugh.

"Hiryu!" came a loud, staccato reprove from the doorway. "What are you doing here?"

Alaris halted mid-explore. Bayer saw the curses racing through his eyes as he slowly turned to meet the large carnivore that swept into the room. A tall, muscular jaguar, covered in battle scars, eyed them with great suspicion.

"I thought you were assigned to Xayall for another two months," the jaguar remarked, his voice educated and painted with age. "Rather surprised to see you back now after you were so keen about its protection."

Without a pause, the pangolin answered: "Major-General Dion, glad to see you again. But yes – General Gallis sent an order for me to return. I thought it unusual, but given the circumstances he outlined in his dispatch I didn't want to ignore it."

"Gallis?" Dion's eyes narrowed. "I wasn't aware he was currently stationed here."

Alaris shrugged. "The order came from here; apparently recent events called for his return, sir."

The jaguar rolled his eyes, casting his head back with perfect exasperation. "Interfering so-and-so," he grumbled. "Seems to have his fat claws stuck in as many holes as he can these days. Regardless, he should not command my subordinates like that. I apologise for your inconvenience, Hiryu."

Alaris shook his head. "Not at all, Major-General. It turns out I may have an assignment here after all."

Bayer shot him a warning glance; Alaris kept his attention on Dion, who stroked a thin, well-groomed tuft of fur at the tip of his lower jaw. He looked about as proud of it as his armour. "Is this something I need to be made aware of? It's not from Gallis, is it?"

The pangolin shook his head. "No, not from Gallis, sir. I don't work for him."

A pause followed, overflowing with silent expectation. Dion's eyes once again narrowed with suspicion. "I assume you have a reason for your evasion, Hiryu. I hope I can trust you."

Alaris bowed his head respectfully, then stepped in

closer with his voice lowered. "Should anyone ask, sir, officially you cannot trust me. Above all else, and in the greater interests of our duty, I promise you *can* – just unofficially. But unfortunately I will not be reporting for duty for a while."

Dion took in a deep breath through his nose, frowning with deliberation. "All right then," he said eventually. "I must leave. Grand Councillor Vol is holding a conference to increase the military manoeuvres on Tremaine's borders. A waste of good troops and a poke in the eye for calm tempers. You shall have to tell me about Xayall some other time. I have often wanted to visit."

A smile spread across the pangolin's face. "Better to see it when it's in one piece, sir. I'll owe you a long drink on our return."

"Excellent!" Dion beamed, raising a claw with triumph. "Any story is best served with alcohol. Fare you well, Hiryu. And don't get into trouble." He turned sharply and began leaving the room A few strides away he swept round grandly. "And hurry up, for goodness' sake! You're my best Captain, and the current replacements just don't cut it. My new battle teeth arrive soon and I will need a worthy sparring partner. I'll find a way to crack your scales yet."

"Of course, sir! Good hunting."

Dion waved a claw over his shoulder and disappeared in the crowd.

Alaris gave Bayer a secretive grimace. "Sorry, Bayer, I was hoping to avoid him. But it may play to our advantage – he's loyal to his soldiers. I'm lucky to be one of them."

He turned back to the drawers, and, with a grunt of frustration, seemed to find what he was looking for. The pangolin tucked it away in his bag before Bayer could see. The blatant manipulation of the system was beginning to fray the feline's nerves a little. "I thought this was supposed to be a secure, structured system," he murmured. "Yet here you are doing favours for another sovereign and being completely undisciplined by your commander. No wonder Kyrryk was left in a mess."

Alaris sighed as they left the room and he slammed the door shut behind them. "I'll admit, Andarn has severe failings as a military machine unless there's a clear cause. In a battle proper, we're virtually unmatched for our infantry tactics and sheer force. Survival of the many is a clear focus to all of us. But outside of combat, egos and status run wild; it's as if everyone believes their rank is highest and only balk when threatened with demotion. What starts as a genuine act of support on the battlefield becomes leverage in the courts and hallways. It's... a little anarchic at times."

Bayer frowned. "So what about Major-General Dion, then? How can he be so lax?"

They rounded a corner, arriving at a large set of double doors flanked by two sets of guards. Alaris saluted them and tapped the Captain's insignia on his left pauldron.

"New transfer from Pthiris to suit up."

"Requisition order, sir?"

Alaris fished around in his belt pouch and pulled out one of the most crumpled pieces of paper Bayer had ever seen. Dirty, torn at the edges, and creased on every inch of its surface.

The porcupine soldier who took the paper raised his eyebrows and let out an incredulous scoff. "This is terrible," he said, trying to pull it straight. "It looks used."

Alaris raised his hand authoritatively. "I haven't taken good care of it, I'll admit; I was given the requisition before leaving, and was stationed away for a few months in poor weather. Meanwhile, this officer has been waiting patiently at Pthiris' expense for my return to enlist as an exchange. There's no final confirmation seal, as you can see."

The porcupine strained his eyes to check for signs of paper tampering. Sure enough, where the 'received' area was scrawled on the parchment, no mark denoted its completion.

"Very well, sir," he replied. "But I would be careful next time – in a condition like this it's liable to be denied, or considered a forgery. We're having to be very careful these days."

"I'll bear that in mind. Thank you."

The pair obediently pulled open the door and stepped within. Racks and racks of armour, weapons, and all manner of military gear he had never even considered immediately met Bayer. His eyes widened, and unknowingly his expression turned to that of a starving creature faced with a free plate at a buffet.

Sitting at desks either side of the doorway were two officious-looking Requisition Officers, surrounded with books, scrolls and loose parchments. One was an old fox, and the other a younger squirrel. Each had a queue of soldiers standing with scrawled orders, accompanied with armfuls of weapons, or small handcarts laden with armour. The unfortunate ones were sent to pick up orders for an entire company, usually as some sort of hazing ritual or punishment.

"I had a feeling this would come in handy one day,"

Alaris beamed, once the door closed again and they were out of earshot of anyone nearby. "It was an old requisition I had been given for a Warrant Officer, but he…" He trailed off as he noticed Bayer's building, excited hunger.

"Not as cosy as Xayall's, is it?"

"Definitely," Bayer gulped faintly, his gaze darting from one blade to the next. "I knew your army was big, but it's easy to forget that it has to be supplied as well."

Alaris nodded. "And this is only one of four armouries. It's not artisan stuff, but it's impressive all the same. Most of the officers, or soldiers with unusual shapes, have custom suits made by Atheus Corraint, on the main southern street. He's, er… expensive."

Bayer looked his companion over as they stepped between two racks, noticing his armour wasn't exactly uniform in comparison to the rows of metal on the wooden railings beside them.

"Yours is custom, I take it?"

"Yes," he replied delicately, flicking a few splinters from his chestplate. "Didn't get it until I was made Captain – I had a leather set before then, as it's easier to make, and cheaper. I had to prove I was worth the extra investment."

"Does yours have an armourer's mark on it?"

Alaris pointed to a small carving on the lower right of his breastplate. "There's a stamp down there. That's normally all there is for custom harnesses. Why do you ask?"

Bayer shook his head. "Just something I saw in the fight. One of the Andarn soldiers had this weird sigil inside his pauldron. I'm not sure what it was."

"Couldn't tell you, I'm afraid."

Bayer studied every sharpened edge and peined surface.

Most of the rank-and-file armour was divided into sets of unfinished, shaped plates awaiting final adjustments and riveting to a harness. There were endless amounts of leather vambraces, thick padded arming jacks and gambesons, neck plates, one-size-fits-most chain mail shirts and trousers, and T-shaped metal bars – a skeletal rest for fresh helmets. He and Kier had broken into the armoury in Xayall when they were younger and it had seemed just as wondrous, but as they grew older and saw more military and protective duties it had lost its fantastic edge. At the same time, Xayall's military policy plateaued into guarding and patrolling the city, withdrawing from border enforcement and military intervention, so the need for new equipment faltered into maintenance only. There had never been a Xayall conscription.

Alaris allowed Bayer a little time to indulge his eye, heading for a smaller section towards the centre of the long, high hall, separated by a tall iron fence. A black pika, looking as bored as he was short, stood by a bolted doorway leading through the railing. Bayer caught up to the pangolin when he saw their progression to a new section, and did his best to look formal, but unassuming. The pika, completely disinterested in either of them, simply held out his hand for the requisition, which Alaris dutifully handed over. The lagomorph chewed on a frown for a couple of seconds, then gave a huff and flicked open the bolt, kicking the door ajar with his heel.

The two entered, giving the sentry polite nods of acknowledgement, hazarding that any greater gesture might result in an unfortunately testy comment. Once inside, excitement flashed in Bayer's eyes again – in here were the specialist pieces of armour – suits already made for officers, and more specialist, unique weapons and equipment. Here, the armour wore a brilliant finish of mirrored silver and white. A shine reminiscent of the honour he used to hold for the warriors he dreamed would protect him, that he could one day have become.

"It's amazing, but not exactly stealthy, is it?" he mused, gently tilting a helmet on its stand. "Must be hard to hide sometimes."

Alaris shrugged, checking the inventory tags on the suits of armour stood on wooden frames along the edges of the railing. "Sometimes intimidation is a greater asset. But," he said, pointing into a corner on the other side of the division, "we have lightweight livery coats for night or forest infiltration. We'll need to go over there, too."

Bayer stood still for a moment, staring at armour sat on its skeletal, mannequin-like doll, devoid of a real body, hanging there like some restrained, shining ghost. It was oddly chilling. If he looked hard enough, he could almost see a shadow of a figure within the armour, arms outstretched, body hanging limply beneath and head hung low. A rift formed within Bayer between his prejudices and his conscience: the echo of a prostrate soldier, shackled to the huge and unfeeling city walls. The soldiers here were alike any other he might see – with no ingrained, xenophobic hatred other than that born from circumstance, much like himself prior to escaping Kyrryk. The difference was the avarice in the chain of command; soldiers had no choice but to be indifferent and invasive. He ground his teeth in frustration and reminded himself of the insecurities that the armour represented. He would not forfeit his misgivings so soon.

An interruption – Alaris pulled a chest harness from the railing and beckoned him over. "This one looks your size."

The ocelot shook his head. The chest was far too wide for his slender frame. "I'll look."

"Sure. We don't have much choice though: most officers' arms are bespoke. We may need to piece something together for the rank."

They sifted through the racks and eventually came to a chest plate in a reasonable size, while Alaris selected the shaped pauldrons and sky-blue harness trim denoting the Warrant Officer rank. With great reluctance Bayer shed his familiar armour and mounted it onto the empty frame, pushing it into a large locker reserved for items to be retrieved later. His own sword he kept at his side. Weapons were granted more freedom of individuality among the officers. The new armour, although clean, stifled Bayer as he strapped himself in. He did not want to know whose it was supposed to be, and tried to push uncomfortable fantasies from his mind. It fit eerily well, a set of articulated plates with a reinforced single piece over the top. Designed with formidable defence as its prime objective, it served as both a comfort and a warning. Alaris regarded them thoughtfully.

"Oh, we match," he mused, gesturing to his own organic plated scale. Bayer nodded, with a soft laugh. It was an ominous statement to agree with, given the circumstances.

After a brief, pregnant pause, Alaris turned to the front of the vault, then looked Bayer up and down. He seemed satisfied, but regarded the iron doors with increasing urgency; their window of opportunity to leave secretly was rapidly diminishing. After Bayer had finished his final adjustments, they marched the tense path down to the Requisition Officers.

They debated quietly which of the two might be more lenient, and laid arguments and counter-arguments as to whether the younger squirrel or older fox would be more attentive to their duty. In the end they opted for youth over experience, discerning that the older fox was giving them a wary eye at their chattering, and would be more suspicious.

The encounter ended up far less painful than they feared: the squirrel quickly read over the requisition, counted the items they held, then gave the order a hearty stamp with his inked seal, handing the completed order back to them with a bright smile.

"Thank you, sirs," he said politely, marking off an inventory list with incredible efficiency. The pride he took in his work was alien to the solemn conduct the other clerks displayed, but it was certainly not unwelcome.

Wasting no more time, Alaris led Bayer hastily away from the armoury, darting into whichever side corridor they could to avoid scrutiny, while collecting more provisions in less-than-official ways.

"You never answered my question," Bayer said once they had left the barracks and were marching swiftly towards the city's northern entrance.

"Which?" Alaris asked distractedly.

"About Dion and his lack of military discipline."

The pangolin tapped his forehead in thought. "What is it you said, 'a duty may change in its scope, but it will always be a duty'? It's similar to that. The Major-General and I have both seen a lot of unusual situations that have required more than an 'official' military response. He's seen diplomatic relations, support networks, units, and soldiers crumble for adhering to overbearing policy, and I've experienced more in the last few months than I ever realised I could as a soldier. He and I both understand there's a greater world than the insignia soldiers are branded with. An occupation, rescue effort, or negotiation can live or die by the kindness of a soldier acting outside his or her orders." He scratched his neck for a second, looking uncomfortable. "But we've been pretty farcical with discipline recently, haven't we? Our whole adventure so far has succeeded by exploiting kind or apathetic soldiers, who choose to undermine their duties for completely different reasons. The whole system needs to be rebuilt, ideally. Nobody has overall control, and we shouldn't, officially, be allowed to roam free like this. But we're too combative as a nation. If this works out and we can eliminate some of our violent nature... then I'd like to think this exception will count for something." Bayer nodded, looking ahead at the city's exit, and to the hillsides barely visible beyond its shadowy mouth. "Let's hope so."

Chapter Ten

The curtains were still drawn, bathing the small, quiet chamber in a soft yellow light while the winter sun waited patiently behind them, keeping a respectful distance from the sleeping figure inside. He was rarely alone; whether it was his daily physician visit, a nurse or a friend, someone kept a watchful eye on him, should he awaken from the deep slumber he had succumbed to for a long time. He had changed little in the last few weeks, however, and little more could be done except tend to his slowly healing wounds and replenish his fluids. For someone once so full of life, the quiet loneliness was a devastating contrast.

In his torpor he could not even hear the figure approaching from the curtained doorway with movements that were anything but subtle. The athletic, silver-furred wolf walked quietly to the bedside and gave a gruff sigh, discovering once again that the raccoon was still asleep. Fur had not yet fully grown back over the scars. The injured creature's augmented metal reflected dimly in the light, a greater testament to his painful history than his catatonic flesh. The grey plating was dented and scratched, but more harrowing were the punctures left by his attacker's nightmare claws. The Xayall doctors could not remove his metal plates, having limited knowledge of the process by which they were bound to his young frame, so the scars stayed, each one a three-layered indication of his painful journey: the accident in his youth, the Dhrakan tampering, and his current grievous injuries.

Kyru, although present at the raccoon's sacrifice, had been under hypnosis during the battle in the Tor, and did not consciously witness Tierenan's horrible fate. When he first learned of it, he had fallen silent for a long time, and stayed in his young friend's room for almost two full days, waiting for him to wake up. Since then he had returned daily, hoping for some sign of improvement. Initially, after the raccoon's critical condition eased, there was hope that he would return steadily to consciousness, but his healing plateaued. Even with his silence, the loyalty of those who cared for him never diminished despite harbouring their own injuries. Kyru himself had been nearly killed by Aeryn's shattering of the crystal in his back, but he dismissed it, being too quietened by the involuntary betrayal he was forced to play against Faria, his friends, and his love. Both Faria and Aeryn had forgiven him, relieved to see him returned to normal, but he had yet to forgive himself. Between his emotions and those of his partner Aeryn, conversations sometimes ran high with tension. Seeing Tierenan so badly injured only added to everyone's sense of loss; the first week or so after the siege was slow and devastating. But as long as Tierenan remained alive, hope bloomed, and Kyru was not about to let go.

"You're supposed to be waking *me* up, you know," the wolf said pointedly, almost ruefully, folding his arms. "If *I* don't get to lie around after our battles, then you've no excuse." He waited for a few seconds, as if expecting a response. A flash of despondency lit his indigo eyes and he spun on his heel to face the door, taking a stride towards it. "Lazy bugger," he grunted.

He made it two steps before stopping again, staring at the floor, arms by his sides. "You... did a good job though. You did great, in fact. Especially since I... So... thank you. Faria would have been lost without you." He cleared his throat, trying to let his voice escape freely. "We all might have been."

He looked back over his shoulder at the raccoon, who still breathed silently, steadily. Turning round again, he walked back to the raccoon's bedside and watched him for a few more seconds. He flicked his claws, racking his brain for anything that might rouse the cybernetic patient. Carefully, he leant in and prodded Tierenan's cheek. His head rocked slightly, but it wasn't a conscious action. Pursing his lips, Kyru picked up one of the small wooden medical tools and began touching it to the racoon's non-metal ear cavity, trying to irritate him awake by tickling the hairs. He moved to the metal ear, tapping it against the edges like a small musical triangle.

"Come on, Tierenan, you should be chasing me around the room by now!"

He grabbed his cheeks and began wiggling them around, when—

"Is this some Ohéan healing method that I'm not aware

of?" came a stern voice.

Kyru leapt up and spun round, hair standing on end. "Just trying something different," he said quickly.

The falcon, Maaka, swept in, giving him a critical eye. "Playing with my patient, yes?"

Kyru's excuses diminished in his throat as Maaka began assessing the racoon's progress, and as the familiar faces of Aeryn and Faria appeared through the door. The female wolf's auburn and white fur and her yellow eyes appeared even richer in the room's muted light. She shook her head at Kyru's poorly-hidden embarrassment, pushing Faria into the room on an ornate wheelchair. The fox was virtually cemented in place with blankets below her shoulders, and would have been shifting uncomfortably if she had the ability to do so. Her arms weren't pinned in, but the wheels on the chair were too small to reach, and didn't have handles she could turn, robbing her of any chance to roam the Tor under her own steam. She gave Kyru an enervated wave and a tired smile.

He clasped his hands in front of him dutifully and politely greeted them, as a bodyguard should; although he was well familiar with them both, his guilt caused a great deal of self-admonishment in their presence, amplified by Maaka catching him out. Aeryn and Faria were both trying to cure him of the emotion, not least because it didn't suit his familiar brusque-but-honourable nature.

"It's good to see you out, Faria," he said quietly.

"Glad to leave my room every now and again," she replied. "I was starting to hallucinate with boredom."

He shrugged. "Hallucinations are all right if they're not scary. Something to keep you occupied, anyway."

Aeryn raised an eyebrow. "You'd know all about hallucinations, wouldn't you? What was it you used to smoke in Ohé?"

"Hey, I didn't smoke that crap! I just *happened* to share the tent. Stuff gave me a headache." He shrugged. "Did make for some vivid nights, though."

The she-wolf, after pushing Faria to Tierenan's side, stood by her partner with her arms folded. "Not forgetting the times you've been drunk, of course."

He gave her an incredulous look. "I never got *that* bad. At least I can handle what I take in. How many times did you fall off your stool that evening outside Al-Mayena? You must have seen some crazy stuff, because the conversations you were having with that gutter were something else."

Aeryn blushed, turning directly to Maaka in a bid to end the conversation quickly.

"Any change?" she asked, more loudly than she meant to. Faria stifled a laugh as Kyru gave her a glib wink.

"I'll tell you about that sometime," he murmured secretively.

"I need some peace for a moment," Maaka said curtly as the feathers on his neck bristled and puffed.

Kyru stood next to the falcon, watching him work. "I didn't see any change or reaction. He could be messing with me for all I know, but... I'm not a doctor."

"You've made that evident several times," the physician muttered, his feathers still ruffled in ire. "Insistent on self-diagnosis, self-treatment, *and* you harassed all of my patients at some time or another. You should be lucky I don't slip you some laxative to keep you out of my feathers."

"Wouldn't need to badger your patients so much if you

could fix them," he retorted. Aeryn gave him an elbow to the ribs, and he growled something inaudible in reply. Maaka ignored him, used to gripes and complaints from the injured.

Faria allowed herself a smile at Kyru's expense, but couldn't help relating to his frustration. It wasn't Maaka's fault; they had suffered some weird and extensive injuries, a number of which involved developing new surgical techniques. They were lucky to have him; the falcon was one of the best physicians she'd ever seen, and to be on Osiris' crew was testament itself to his skill. But Tierenan's slow progress had been disheartening all the same. Motivated by Aeryn and Kyru's swift recoveries despite their deep wounds, Faria had challenged herself to recuperate as fast as possible. The resonance had started eating away at her muscles and she suffered from atrophy and anaemia, but thankfully the crystal's energy hadn't penetrated deeper into her body. She had been lucky to stop Raikali relatively quickly, before her powers were dissolved within the crystal below Nazreal's surface. She was now victim to the tiredness she had always seen in her father's eyes, although he had suffered a far, far greater disaster, and for significantly longer, before his death.

Having the wolves around had given Faria confidence to continue through her tiredness and look to the future. Her ambitions to bring the world to peace and stability were strong, and she was eager to spend her days without falling into a semi-conscious stupor every few hours.

Tierenan's silence, however, was devastating. Faria wondered if he knew how many people cared for him. It wouldn't matter, she surmised. He would be happy just to see everyone safe, then get busy checking on everybody else's injuries and gathering stories he'd missed. While she hoped against hope that he would wake up at any time, a looming question pawed at her mind, and no doubt everyone else's. She had so dreaded the answer that she hadn't given voice to it until now.

"How... how likely is it that he'll recover?" she asked quietly, touching his cold, metal claws.

With his beak, Maaka rotated one of the hand-like surgical devices attached to his wing and delicately inspected Tierenan's head wounds. "It's hard to say. These aren't the first head injuries he received, obviously, given the plating."

Faria nodded. "I was wondering if... maybe if the metal was damaged, if that could be affecting him rather than the wounds themselves."

The falcon gave a contemplative click of his tongue. "The brain is incredibly fragile. One injury in the wrong place and you can be in this state for the rest of your life, or whatever you would call it." He straightened, nudging the small eyeglasses further up his beak. "I honestly don't know what they did to him in Skyria when he was young. While I studied most of their medical knowledge, it's obvious they have technologies and methods that they won't reveal to anyone else, especially where artificial limbs and metal-to-flesh bonding are concerned. They may have expedited his recovery through some additional procedure, and the Dhrakans may have added to that even more so. They may still have access to weapons and tools that we are not aware of."

"Like the control chips, you mean?" She remembered the small electronic piece that Maaka had pulled from her friend's head on the Coriolis.

"Yes. The influences on his mind aren't just biological, so you may be right. I do not want to risk him further damage by taking apart the metal pieces, as I have no knowledge of those. Either way, it takes a long time to fully recover from cranial trauma that severe, so even if everything augmenting him was in full working order, he may just need a long recuperation period."

Faria wrung her hands. "Osiris mentioned… that he'll need to go back home to be properly healed…" she trailed off sadly. Aeryn laid a hand on her shoulder and gave it a gentle squeeze.

"You are correct," Maaka said. "Osiris and I had been discussing that eventuality, but we needed to wait until he was stable." He shifted his weight, taking a moment to look at Faria a little more gently. "I have already contacted Skyria, and they will await our departure on the Coriolis. Osiris was insistent we get him there quickly and safely."

"I understand. Thank you, Maaka."

She regarded the raccoon sadly. Ideally she would remain beside him, to be there when he recovered or to try and help in some way, but she knew it was beyond her power. "Do what you can for him, please."

Maaka bowed his head respectfully. "Of course, Faria. I would ask in return that you don't over exert yourself. You are recovering also."

She nodded, somewhat impatiently. "Thank you. I will recover in my own time, though, be it fast or slow – the lives of those I care for are my concern currently. I've had enough of lying down."

Kyru and Aeryn swapped encouraging looks, like proud older siblings. Faria caught sight of them out of the corner of her eye, and immediately looked away to avoid a rush of self-consciousness. Although some of her authority had begun to manifest naturally, she had to construct the rest of it herself in order to sound like a leader. She wanted to inspire confidence from the officials and councillors she had yet to meet in her new capacity as Empress, and the citizens too. She just hoped she didn't come off as demanding or insincere, and had to trust others would keep her in check if she ever became unreasonable.

Thankfully, Maaka appeared understanding. He gave Tierenan one last check and marched towards the door, stopping only to shoot Kyru a reproachful look. "Don't touch my patient."

The wolf almost said something rude in response, but seeing that both Faria and Aeryn were watching him, he simply made a dismissive grunt.

A few seconds later, once Maaka's clawsteps had diminished down the hallway, Faria removed something from under her blankets. A small pile of twisted metal parts appeared in her paw, barely recognisable from the small, flittering shape it once held as Tikku, the mechanical bird that had attached itself to Tierenan.

"Are you sure you don't want Maaka to know about this?" Aeryn asked quietly. "If something goes wrong, we'll need him to make sure Tierenan's all right."

Faria shook her head. "It's just an idea, and probably too broken to work anyway, but… it's worth a try." She held the tiny, shredded body tightly in her hand, remembering her friendship with the raccoon. "I'll try anything if it helps him." She paused for a second, flashing them a nervous smile. "Although unlike last time, I won't resort to electrocution just yet."

Carefully, she placed the bird in his metal claw and waited. They all watched for any signs of movement in either creature. The longer they waited, the heavier the air became with disappointment. Faria took the bird again and held it close to him, anticipating a response, then, met with nothing, rested it on his pillow, making sure that it touched the metal plating on his head. She thought she felt a small electrical spark between the two, but even after a minute of apprehensive waiting, only his calm, quiet breathing met their ears.

Kyru patted her on the shoulder. "A good try. He'll come round soon. Little git's more resilient than any of us would have given credit for."

"I know," Faria whispered, sadly. For him to bear these injuries twice and still be alive, she could only guess at his internal strength. He deserved some rest for protecting her so bravely and for enduring whatever torture the Dhrakans put him through after kidnapping him. But that didn't stop her from missing him terribly.

Aeryn took hold of the wheelchair and gently pulled her away from the bed. "Come on, let's take you outside."

Pushing through the curtains, a shape came from nowhere, almost colliding with the wheelchair were it not for a sidestep to the wall. The three peered around the curtain to see who they'd encountered, and were met with Kier presenting himself with a formal bow.

"Kier!" Aeryn called. "It's a pleasure. I presume you need Faria?"

Kyru gave the fox a polite salute, and Faria responded to his presence with a warm smile. Kier's tail bushed out at the observation of all three, and he dusted off his shoulder.

"I do, if you wouldn't mind."

Faria tilted her head slightly, a movement that sent Kier looking suddenly every which way but at her. "Is everything all right?" she asked softly.

"Yes, it is, yes. Well, I had been looking for you, Your High- er, Faria," he flustered. "I just needed to deliver a report."

Faria nodded and squirmed her way into a more upright position in her chair. It was difficult to look regal when swamped with wool. "Yes, please do. Is it all right if we talk on our way to the gardens?"

Kier nodded, but as he turned to walk alongside them, Aeryn took his shoulder. "Actually, Kier, we'll let you escort her. Senate business is important for the two of you to discuss freely, and we don't want to be a distraction." She looked to Kyru. "Well, we don't want Kyru to be a distraction."

"I hate politics," he said blankly.

She bowed her head and presented Faria's chair to Kier. "Report away. Kyru and I will go and conduct some training observations. Don't be too rough with her."

While Kier emptied desperate, silent protests from his wide eyes, Aeryn and Kyru turned briskly away and strode unstoppably down the corridor.

"That went well," Kyru whispered.

"Lucky coincidence. He needs some encouragement," she cooed to her partner.

"You're a mischief, Aeryn."

"I am *not* a mischief, I'm just chaotically proactive. Used to do the same thing in Andarn when two officers who needed to coordinate insisted on talking through their Lieutenants," she returned as they rounded the corner. "Whether they admit it or not, those two need each other, and if all they're going to do is exchange stiff conversation and walk in opposing circles then someone needs to make them break the ice."

"So is this about their duty or their personal lives?" Kyru looked at her askance.

Aeryn shot back a piercing stare. "What do you take me for? I'm not some teenage bard writing gooey romance plays. Kier can teach her about the Senate. Osiris can't do that because he's been isolating himself from politics for too long to understand recent histories. He's an ancient creature, a great one, but a terrible diplomat because of his aggressive lack of trust. We need allies now more than ever. Faria, on the other hand, can teach Kier about her resonance, needs, and personability. They can share with each other what they know about her father." She looked at the window and the soft light breaking through it. "We're only bodyguards. We can protect them all we want but it won't help her rebuild Xayall's reputation in the Senate, or fill in the knowledge void Aidan left. The fight goes past the blood on the ground."

Kyru look at her for a second. "You spent a long time justifying this, didn't you?"

She punched him hard in the arm. He smiled at her, and she couldn't help but smile back. "You know I'm right," she said.

"Just nice how it works out, isn't it?"

"Yep."

Kier and Faria were left in silence. She looked around expectantly, waiting for them to start their journey. For a second Kier seemed distracted, pulling at the sleeves of his jacket. She looked back at her blankets and ran her fingers over the sculpted wooden curls of her armrests, until eventually, he spoke.

"Where would you like to go, Faria?"

She smiled. "The gardens would be wonderful. Thank you, Kier."

He gently took hold of the handles and together they moved onward.

Chapter Eleven

For being so small, Kyrryk's boundaries were well-defined. It nested in the fork of two mountain ranges, to the south of which lay the ever-expanding Andarn. An encirclement of gorges, threaded by a wide river, bordered the sovereign to the north, and above this were several small city-states, and the larger nation Hadris towards the coast. Even those who honestly knew nothing about the internal conflict were warned away from both the land itself and the direct route to Hadris by the harsh mountains.

Unnervingly direct, Kyrryk's mountain path took Bayer and Alaris around half a day to reach the jagged range, even on foot. Although still relatively close to Andarn, the seasons were markedly different here: the chill in the air a product of the altitude, not the climate outright.

Halfway along the wide, levelled mountain pathway, they came across an inn carved into the rock face, probably one of the few places between the sovereigns still finding steady business by making good use of the frequent military travellers. Assuming, of course, their takings weren't being confiscated by the occupying command.

"High Peak. Appropriate name," Alaris mused.

Bayer frowned. "It's the peak of something, all right." He shuddered and tightened his grip on the satchel around his shoulder. Alaris rapped his claw on Bayer's pauldron.

"Don't predict problems before they've happened. We should stop in and see what we can find out."

Bayer's ears flattened. All Alaris could offer in compensation was a shrug. "It's not ideal, but it's easier to get information from someone with a drink in your hand than a sword."

They pushed open the heavy door and were immediately faced with a significant number of Andarn troops, turning drink into yells and laughter, tables into dance stages, blazing forums, or blunt weaponry, and sometimes a sequence of the three. Whether they were entering or leaving the embattled sovereign, Bayer understood the need to justify either direction with a stiff drink or six.

The staff seemed to be holding their own, however – and even with the raucous behaviour at the tables, there was no sense of danger – at least, none of the bar or waiting staff looked particularly beleaguered.

Most of the soldiers were thankfully too involved in their own tales to notice the two enter. By the time they'd made their way to the bar, however, they had gathered a few glances and salutes, to which Alaris responded casually; although not enthusiastically enough to warrant an invitation to sit down.

The bartender, a black panther with a set of old scars running up his muzzle to between his ears, folding a rag, acknowledged them with a nod. "You on your way in or out?" he rumbled.

"In," Alaris replied, in a similar tone. He gestured to the rows of barrels behind the bar. "Two of whatever's your favourite."

The panther bowed his head, whipped the rag onto his shoulder, and turned to fill them each a tankard.

"You'll want more than one each if you're heading in," came a hoarse voice from behind them. A bandicoot, wearing half his armour, had lumbered up. "Must be new." He looked them both up and down, which must have been difficult for how much he was swaying. "You're a shiny fella," he said to Bayer, flicking his new suit of armour with his claw. "Super new."

"Armour's new, service isn't," Bayer growled.

The bandicoot shrugged. "Doesn't make a difference to me, we're all dirt to the commanders."

Alaris raised an eyebrow. "That bad, is it?"

The bandicoot flailed a dismissive arm. "Nobody gives a damn about this place. There's nothing to do except sit and drink and sleep and piss up the walls."

Bayer took his tankard from the panther. "I thought we're suppressing a war."

"Don't be daft," their impromptu concierge spluttered. "The only thing we're suppressing is our will to live, and the blighters who live 'ere. Saving grace is they're the only ones the commanders care about less than you."

Alaris took his tankard and laid some coins on the bar, which the panther quickly slid into his apron. "So what are all these troops here for?"

"I don't know; something important must be happening

somewhere. I'm just paid to be here, and I'm glad to be on my way out."

Bayer's tail was rigid, almost gnarled. His lip curled. "What the hell is going on here?" he seethed.

The bandicoot leaned in to get a better look at Bayer's face, seeing him hunch further over his beer, but Alaris hooked a claw onto his shoulder to bring him upright and avoid an explosive encounter.

"Listen," he said quickly. "We weren't given clear instructions – do you know where the main command centre is?"

The bandicoot rolled his arm out of Alaris' grip with a petulant scowl. "S'in the capital, in the northwest."

Bayer straightened slightly, realising his claws had marked the tankard. "What about the locals? Are they still there?"

The bandicoot spat on the ground. "Yeah, but you can ignore them. They've got no government but their village elders, and they hate us, tell their people that we'll kill them if they get in the way. So it's quiet."

Bayer fell silent again. The elders still had some say over their own people: a small consolation. He was in no place to dictate their actions, but turtling themselves in their homes would only perpetuate their lack of growth. There had to be a way to help. Maybe ousting this insurrection would carve a path for a less corrupt influence to take control.

Alaris gave the bandicoot a thankful nudge, and their guest sank into the tables further inside the bar. They continued their drinks in silence, pausing only to check over their shoulders when others came too close. Bayer finished first and immediately left, tearing open the door. Alaris saluted the bartender and followed swiftly behind him.

Bayer's feet crunched against the loose stones of the mountainside. Now on a downhill course from the mountain path's highest point, Bayer caught the first glimpse of the land he'd deserted so long ago. With the climate isolated by the tall mountain ranges and a strong, warm wind coming from the north, it would have been pleasant, were it not for the pit of his stomach sending a cold sprawl over his body.

He felt a tap on his arm – Alaris, champion of interrupting his trains of thought.

"Are you sure you're up to this?"

Bayer sucked in a deep breath, feeling the air wash down his throat. "I have to be. I should always have been, as much as I tried to deny it."

Alaris nodded. "I'm sorry you have to see it again in such a mess. Your presence is greatly appreciated though. I imagine you welcomed the prospect even less than I did."

"Yeah," Bayer responded, a little coldly. 'Welcome' was definitely a loose term at present, especially when placed in the context of his former sovereign.

With war as an enigmatic shadow, Kyrryk was deceptively barren of the smoke and devastation Bayer had been expecting. But then, the civil war had grown stale by now, and had long been directed more passively towards the antagonistic and incessant presence of Andarn's troops. With the warlords either dead or under close guard by the invading police, the fighting was more subversive – there were no battlefields here. Had the civil atmosphere in

Kyrryk not been so poor for such a long time, it would have found itself prospering under virtue of being a more direct travel route up the continent. Its containment forced other sovereigns elsewhere. Hadris particularly, a peninsular sovereign with plentiful resources and a well-controlled population, found itself in no need of pressuring Kyrryk's subjugators to ease restrictions or provide relief.

The land lacked the degree of colour and richness that Bayer remembered. In the distance, the layered fields had shown signs of activity, or at least maintenance, but they were dull and tired, perhaps exhausted, or simply lacking the population to take care of them. The speculation as to the sovereign's devastation whirled around his head in a strengthening vortex of assumptions and ire; it took Alaris to set his focus straight again.

"So, we have a long walk ahead," Alaris breathed.

Bayer nodded. "Two days away, probably less."

"All right. What do you know of the land around the capital – are there many places to hide an army?"

Bayer shrugged. "To be honest, if you're populating a sovereign with thousands of troops anyway, why bother to hide it? None of the locals will regard them as anything other than the same kind of intruder, and they certainly won't be interested in engaging them, if what that bandicoot said is true. And it's not like the soldiers will question the presence of other troops, regardless of whether they're doing anything constructive or not."

The pangolin scratched his head. "Good point. But we don't know where these troops have come from – you're inferring they're from Andarn, right?"

"Not necessarily," he partly lied. "But since Kyrryk is

under Andarn's control, if I were hiding an army here I'd dress them all up in your colours. That way it raises fewer questions, and your army is so big, seeing unknown soldiers or detachments isn't going to be uncommon."

Alaris clicked his tongue and gave a slow nod. "Can't argue with that. I can see this is something you've given a lot of thought to. I apologise that we appear so untrustworthy."

Bayer shrugged. "It's... nothing personal." A strong breeze swept across the path, stirring the stone dust around them. To Bayer it felt like a warning. Below them lay the foothills, amassed around the mountain's base as if gathering for warmth or protection. Almost like the land was trying to escape itself. Bayer sighed for thinking so bleakly, but he was looking forward to little of this, except, perhaps, the slim chance of bringing a breath of restitution to his homeland. So many difficult memories pinched at his mind that periodically he had to force himself to look ahead. He set his leather satchel on the ground and stood on a rock to scan the horizons of his former land.

"One of the warlords used to do something similar – dress his soldiers in the livery of another, and when the guards swapped duties, they would turn their weapons inwards and either hold him hostage, or kill him. His tactics became pretty infamous; they called him 'The Earthquake' because he sprang without warning and destroyed everything in his path."

Alaris rested on the hilt of his huge, double-handed sword, playing over possibilities in his mind. "Interesting. What happened to him?"

"Rumours flew all over the place back then; it's hard to tell which were worth listening to. He killed a thousand soldiers in one story, and laid down his arms in another. He could have done both. War isn't a good time for breeding accuracy."

Alaris acknowledged his sentiment but didn't reply, keeping his gaze over the distance. "Do you think we can do it, Bayer? We've got no support out here."

The ocelot took in a deep breath, leaning forwards, feeling the wind in his fur. "Greater numbers would look suspicious. We're free to use our own methods like this. Isn't that what you like as a soldier?"

"In part. I've never been completely autonomous, though."

Bayer let out a small laugh. "You could have fooled me. I'm surprised you still have your rank with your roguish tendencies." He flicked his claws in thought. "I think we can uncover something between us, but once we do, our escape will be on incredibly short terms."

Alaris nodded. "Agreed. Let's make sure this isn't a one-way trip. I want the rest of my life to be long, and not staring at a grate in the ceiling of Andarn's military prison."

"Likewise." Bayer clapped his hands together, allowing the wind to brace his back with a cold rush. "So we need to find an army? Let's start where we *know* one is right now."

Chapter Twelve

Restoring the Tor's rich gardens had not been a priority, and winter's grey veil had painted the remains a shadow of its former warmth and comfort. Large rocks, pieces of the Tor's former crest and top floors, lay embedded in the ground or on top of crushed, split trees. Faria remembered the last time she was here in the gardens; even in the moonlight of that fateful evening it had felt so calm and comforting. The shadows had been her friends back then, and silence her mantle. Now, whatever quiet she met with brought an unfamiliar emptiness, an infinite nothing that she wanted desperately to escape. Even the sounds of her own city, heavy with the noise of construction and shouts of marshalling soldiers, were not currently soothing her mood. Aeryn and Kyru had done well to cheer her with their visits, but any advice to focus on herself rather than the governance of the sovereign filled her with solitude.

Her thoughts had turned so deep that she'd forgotten Kier was pushing her wheelchair. She regarded a flowerbed they strolled past where a single circle of flowers, winter bloomers, stood defiantly next to a large piece of sandstone and its craterous impact. The small blooms, five white petals flecked with a deep burgundy in the centre, waved in the breeze.

"These are going all over the city when I'm in charge."

"You *are* in charge. But I think they're quite rare."

She jumped at his voice, and turned a shade of red so deep it became visible through her fur.

"Oh, Kier, you gave me a start. I'm sorry, I was in my own world."

He smiled. "You needn't apologise. I escape into mine, too."

"Ah," she said quietly, looking down at her hands before cocooning them in the blanket over her waist. "Still, we can have a city full of rare flowers. That can be my single unreasonable demand as a mad Empress. Does that sound all right?"

Kier chuckled. "I'd much rather deal with flowers than assassins," he replied, prompting a smile from Faria. She rubbed the soft, textured surface of her blankets as she anxiously tried to form a question. Now she had escaped her wandering thoughts, she was incredibly aware of the other fox's presence and did not want him feeling ignored. Besides, she liked him anyway, and didn't want to squander a chance for conversation, especially as he'd been her father's protector for some years now and had been absent about as often.

"Did… how did my father run the sovereign, Kier?"

The wheelchair stopped for a second. "Well, he… without meaning to sound obvious, he would always listen to others' requests, even if he knew they were unreasonable or demanding. That was one of his most important rules – even if you couldn't fulfil a demand, communicating well with other sovereigns made them a lot easier to negotiate with. He said that they needed a good moan, like anyone else. A lot of the other Representatives expect an argument from the very beginning, so you can disarm them with... not placidity, as such, but calm rationality. He'd never trust them outright, though. That was key. Discuss what you can freely, but never reveal what resources you have, and don't trust that you'll receive anything in return until you have a guarantee, or leverage, or something in escrow."

Faria grimaced. "All right, that seems sensible enough. Was it difficult, though? Do you have to be really impersonal with them?"

Kier tilted his head from side to side and sucked his teeth, trying to decide the accuracy of his answer. "Yes and no. If they think you're emotional then their emotions will rise too; they'll either try and walk over you, or get angry, or leave. For being diplomats they can have incredibly poor social skills." They passed a particularly large chunk of stone embedded in the ground, the wheelchair making a sweeping detour around it before righting its course. "Logic helps them ascertain their goals, I suppose. If you remember that everything you do is to protect your nation and the people within it, it's easy to be objective, especially when another sovereign's demands are unreasonable."

She nodded. "I see. Yeah, I can do that. I'd certainly never want to sell us out."

"No. I don't think you would," he said, idly fiddling with the handles of the chair. "You're braver and smarter than you give yourself credit for," he said quietly.

"That's kind of you," she breathed, a warm smile lighting her face. "I just worry. There's so much I need to learn; I want to do my father justice. Everyone. The city, too. I don't want to be a disappointment or a danger."

Kier felt his face turning hot. "You won't be alone, Faria. I'll be with you." He could see his breath clouding the air before him, and tried to restrain his emotions. When she leant back to see him, he caught her gaze and fell quiet while she presented him with a grateful smile.

"Thank you, Kier. That means the world to me."

He bowed his head, shying back a little. "Of course, Your High- F- I mean, Faria. I'll always serve you as I can," he stammered.

She watched him for a second, a hint of sadness creeping into her smile. He kept his head bowed and looked away over the gardens; deliberately, she thought, but she didn't judge him for it. He had been shy about her since she'd known him, and their interaction would always be complex, especially with her father gone. She hoped at least that he would be a friend, like Aeryn, Kyru, and Tierenan.

"How are the outer walls?" she asked quietly.

He turned the wheelchair towards the nearest archway leading to the city. "Progressing, slowly. I can show you if you'd like."

She shivered as the wind picked up, ruffling her blankets. She pulled them tight around her neck. "Yes, thank you."

Kier skirted the chair around more rubble and pushed her out onto the streets of Xayall. The wheels rattled on the hard stones, and on the older streets nearer the Tor where the paving wasn't smooth, it became a very rough ride. The blankets cushioned Faria to a degree, but she found herself shutting her eyes and bracing herself whenever she spied a large cobble about to run under her vehicle.

She gripped the armrests. "I hope never to be in one of these again after this."

Kier stopped suddenly. "Is everything all right? Do you need me to turn back?"

She waved her hand. "No, Kier, it's fine. I'm not used to being a passenger like this. Carriages are one thing, but in this the roads are a little more… direct."

"Ah, I see. I'll try to be more gentle. Or I can find another route if you'd prefer."

She rested her head against the chair's back. "No, I didn't mean it that way; it's not your fault. I just… this is what it is, and I'm complaining. I'm not asking for a rescue or policy change or anything. I don't want to be one of those prissy princesses that demands all the roads to be repaved in case she might possibly have an uncomfortable journey."

"Ah… I'm sorry."

She dropped her shoulders. "There's nothing for you to be sorry for, Kier. You're the one going out of your way to hand-deliver me to a broken part of the city to alleviate my boredom." She rubbed her face. "Ugh, I sound like one of those princesses already."

He gave the chair a push, trying to aim the wheels between the stones instead of over them. "Ignoring the technicalities of titles you don't have, I've never known you to be demanding. You're generous and attentive, something most sovereigns would die for in their government."

"Well, if the sovereign can hold off on dying then I'll do my best," she retorted, pulling her legs up as Kier angled the chair back to mount a step near the city walls. Ahead lay the section of the city walls that the Gargantua had crushed. Both the stone and the metal were being dismantled piece by piece. With the gigantic machine dead, it could be removed no other way.

"The Councillors and I had discussed about trying to make that an extension to the city, but it may be too dangerous."

Faria looked up at the tower's pinnacle, which listed to the East. "It's sinking, isn't it?"

Kier nodded, slowing his pace. "Yes. It diverted the flow of the moat and that's eroding the topsoil underneath it. Thankfully the pyramid shape means it will never properly fall over, but we may need to wait for it to settle completely before we can do anything, unless we just build a wall around it."

They stood opposite the wall, and for the first time Faria saw the giant tracks that drove the enormous creation into their land, resting atop the rubble. To call it a monster wasn't enough. It was a nightmare. Above them she could see flickering torches of the teams of workers on its distant walkways.

"It's very dark inside," she said quietly.

"When you're steady on your feet I'll show you around the areas we've been able to excavate."

Faria stared at it, the dark yawn of a dormant leviathan. "I've been there before. Is there anything we can use for our defences?" She pulled the blanket over her shoulders again, feeling the cold. "How many died in there?"

Kier looked away. "A lot, but we can't get to them. There's a clay-like substance filling the lower levels. It spilled out of tanks above the reactor, apparently a failsafe designed to absorb radiation, Osiris said. There... there were reports of non-Dhrakan scholars and scientists on board... and we haven't been able to recover their bodies yet." The setting sun hued the clouds overhead in a deepening blue. She looked back to Kier, who dutifully returned to her chair. "Could we go inside?" she asked quietly. "It's cold."

A semi-circle of Andarn guards standing outside the Tor's entrance greeted Faria and Kier on their return. The two foxes stopped at the base of the building's steps, the soldiers all standing above them, at attention, their collective stare fixed ahead. At the centre stood a porcupine, dressed in near-regal finery of gold and red, his nose turned up to the sky and a series of scrolls tucked neatly into a knapsack by his side. Kier and Faria let out a collaborative sigh.

"Damn it," Kier wheezed.

"Are you Faria Phiraco?" the porcupine asked, lowering his gaze but not his head.

Kier stepped forwards before Faria could answer. "This is the Empress of Xayall. It would be polite for a guest to offer courtesy to Her Imperial Highness, especially in light of his unannounced arrival and lack of introduction," he replied, stern warning in his voice. She cast him a pointed look and gripped her hands under the blankets.

The porcupine descended the steps with haughty deliberation, watching them for his entire journey before reaching Faria's chair. He inhaled a lengthy sniff through his nostrils, then bowed deeply. "Your Imperial Highness. Please pardon my unscheduled attendance. I am Barra Thrain, Senate Administrator for Representative Succession. I was hoping for an audience with your father, the Emperor. Although I am told he is no longer in office; is this true?"

Kier raised his arm to make an offended reply, but Faria stayed him with her own hand. "Correct, Thrain, he is not," she barked. "Emperor Phiraco is dead, and, as his daughter, I am to take his place as head of state and as Xayall's Representative in accordance with law and tradition. I request that you address me as Empress Arc'hantael from this point forward, or I would find you in contempt of my presence, and there would be no further meetings until an apology is issued and we are contacted appropriately."

Barra's eyes flickered for a moment, but his imperious expression remained otherwise unchanged. "Well, I am sorry for your loss, Empress. We at the Senate were concerned with Xayall's lack of communication and wished to expunge some of the rumours that have been circulating."

"What lack of communication?" Kier seethed. "We've sent out reports daily. As soon as our gates were secured I notified the Senate of our circumstances, and I know the Andarn commander has done the same with his superiors."

"What rumours?" Faria added, almost in the same sentence as Kier.

"We have received nothing from your sovereign," Barra affirmed, drawing back a little from Kier's increasing temper. "And as for the speculation, it would be inappropriate for me to divulge them in so informal a manner, especially given the unfortunate and apparently untimely departure of your father."

"What has been said, Sir Barra?" Faria punctuated.

He waited for a few seconds, gauging their suspicious responses. "There has been conjecture that a coup was held in Xayall to unseat the Emperor from his position, and that a conflict had broken out as a result, leaving the city in ruin. Given the recent upheaval all over Cadon I thought it prudent to investigate your situation in person, as our official lines have suffered from… inconsistencies of late," he finished, glancing at the remains of the Gargantua.

"That's absurd! It's not an occurrence 'of late'," Kier retorted. "We had difficulty assuring our Senate communications before we were besieged the first time *by the Dhrakans*! This wasn't a coup from within, and we have Dhrakan prisoners who have already confessed to their sovereign's actions. All of these details I have sent to the Senate multiple times, and occasionally I even resorted to hand-delivering messages directly to Representatives to guarantee any degree of reliability."

"And this discontinued why?" Barra quipped. "If you knew the importance of these messages then surely their acceptance is paramount to ensure Senate cooperation?" He looked down his nose at Faria. "We almost held a referendum to impose sanctions in your absence as we could not assure your continued involvement in Senate gatherings. As one of the longest-standing members, I'm sure you are already aware of the laws, even with your recent… appointment."

Faria saw Kier clenching his fist. She looked to Barra, making herself as tall as she could in her chair. "Kier has been governing Xayall's recovery and communicating with

Andarn to help us rebuild, and until my official return to office he has additionally been acting as Representative. As a follower of Senate bureaucracy yourself, I'm sure you understand a Representative does not simply wander off by themselves to hand-deliver letters, especially when more important matters, like citizen's lives and the reformation of order are at stake."

Barra bowed his head. "Yes, Your Imperial Highness, that is correct. As I said, I merely had concerns that—"

"Your concern is appreciated," Faria said quickly, "but I assure you Xayall will cooperate with the Senate as long as we are informed of our standing and adequately communicated with, and not just presumed to be delinquent. We are in the midst of recovering from *two* brutal sieges by the Dhrakans, and will give a full presentation as we can at the next meeting."

Barra raised an eyebrow. "You have already missed four Senate meetings, if you would pardon my boldness to say so. This is why we deemed it prudent to investigate."

"We haven't been given a summons in months," Kier grunted. "We thought the Senate had been affected by the battles as we had." He gave the porcupine a piercing stare to punctuate the end of his statement. "Evidently not."

Barra shifted slightly, almost uncomfortably so, but retained his formal indignation at the two.

"It is clear that there has been far more going on in Xayall than we anticipated," he said slowly, deliberately, throwing a derisive glare back at the fox. "I hope the rumours of corruption prove to be untrue. I look forward to your complete and total understanding investigating these matters."

He gave a swift bow to Faria and turned on his heel, sweeping into the Tor, quills bristling as he walked. The company of troops followed him inside, leaving the two foxes alone at the steps. Faria sat back in her chair and rubbed her forehead, sighing heavily.

"I don't like this. Why haven't our reports been getting through?"

Kier shook his head. "Even without the Dhrakans bringing down our walls, whoever they had sending out fake quarantine despatches may still be trying to run us into the ground diplomatically. I haven't had a chance to survey our messenger lines or send a council member to the Senate to liaise. I just... presumed the Senate was taking note and being indifferent by not responding. I'm sorry, Faria."

"I don't blame you, Kier. It's not unusual for them to respond late." She rested her muzzle in her hands, pressing her cheeks down her face in a massage of frustration. "I should have been more active. Just one battle after another, isn't it?" she groaned.

He knelt beside her, his jinbaori rippling in the breeze. "Are you all right, Faria?"

She shook her head. Her hand trembled slightly. "I'll live with it. This is all part of what my father had to do, right?"

Kier nodded. "I'll be here, and I'll help all I can. I don't trust that quill-pusher enough for you to be alone with him."

"Me neither. Thank you, Kier." She let out a tired laugh. "I wish Osiris wasn't in the desert. He's really good at deterring miserly officials."

"He's better at upsetting them, which may not work in our favour if we're already marked."

She looked up at the Tor, still beheaded, with skeletal scaffolding poking into the sky. "It would be too simple for this to just be over, wouldn't it?" She hadn't even started her reign yet, and already all she could see ahead was an endless series of hoops to jump through, a bureaucratic obstacle course completely removed from the issues she would rather be concerned with. Even with Raikali and Fulkore gone, she had no idea where the Dhrakans were or if they were planning to attack again; even with her city in tatters, suddenly it was clear that the attack on Xayall would be neither the end of the battle, and that something could be reaching far deeper into the fragile network of the continent's allegiances.

"We'll give him what he wants, but we have to be careful," she said quietly, as Kier began pushing her up the makeshift ramp by the side of the stairs. "The bare minimum. I won't give up anything of Nazreal."

"Do you want me to send more guards out there?"

She shook her head. "I don't want to arouse too much suspicion – one patrol at a time should be enough. Osiris has his crew at the Coriolis, and they're used to protecting ancient secrets. We'll just have to hope it's enough for now."

They reached the top of the stairs and paused, both reticent to enter.

"So…" Kier began, fidgeting with his ear, "should we…?"

Faria flicked her claws. "I suppose so. The sooner we can get rid of him, the better."

In a very short space of time Barra proved he had no

intention of making his stay either short or smooth. He spent hours poring over requisition papers and cross-referencing authorisation signatures. Another two-foot pile of papers to sort through still stood to attention as it grew dark. The candlelight washed the room with a soft, orange colour that would have been comforting if the candles themselves weren't inviting the temptation of a convenient and devastating fire that would eliminate the detested parchment and finish this painful drudge.

Barra had said nothing to either of them for several minutes, but sipped at a glass of water, squinting at a long parchment under perilously furrowed eyebrows.

Faria's head was getting closer to the table with each heavy second, and Kier had gone from standing rigidly by her side to draped in a chair at the table's edge, only moving himself to a more stately position when a document to be explained passed his way. They had initially dismissed the staff who came in to offer refreshments, in the hope it would encourage the aggressively fastidious porcupine to hasten, but sent for them later when hunger and irritation grew too palpable.

Kier turned his head to Faria, whose fixed gaze rested unwaveringly on the slowly dwindling pile before Barra, and gave her a timid nudge on the shoulder.

"I can stay until this is finished if you'd prefer to rest, Faria."

She leant on her arms, pushing herself slightly more upright. "No," she croaked. "I'll sleep when it's done. This is my duty, and I won't ignore it."

Kier nodded, albeit after a reluctant pause. "I understand. But tell me if you change your mind."

She smiled, slightly, then immediately her expression sank again and she pushed her face into her fists, hissing through her nose.

Suddenly, Barra shifted in his chair with a long, officious intake of breath. Kier and Faria both sat upright, expecting a ream of paper to be thrust at them. "Well, I believe we can be granted a recess for some hours," the porcupine whistled gravely, not even making eye contact with the two foxes as he stood up and walked to the doorway. He did, however, give a perfunctory bow as he reached the handle. "Thank you for your cooperation. I expect tomorrow shall be a long day."

He left, and the door shut. Faria balled her fists, which quivered impotently above the table. Kier's lip twitched into a slow sneer. Faria punched her hands into the blanket and growled. The fur on the back of her neck bristled in waves.

"Don't let him back in this room," she seethed. "I don't care what it takes, just... don't."

Kier nodded, gently moving her chair from the table. "I'll do what I can. Let's sleep for now."

She clenched her fists, scowling. "Why did he have to come *now*, when we're in the middle of all this? Doesn't the Senate have any idea what we've been through? Doesn't it mean anything to them?" She looked to him over her hunched shoulders. "Tell me this is worth it, please."

Kier sighed. "You saved the world once, and if all you ever need to do is paperwork to save it again, it's probably a small price to pay."

She rolled her eyes, scoffing. "I can handle battles; this is far worse."

Behind her, the servants snuffed out the conference room's candles and began setting the Tor to sleep.

Chapter Thirteen

Rippling currents washed over the grass fields of Kyrryk's flatlands, their harvest already reaped for this season. Bayer considered the landscape's calm desolation, the eerie feeling not unlike venturing out after a curfew had been enforced. Over the last day and a half's travel they had seen few civilians outside of their villages, which were heavily guarded and fiercely cautious of any soldiers passing by. Several Kyrryk citizens on the paths had disappeared into the trees or turned to walk swiftly in the opposite direction on their approach, a clear sign of Andarn's intimidation. Once away from the mountains, the roads had been altered from their natural curve to arrow-straight pathways, well-worn with carriage tracks and the tramping of armoured feet. Any crossroad they came to had been stripped of bordering trees, rocks or shelter of any kind, to ward off the threat of ambush. They had seen numerous Andarn patrols on their journey; thankfully none had actually intercepted them thus far. A few had given half-hearted salutes, but mainly the pair were ignored. The lack of consideration for unknown soldiers wandering a path was a far cry from the suspicion strangling Xayall at present.

The closer they got to the city, however, the more soldiers they began to see, and the warier their oncoming looks became.

Smaller patrols of two or three soldiers could be avoided fairly easily – most of those were unaccompanied by officers and the infantry seemed unwilling to add to their trials by questioning soldiers they hadn't met before. Towards the outskirts of Kyrryk's capital city, however, they faced an entire platoon marching towards them, with a staunch looking wolf, a Lieutenant, at its head. Scratches and scrapes, not impacts from heavy battles but a series of brawls and tussles, dulled his armour. He looked like he'd been thrown to the ground a few times, but the hardness in his face suggested he could give as best as he received.

Once the wolf caught sight of the two, he accelerated his pace, waving his arm for them to come forward. Bayer and Alaris exchanged quick glances, hands covering their weapons, but they obeyed nonetheless. Bayer followed a few steps behind Alaris, a steely gaze fixed on the approaching Lieutenant.

"Which squad are you?" the wolf snapped.

"None yet," Alaris replied, tapping his shoulders to denote his rank. "Perhaps you could direct us to the barracks and the commander-in-chief? I have a Warrant Officer to deliver."

The wolf hesitated upon seeing Alaris' rank, and stiffened, giving him a discerning eye. "Pardon my rudeness, Captain, but things are not easy up here. We're given little support and our supplies are low."

Alaris nodded, maintaining strict eye contact with the wolf. "Understood. That's what we're here to investigate; we believe the locals have been raiding supply carts meant for your station. I am Captain Hiryu, and Warrant Officer Kanjita here is an expert on Kyrrykian culture and localities. We're here to help, if we can."

The wolf gave a sharp but brief salute, looking to the road ahead as if already hoping for this meeting to be over. "Lieutenant Burr. Our Captain is currently in the southern outpost, but Brigadier Donamin is at the barracks. He's the resident commander of the Kyrryk operations."

"Thank you, Burr. Can you direct us?"

Burr clicked his fingers at the nearest soldier, a cheetah, and flicked his thumb back in the direction of the city. Wordlessly, the cheetah nodded and began marching back down the road past the platoon line as Burr signalled for the rest of the troops to continue. Alaris and Bayer had to quickly make way for the soldiers; the ocelot saw how stretched and disillusioned the troops were.

"They look terrible," he muttered.

The fatigue and irritation showed in the company's hunched shoulders and sour faces. It seemed like the occupation was taking its toll on both sides; not what Bayer expected. Watching the cheetah burn on his sprightly march, they followed him towards the city.

"We shouldn't be here," Alaris said quietly. "Nobody but Kyrryk should be. Our army... it's too big to fit within its own walls now. We almost need war and occupation to survive, and that's a disgrace."

Bayer felt a slight twinge in his shoulder. He slipped his

hand under the leather harness and pressed against it; memories of his injuries in Xayall danced across his mind. "Maybe... maybe they just don't know where to fight yet. Soldiers get restless without a cause, so it's up to us to show them the right one."

Bayer chanced a gentle nudge with his elbow against Alaris' arm. Alaris looked a little surprised at first, but smiled.

"You sound like me."

Bayer let out a small laugh. "Despite my best intentions I've surrounded myself with optimists. You haven't won me over yet, though, so don't go celebrating. If this sovereign can ever be free... then I'll consider changing my outlook."

Alaris laughed. "No problem. We're already partway there."

The city of Kyrryk, by comparison to other capital cities on the continent of Cadon, looked old almost to the point of being primitive. The perimeter walls were tall wooden stakes, and of the buildings within, fewer than half were made of stone, constructed instead out of clay or wood. The city lacked the vertical height and grandeur of many of the other major cities, but currently the sovereign was not in a position to make improvements. Large buildings, those previously owned by the warlords and vassals, had ornate roofs of slate and carved beams, but these were shut behind firmly locked gates; forbidden to all as symbols of the roles they played in the civil war. The conflict had rent its populace so deeply that an overwhelming atmosphere of mistrust fogged the air, and in commons goals were impossible to achieve in such a divided time. Financially, meanwhile, the all-but-bankrupt sovereign barely sustained itself with its crops, while losing huge subsidies to the occupying troops and as taxes to Andarn. A matter made all the more desperate by the numbers abandoning Kyrryk for better lives elsewhere, leaving many farms and markets void of workers. The villages of Kyrryk seemed to have a stronger foundation as defensive, isolated, self-contained units.

The streets were missing most of their paving stones, having had them torn up over the course of the war to provide extra defences to the warlord's houses, or in rebuilding bridges that had been destroyed. All that remained in the muddy gullies were broken corners and splintered rocks, which rain and surface water would expose further and drag down the slopes to a craggy pile near the city gates.

Despite the desolation, shops and stallholders still carried on their trade, although with the borders effectively closed to all but the occupying soldiers, many had foregone the use of gold and traded services and goods directly instead. Bayer could see the suspicion on their faces as they passed through, and wondered how many had been taken advantage of by the white-clad invaders. He felt disgusted to be wearing the armour, seeing how contemptuously the citizens, his former people, stared at him. They could see through his metal and flesh, scrutinise his soul as a weak deserter, he was sure of it. Maybe someone even caught a fleeting shadow of the young feline who broke from the line of refugees and disappeared in the long grass years ago, abandoning his village. The further they walked, the more his head sunk between his shoulders and the heavier his scowl became. He hadn't realised how much he had hunched until Alaris elbowed him – quickly he righted himself. No, it wouldn't do to show his emotions so readily during a covert mission. He had carried his past within him for this long, and he could carry it further yet. While he could not change it, he could at least save others from reliving it. Even while holding his head straight as they entered the barracks, he still feared the gaze of those around him.

The makeshift Andarn barracks was in one of the few stone buildings left in the city. Its original purpose – a warlord's house perhaps, or a hospital – had been stripped to the walls; whatever it had been, the space could not house all of the soldiers who were stationed there. At the very least, it was moderately defensible.

"They would put themselves in the safest place, wouldn't they?" Bayer scoffed.

"Have you ever lived inside hostile territory?" Alaris replied.

"I lived here long enough," he retorted with a steely look.

Against the walls were mismatched bookshelves, presumably taken from whichever rooms or adjoining buildings had some to spare. In front of these sat filing clerks and junior officers, sorting through papers or scribbling out notes, reports and dispatches to sign. They didn't even notice the three walking in. Led straight to a double door at the back of the room, the cheetah braced himself and rapped on the door with his gauntlet. A weary sigh escaped through the gap.

"What?"

"Brigadier, Sir, I have two—"

"Just come in. I don't have time to play 'whisper down the alley' through that blessed door."

Alaris gave a conversant smile and gestured for the cheetah to return to his post. "We'll take it from here. Thank you."

The spry cat saluted gratefully and skittered back outside.

Opening the door, Alaris and Bayer were met with the sight of a wiry chameleon, shifting papers from one side of his desk to the other sheet by sheet, striking a signature on each that was all but a single line with his ragged quill. He had three whole pots of new feathers on the shelf behind him, and a pile of expired ones on the floor near his feet. His skin colour undulated in slow ripples from dark green to black, suggesting he was either cold or angry, but likely both. He didn't acknowledge them as they marched towards the desk.

Alaris gave a smart salute, and Bayer followed his lead. "Brigadier Donamin. My name is Captain Alaris Hiryu. I'm here to investigate your supply issues."

Donamin raised one of his eyes for a quick glance, still bustling through papers, then turned it back to his desk, saying nothing. Bayer looked around cautiously, waiting for a cue from the commander.

"Is that it?" Donamin muttered.

"Pardon me, sir, I was expecting more of a briefing," Alaris replied. "I understand things are tight here."

Donamin raised his head, his scales flashing a dark brown. "Yes, they are. I don't care why you're here, just get on with it and give me your report later. I'll sign the papers when I find them. *If* you're lucky enough to find weapons or locate some of my officers and bring them back here to do some bloody work then I might give you a little introduction, but as you can see," he pointed angrily at the shelves behind him, "I'm battling more with bureaucracy than the locals right now. You want to really help? Sit at those desks and get the damned Senate off my back so we can do some military work! Or better yet, grab Councillor Vol by the throat and tell him to give me back the soldiers he stole for his personal guard. Otherwise leave me alone."

Alaris bowed his head. "Of course, sir, we'll be out of your hair."

"Scales," Bayer said quickly.

"Not even supposed to be a Brigadier – I'm a sodding chaplain." Donamin grumbled as they turned to leave. Fearing the situation's explosive nature balanced on a hair trigger, Bayer and Alaris exited as quickly and swiftly as possible, directing themselves straight onto the streets once again.

Bayer looked idly at the buildings ahead. "Well, that was…"

"Better and worse than expected," Alaris breathed. "No question of our presence, but no information, either. Let's patrol and see if we can interview some locals."

Finding a willing speaker proved easier said than done. When approached, many citizens walked away, while those further from their path skulked and glowered in resentment. When they did find someone brave or friendly enough to speak, they did not want to talk about the soldiers. The moment that Alaris or Bayer mentioned they were trying to find some wayward troops and missing supplies, they were met with sudden silence, followed by quick dismissals or fervent denials. Merchants were guarded to address anything other than their wares, and hovered over them defensively as if pre-empting a raid. Eventually, after watching their meandering and fruitless trail up the reluctant street, an old marten selling armour fittings ushered them into the back of his shop.

"You have a death wish to be asking questions so brazenly," he scorned quietly, keeping an eye on the open doorway behind them. "A false word will be a knife in your throat while you sleep, especially around here."

Bayer moved closer. "Who would do that? What's been happening around here?"

The marten looked between the two for a few seconds in dubious study. "You obviously haven't been here long. Nor should you be, if you have need to ask questions like that." He straightened, stepping back. "Nor will you be, if I answer you; it'll be your death, and mine. Better for you to leave unknowing than not leave at all."

Sensing their first real lead slipping away, Bayer thought back to the few confrontations from which he'd managed to conjure a friendly response. It wasn't something that came naturally to him, as he'd had very few people to care about since his brother died. Kier, of course, but their childhoods weren't exactly ordinary, and hadn't lead to ordinary situations or arguments; that worked to his advantage in rare occasions where 'normal' hadn't seen the light of day in a long time.

Channelling into a realm of empathy hardest for him to reach in his current state of mind, Bayer took the marten by the shoulder in a firm but calm grip. "I understand your hesitance. I grew up in Kyrryk, and lived through the civil war…" he paused, clenching his jaw, "well, I left after Andarn arrived, if you can call that a blessing. But we are not here to die, nor to send anyone else to their deaths. Something sinister is going on and we need to stop it before this sovereign becomes another wasteland."

The marten shook his arm free. "Don't think you can placate me with false hopes, boy. The war was the end of the world, but this… this is what comes after. It's evil's domain now. You won't find anything to help you, only death."

Bayer stood back slightly, realising how close he'd leaned to the marten. These people had been intimidated enough; they weren't going to be won over by force. "We have one chance to unearth the corruption here, and we won't if you don't help us. The blood is being sucked from this sovereign and spilt in the streets far outside its walls. The Senate is already painted red with the knives in Kyrryk's back. If you know something, tell us now, and we *will* fight to free you."

The marten shook his head, looking down at the floor. Alaris stepped around Bayer, careful not to advance on the creature too forcefully.

"We're not going to take anything from you but your word, and as soon as we know something we'll be back with reinforcements to root out this bad seed. I promise that you can trust us."

The marten shot him a stern look. "For your heart I'll give you some credit, but ones like you don't last long around here. Like that barracks you came from – the soldiers there aren't the same as the others who patrol the streets at night and raid our villages. There's another power in Kyrryk, and they're strangling the life out of everything, even your own men."

Alaris gave a low rumble in his throat. "That's what we feared. Can you tell us anything more?"

He was met with a grave stare. "There's more than the soldiers in white around here. Used to be dragons, there and everywhere, but nobody's seen them in the last two seasons. That's one small redemption for us, but they weren't as bad as the others here."

Bayer pressed forwards. "What do you mean, 'more than the soldiers in white'?"

"All soldiers!" the marten hissed, throwing his arms wide. "All of them, the whole land's trying to take us over! An army of every nation sits under the mountains by Tremaine, and they're breeding evil here to send it back where *they* came from, too, you can set your neck on it."

"From every nation?" The scales on Alaris' head flared. "Are they from the Senate?"

The marten's eyes flashed widely. "I don't give a damn about your toothless Senate – they haven't existed here for years, and they threw us out as soon as the war started! You're a damn fool if you think they'd ever show up to help us. This is... different."

The pangolin watched him expectantly. The armourer shifted uncomfortably, his eyes fixed on the open doorway. His voice lowered, and even as he spoke there a hint of defeat coloured his words, like the admission was enough to sentence him to a cruel and undeserved fate.

"There's a mark," he muttered. "I've seen it a few times, having to fix their harnesses. It's always on the left arm somewhere – pauldron or vambrace. I pretended not to listen, but they call it the Shadow's Claw." He turned and lifted a piece of charcoal from his spent fireplace and quickly scratched the symbol onto the dirt floor. Three curved blades, like sickles, arranged in a fan, joined at the base by a skeletal wrist, encompassed in a double ring. Immediately Bayer recognised it – the sigil carved on the armour of the soldier in the plaza brawl in Andarn. A second later the marten wiped it away with his paw, frantically brushing the black smudge to oblivion.

They stood in silence for a moment, staring at the floor.

"Which mountain are they hiding under?"

The marten looked to Bayer, fixing him in a stern glare. "I'm sending you to your death if I tell you."

Bayer kept his eyes on the marten. "Better an honourable death than a cowardly life."

The marten scoffed, but broke his gaze. "Out of this city along the road to Tremaine, over the second river, look to the west and you'll see a mountain with three peaks – it's called Eagle's Flight, if you need to ask anyone. You better not, though. Head directly to it, following the line of the forest, and eventually you'll reach a dirt path with two broken obelisks either side of it. The path will end, and directly across the grassland there's a cave."

He shook his head, glancing fretfully at the soldiers before him. "I don't know what's inside and I hope to never find out. Never find me again, if you even survive. There's evil wandering these lands, and its eyes are everywhere."

Alaris took in a deep sigh. "We're grateful for your risk. We have some hope now."

"Enough," he hissed, flicking his claw dismissively. "Get out. Just go. You've stayed too long. If I'm safe after you've gone, it'll be a bloody miracle. I hope you survive your damned investigation, but forgive me for not believing that you will."

"We understand," Alaris said, turning to the doorway. "Thank you."

The marten said nothing, turning to his desk of tools, throwing them around noisily and with general disregard for their integrity.

The two left in silence, the words lost between them a sign enough of the occupation's severity.

Checking for watchers, they made haste towards the pathway the marten had described. Bayer dug his claws into his palms. This wasn't the journey he was intending on taking, and he could feel dark shadows of his past waiting for him, looming on the horizon. Returning to Kyrryk set a cold fire in his legs that burned to take over his entire body and march him to some unknown safety.

This time, he would not run away.

Now, he would tear to the ground those who were strangling his sovereign to death.

Chapter Fourteen

I t had not been dark for long, but silence fell quickly upon Xayall during winter nights. Torches along the corridors were now completely burnt down, with only faint embers pulsing in the night like tiny, glowing heartbeats. The dark held a rich, thick quality that padded the air with calm in the absence of so many citizens. Fireplaces burned in the city, keeping the hushed buildings warm, and softly twisting smoke into the darkness.

A figure trod the cold stone passageways, his soft footsteps disturbing the frozen quiet. He stopped outside one of the smaller rooms in the Tor, where inside lay one of the targets of his mission: asleep, alone, and awaiting his recovery.

Barra had been set a simple task. He had spent the day biding time since his arrival, assessing the Tor, making preparations, getting troops in order, and now came the plan's execution. He knew he would be well rewarded – this city could well become his, in fact. He tried to curtail his excitement at such fantasies, but the promise of a city to himself, and not just an adjudicating role in the Senate, rushed through his blood and set his claws alight with anticipation. Now the time to carry it out had hit, he almost shook with anticipation of the outcome.

He stepped into the room. Small candles sent shadows dancing over the walls; the flame refracting in glass medical bottles and tubes made the room appear to undulate like ripples of orange water. In the centre lay the raccoon Tierenan, his metal parts glinting in the candlelight. Barra's first target. The 'object' he'd been told to recover.

From a pocket in his robe, Barra pulled out a small metallic orb and set it down on the raccoon's head. As soon as it touched the metal, it unfurled into a mechanical red bird. It stood upright, chirruped, and started inspecting the plates beneath its feet, giving exploratory pecks at various screws and joins. After a few seconds it stopped over a small section under Tierenan's left ear and tapped at a screw, carefully loosening it until it came off in its beak. Holding the screw firmly, the bird flicked the panel open with its claw. Underneath was wet, cracked bone, which revealed an embedded octagonal chip. Barra shook his head in disbelief at the complexity of the machine. He'd never seen anything other than armour and sword shaped in steel, but to have living flesh bonded with metal… it was both incredible and sickening.

At the chip's centre was a star of eight tiny crystals, six purple, two blue, pulsing dimly with the rhythm of Tierenan's heartbeat. The bird inspected the chip closely with each eye, then carefully positioned the crown of its head over the centre. A tiny, almost inaudible whine resounded, varying in pitch and tone. The crystals in the chip all flashed at once several times, then began pulsating in sequence – first blue, then purple, in response to noises around them. The bird inspected the array again with both eyes, then flipped the panel closed and replaced the screw.

Barra watched the tiny surgeon with great interest. He had been told only a small amount of these augmented creatures' origin, and most of it still sat above his knowledge. Nobody had told him clearly why this freakish raccoon was even important, only that he was and should be secured at all costs for 'information vital to the next stage of the plan'. Fulfilling his superiors' orders and securing his position in this city mattered most to Barra – nothing else was of consequence, and he would have time for exposition later.

The bird flitted around the room for a moment, then landed back in Barra's pocket. He looked expectantly at the raccoon.

"I'm not carrying you. Get up."

Tierenan's eyes slid open. Blank. Unresponsive. He lurched upwards, his body stiffened by months of rest. His joints resisted as atrophied limbs moved for the first time since his grievous injuries. He swayed uneasily in the bed as his metal ear twitched and swivelled attentively.

"Good," Barra growled. "Now follow me."

Barra led the raccoon along the silent corridors, pausing every now and again when the uneasy creature stumbled against the wall. It was perverse, a living automaton afflicted by the imbalance of being woken up too soon. Barra scoffed at the raccoon's diligent but clumsy pursuit, and strode swiftly ahead. In little time they reached the upper floors, and the larger staterooms. The torches were empty, and there were no guards in sight. Shadows, thick and deep, would hide him well.

"Perfect."

Barra stopped outside the large doors leading to the Empress' chamber, and from his robe drew a long, curved blade. Pausing to take his breath for a moment and quell the excitement burning up his spine, he reached for the handle.

A cold, sharp edge at his throat halted him; he froze immediately.

"Wh-who is that?" he croaked.

Camiyan slipped a paw under the porcupine's chin, grasping his jaw like a vice.

"Your death, Barra."

"N-no, wait! You don't understand, I can explain!" he pleaded, his own blade quivering in his grasp.

Camiyan drew the porcupine's head backwards. "I don't think you can, Thrain. But that's to our advantage, isn't it?"

Barra tried to twist against his captor's hold, but the officer was too strong for him. "What do you mean? Are you... are you with The Cla—?"

The otter draw clamped Barra's mouth shut, exposing his neck further to the blade pressed against it. "Part of Kura's command, here to complete the assignment. You have acted out your part perfectly, Thrain. Unfortunately for you, we had to omit the real reason for your trip here. You see," he hissed, pulling the blade inwards, "according to my report, tomorrow you will be found dead in your chamber, evidence of the Empress' continued coup against the Senate and alliance with Andarn defectors. In the ensuing battle, the loyal and heroic Andarn troops quelled the uprising. But the poor Empress will have killed herself in her bedroom, humiliated, discovered, and unable to continue the fight any longer." He flicked his claws on the blade's handle. "With you murdered at their hand, Andarn will have no choice but to intervene with the sovereign's government and take full control of all of Xayall's assets."

Barra struggled fiercely. "No, no! Haru sent me himself, he knew what he promised me!"

Camiyan leant in to the terrified creature's ear. "You're right. He knew *absolutely* what he promised you."

He jerked the knife up and back with a sharp twist, then wrenched it from the side of Barra's neck. There was a brief gasp and a hollow rattle from Barra's throat. His blade fell – Camiyan caught the short sword just before it clattered to the stone, letting his victim slump to the reddening stone floor.

Barra shakily reached for the gaping slit in his throat as his strength ebbed away, mouthing a soundless curse to Camiyan as he died.

"The Claw thanks you for your sacrifice, Barra."

Camiyan glanced along the corridor in both directions. He could hear his troops preparing themselves outside the other doors, ready to strike. They had removed most of their armour to aid with their stealth, but their weapon belts still remained, and the movement of so many soldiers was hard to mask on echoing stone. Still, it would be sufficient for a complete massacre.

Casting Barra's blade onto his lifeless body, Camiyan pushed open the door to Faria's chamber. He glared at Tierenan, standing motionless by the opposite window.

"Stay here."

A flowing veil of curtains brushed softly against his face; Camiyan pushed them aside and shifted quietly into the room.

The Empress was asleep in her bed, behind more rippling veils. To his left, near the balcony, Kier was curled over a chair, his duty as Faria's sentry giving way to sleep after Barra's endless administration.

"*Fool,*" Camiyan thought, proceeding towards Faria's bedside. Wasting no time, he wrenched open the veil and saw the young fox lying before him. He had to be quick. As he moved the blade to her throat the deafening buzz of noislessness around him began to press into his mind. Nerves, adrenaline. He shook his head to try and calm his senses. He had killed before, and this would be no different. He could not sacrifice the plan to childish anticipation.

Something was wrong.

She stirred.

Quickly he thrust the blade forwards, but a piercing, electric sound shot through his head, destroying his balance. He stumbled sideways, collapsing into the wall with a thud. As he turned he saw Faria shifting, awakening. He lunged for her again but a crushing impact flattened him to the stone floor, banishing the air from his lungs with a thunderous boom. The veils flew wildly with the force of the pressure wave; Kier launched upon Camiyan from the darkness, and struck him in the temple with a brutal punch.

The otter fell limp. Faria sat up in a wild daze.

"Kier?! What's happening?"

He ran for his sword by the chair. "We're under attack." Pulling Faria against the wall, he ran to the wall next to the balcony.

The boom had alerted Camiyan's troops, already rounding on Faria's chamber. They burst in, weapons ready, brandishing them towards the darkness.

"Captain!" one called. "Where are you? Are you hurt?"

"I can't see a damn thing in here," another hissed. "Why is it so dark – where's the window?"

Faria watched them carefully. They looked all but blind, stepping cautiously into the room, feeling with their feet, arms wavering in front of them. But the balcony was exposed to the soft moonlight and city's ambient glow – she could see perfectly. What was happening?

"She's a resonator, so be careful."

"Faria," Kier whispered.

She started, elbowing him to be quiet.

"She's not on the bed, she's hiding!" a soldier shouted.

"Faria, they can't hear us, it's all right," he said softly, calmly. "Do you have any crystals left here?"

She nodded, still wary to speak, and pointed at her father's metal worktable across the room from them.

"Can you get there?"

"Yes," she whispered.

"Good. Stay with me."

The soldiers had made it about halfway to the balcony from the bed already. They were feet away, jabbing spears randomly into the darkness. One tripped on a pile of books, his descent causing the spearpoint to lunge towards Faria's head. She dived away from Kier; the point cut through the air between them. As soon as she broke away, the guard on the floor heard her.

"She's here!" he roared.

His company moved in his direction, more urgently now

but still hindered by their obscured vision, trying to follow her footsteps. As she reached the desk another spear narrowly missed her side, thrust wildly from one of the soldiers. Kier brought his sword down on the haft, cracking the wood to hang by a few ragged fibres, then swung his pommel into the guard's forehead, rending him instantly unconscious.

Faria wrenched open the drawer and grabbed a fist-sized crystal from it. Holding it against the floor, a ripple of energy spat from its rough, unfinished surface. The stone floor buckled, and spat pillars at the invading guards, hitting many in the chest, and throwing them back towards the door. The resonance energy sparked and fizzed wildly in Faria's hand – she struggled to hold it, and the blue light illuminated the room. More guards rumbled through the door. As Kier battled their attackers, Faria readied the crystal for another burst. She held it to the floor, feeling the electric buzz pass down her arm. The crystal touched the stone, but instead of the floor shaping to her will before her, the blue gem rattled violently and fissured. A surge of blue lightning burst across the floor and up the walls, striking the legs of everyone in the room. Several soldiers fell over and Kier let out a painful shout. Faria fell to her knees. Blue sparks danced up her arm. She screamed and reeled back in pain as the blue light in her hand flashed, sputtered, and disappeared, leaving her contorted hand holding nothing but grey dust.

Kier ran towards her at her cry. Two spear points intercepted his path, jabbing at his side. A soldier reached for Faria.

A soft whistle passed the vixen's ear. A dull thud,

followed instantly by an anguished scream, stopped the soldier's advance. Her whole body pulsed, ached; she could barely breathe. Looking behind her, she saw Aeryn already knocking another arrow to her bow. Kyru landed awkwardly on the balcony platform – the two wolves had jumped from their own balustrade next door to escape the murderous intruders. Aeryn loosed another arrow into the bottlenecked troops, advancing to protect Faria, and Kyru barrelled forwards, swinging his shield into the face of one of the guards – he was missing his sword.

Kier swung his pommel into the chest of another guard with a sickening crack, then leapt back, casting his sword to the floor.

"Kyru, get away."

The wolf glanced briefly over his shoulder. Kier balled his fists, and the crystals on his ears began to shine a brilliant white. Taking no moment to pause, Kyru rolled aside.

Low, subsonic tones shook the room. The stone trembled. Kier opened his mouth, and let out a series of ear-splitting barks. Surging crescents of force flew at the intruders' heads. The soldiers dropped like stones, unconscious. Seeing their vanguard fall, the guards in the corridor turned tail and fled, the noise of Kier's barrage like a salvo of monstrous cannon fire.

When the last soldier had fallen, the hum subsided. Kier opened his fists and allowed himself to breathe normally again. Still shaking, Faria watched him, wide-eyed.

"You're… a resonator?"

He bowed his head. "Yes. I… I'm sorry Faria. I shouldn't have hidden it from you."

"But… how long—"

"Hey!" Kyru yelled – Camiyan had found his feet and leapt over the prostrate bodies of his men. In the darkened corridor, Faria saw Tierenan's ghostly stance.

"Come on!" Camiyan hissed at the raccoon. "With me, hurry!"

Tierenan began a slow run behind him. Faria struggled to her feet, shaking desperately. "Tierenan, no, wait!"

Aeryn and Kyru made it to the doorway first. To their surprise, the young raccoon had stopped in his tracks only a few feet away. Camiyan glanced over his shoulder and saw them, his teeth bared in a raging grimace.

"Get here, now!" he roared.

Tierenan began moving again; a slow, lumbering response gradually quickening as his body realigned itself.

"Tierenan, stop!" Faria called, as Kyru gave chase to Camiyan. "What are you doing?"

The raccoon stopped again, almost stumbling. Kyru raced past him.

Camiyan wheeled around, grabbing a discarded sword from the ground. "Kill them!" he bellowed.

Tierenan hauled his arms upright and fired them at Kyru. The metal claws clicked and burst from his elbows, shuddering through the air, and latched onto Kyru's neck. Metal dug into his throat; he choked, feeling the cables taut behind him. He twisted his right arm, wrapping the cord around it, then with both hands wrenched forwards, pulling Tierenan to the ground, releasing him from the raccoon's piercing grip.

"Tierenan, don't listen to him, please! We're your friends!" Faria cried, trying to reach him. The pulsing ache threw her off balance; her head pounded and her arms burnt. Her vision clouded and spun – every time she blinked her temples throbbed, and she fell against the wall.

"Kill them!" Camiyan roared again. But Tierenan didn't move, lying on the floor, catatonic, blank.

Defeated, Camiyan turned to flee just as an arrow from Aeryn's bow shot through the air and pierced the back of his left thigh. He collapsed to his knees with a yelp. A low boom echoed in the corridor, followed by a rush of air, and before anyone could tell what had happened, Kier was holding his sword at Camiyan's neck, standing on the otter's legs to prevent his escape. The Andarn Captain growled fiercely.

"Damn you all! Should have known resonators would fight dirty."

"And killing us in our sleep is so much more honourable," Kier growled, pressing his blade tighter against the soldier's windpipe.

Faria crawled to Tierenan, shaking his shoulder to try and rouse him. "Tierenan? Are you there? Please, say something!"

Nothing. His empty stare chilled her.

Kyru stepped over to them, a shadow of guilt darkening his face. "Did I hurt him?"

Faria shook her head. "I don't know. He's awake, I think… but… he seemed to listen to me…"

"Or to his orders, at least," Aeryn said, keeping her bow ready to strike Camiyan again if he tried to make a move. "He reacted to any instruction given to him – both yours and Camiyan's."

Kyru waved a hand over the raccoon's eyes. No response. "So he's-"

"A machine again," Faria growled.

She rose to her feet, shakily, advancing on the restrained Camiyan, her fists pulsing, clenched, her teeth chattering in a pained, angered grimace.

"What is the meaning of this, Camiyan? What do you want with him?"

He gave a throaty laugh, accented by the blade at his neck. "I won't tell you."

"Was this on the Senate's order?" she pressed, advancing closer. "Is that why Barra was here, to take us over, or was he a victim of your own opportunity? Answer me!"

The otter struggled against Kier's blade, which drew tighter against him, drawing a tear of blood down his neck. "Idiot girl! Do you think we'd have succeeded this far if we spilled our secrets on our deathbeds?"

She stood in front of him, her fist itching to claw his face to pieces. "I can do more than kill you, *Captain*," she said, her voice a low, guttural rumble. She knelt down to stare him directly in the eye. Her eyes shimmered, conjuring internal energy. The otter tried to turn away, but Kier held him firmly in place. "You spill more blood in my city, you *dare* to kidnap my injured friend, and you attack me in my sleep. You're despicable. You don't know what you're playing with here, and you have no idea what I am capable of. I may be recovering, but I am not a weakling, and I will not be subdued by a disgusting mercenary like you."

Aeryn could see the Empress' fist rising as if to strike. With a spitting sigh, Faria stood up and whirled around.

"Get them out. Get them all out."

"We don't know who's involved," Kier replied.

Her voice raised. "I know, Kier. I want *every* Andarn soldier out of this city. I don't care how many guards we're left with, just get rid of them. We're not safe as long as even one of them stays. Except him – throw him in a cell. We'll get information from him eventually."

She gave a commanding look to her two wolven guards. "Warn Alaris. If they've attacked us then they could be after him, too. Thank him for me, as well, but discharge him from our service. Xayall will accept no more support until we know who's on our side."

Aeryn gave a swift salute. "Yes, Faria. We'll ride out immediately. You never know, he may defect to us."

Faria shrugged. "He'd be welcome, for what little we can offer. I had thought relative safety, but…"

Kyru had carefully picked up Tierenan, cradling him in his arms. The raccoon hung limply, eyes still wide. "I'll take him back to his room," he said quietly. "I know he can walk, but… he still needs rest."

Faria stepped uneasily towards them. "Close your eyes, Tierenan," she said quietly. "Sleep again, until you're ready. But please… come back to us soon."

The raccoon's eyes snapped shut. It may be an artificial sleep for now, but it was better than seeing his lifeless eyes staring vacantly at nothing.

Faria gave a brief, thankful smile as he left. She was trying to control her weakening legs; she had not stood or walked unaided in some time, and her head spun. The sharp snap of the electric bolts in her leg still throbbed and burnt. Trying to use her resonance powers had been too much. She hoped, at least, that her exhaustion had caused the destruction of the crystal, and not that her powers were damaged outright fighting against Raikali. If she couldn't use her resonance anymore, everyone was suddenly in much more danger. Her heart raced as her thoughts began spiralling out of control. Feeling herself swaying, she threw a hand against the wall to steady herself. Aeryn ran to catch her, thinking she was falling, but the fox waved her away.

"I'm fine, Aeryn. Thank you."

The wolf gave her a dubious look. "Will you be safe here?"

"Yes," she replied, without pause. "You two are the only ones I can trust to get to Andarn safely." She gave a look over her shoulder to Kier, who had lifted Camiyan to his feet in order to march him to a prison cell. "I'll be all right. Just promise me you'll both come back. I... can't afford to lose any more friends."

Aeryn nodded. "You have my word, Faria."

Chapter Fifteen

The night sky in Tremaine appeared a deep, rich blue: the brightness of the city's torchlight seemed to illuminate even the highest darkness. Orange, pulsing daylight, swathed the city, completely eliminating shadows from the streets. There would be no place to hide tonight, no place where a citizen should not feel safe during the city's bi-annual parade to celebrate the passing of the seasons.

From an ornate pagoda overlooking the parade route, Third Prince Haru observed the dancers, soldiers and revellers that marched past, at a seat set slightly lower than that of his brother, the First Prince. The audience by the pavement were generally engrossed in the parade, but often he would see heads turning towards them. His jaw wound tight, and his nose twitched irritably; he knew they were not seeking him. All of the performers looked to his elder sibling instead, as if judging their success by his expression. Always magnanimous, Prince Lyris held a stiff, polite smile, even if at some times his cheeks fell and threatened to betray his actual mood. Being largely ignored, Haru could scowl to his heart's content and escape scrutiny, but most often found himself focusing on the chair his brother sat in, staring hungrily at its gilded surface. When he sat there, he would veil his face, and not end up looking like a fawning idiot to meaningless citizens.

For now he was glad the duty wasn't his, even if it withheld his adulation. His current position was perfect for travelling outside the sovereign, and facing fewer questions from Councillors and citizens alike. Lyris had an appearance to keep, after all: the First Seat Prince was the ruler of Tremaine outright. He governed the sovereign and was responsible for the affairs of the city overall, while the Second Seat Prince, Pirrum, had control of the military, and Haru was responsible for diplomacy with other sovereigns. The First Prince had power to veto the decisions of the other two should a plan be considered 'not in Tremaine's best interests'.

Should a Prince or Princess die or otherwise vacate their position, the Seats moved up by one and the position taken by the next-oldest living relative. Some hundred and twenty years ago, the final true King had decided that there would no longer be a 'King' of Tremaine, but that the reigning duties be split between the eldest siblings so that each was given a responsibility reflecting their age, experience, and birth order. It became most complex when there were no more siblings to designate positions to, and sons and daughters of existing princes would be considered next in line. Although the bloodlines officially ceased hostilities with each other for the sake of their kingdom, competition still arose in their promiscuity, trying to sire as many heirs as possible to occupy the highest seats more quickly. The lines of ascension read like drunken knitting, but it was accepted as a matter of course in order to keep the sovereign from falling apart.

Currently, none of the Princes had borne heirs. It was the first time the children of Tremaine's royal bloodline had gone without breeding in a long time, and many saw it as a sign of stability.

A smile crept across Haru's face.

Lyris waved at the crowd, but leant his head to one of the guards flanking the Princes' thrones. "It's a shame to need such security," he tutted. "The pagoda used to be so much closer to the street." The guard shrugged in response.

Rowan, patrolling behind the chairs, snorted quietly under the Prince's earshot. "Only so you can admire the dancers…" A quiet murmur rippled from the soldiers beside him, echoing the same thoughts. He circled around to his royal commander and gave him a quick salute, being careful not to obscure Haru's view. "We want to protect you to the utmost, Your Royal Majesty. We posted guards on the rooftops and by every corner. It's for security, but I can understand it seeming oppressive."

Haru leant in, his hand reaching for something obscured by his robe. "I even sent out declarations refusing aid or gifts from other sovereigns. Given the trouble we've faced recently I thought it best not to tempt fate."

Prince Lyris rolled his eyes. "Right, yes. Personally I think you're overdoing it. I can't see how our neighbours would be so bold. They're all toothless, even if they do whine incessantly."

The Second Prince, Pirrum, curled his head round to

Haru. "You didn't have to change my security detail," he grumbled. "My commanders were pretty confused by your additions. I *had* everything in order."

Haru's face split into a half grin, half grimace. His arm trembled slightly. "You just don't understand, do you? You sit on your thrones and hear nothing of what the sovereigns outside our borders are planning. You don't even attend the meetings I set to discuss it – I'm fed up of talking with your attendants."

Pirrum flicked his arm petulantly. "It's not important. Honestly, you cling to that position like a child when you could have been my attendant and learnt something important. There's no reason sovereigns can't come here if they want to talk. I visit Sinédrion often enough rotating soldiers into their ranks, I could probably conduct the Senate meetings myself while I'm there."

Haru's lips curled. He glanced to the street and a long, cloth-draped dragon undulated its way along the aisles of fire.

Something flicked from the dragon's cape and flew past Rowan's head. Likely taking it to be an errant sparkler or baton thrown wild from one of the dance troop, he turned to retrieve it, when a second and third whistled through the air.

Crossbow bolts.

One disappeared behind them; the second struck a guard in the chest; the third disappeared. Screams erupted from the crowd, and soldiers jumped into action. Haru leapt from his seat and onto Lyris. Rowan hauled Haru away from his brother by his shoulder, uncovering a bolt buried in the First Prince up to its fletchings, right under his ribcage. Lyris twitched and flailed, blood trickling from the side of his gaping mouth. Haru's hands dripped with crimson.

Soldiers in white helmets overturned the cloth serpent in the parade route and stormed the up the stairs to the royal pavilion.

Rowan must have seen them immediately. "Guards, defend the Princes! Take them to safety immediately!" He whirled his spear to face the approaching troops.

Haru did not move. Rowan looked to him, desperation in his gaze.

"Prince Haru, run!"

Haru glanced quickly back at the advancing soldiers and broke into a run behind the Captain. Rowan checked Pirrum, who was already being hurried away, and slowly stepped backwards, bracing himself to face the Andarn warriors. There was a dull thud against his backplate, and he felt a sudden coldness in his back, a deep, penetrating tear that pushed his stomach outwards in front of him.

"Farewell, Captain."

The agonising sharpness rose as the blade withdrew from under his ribcage. He stumbled a foot, then was pushed down to the stone by a kick to his leg. He curled inwards, turning his head to his assailant. Haru flicked the knife back under his robe and vanished among the mass of Tremaine soldiers. Within seconds the Andarn soldiers engulfed Rowan. Panicked citizens began storming towards the pagoda.

Blood poured down the steps. As swords and armour clashed around him, Rowan felt his body grow heavier and his strength slowly drain away.

"Al…aris…"

Chapter Sixteen

The mountain range stretched into the darkness of Kyrryk's night landscape, silhouettes fading into the blackening, purple sky above. They had been walking for hours. Alaris and Bayer gave each other reassuring guesses as to why they weren't lost yet, despite misgivings over the old marten's instructions, vague and ominous as they were.

"The mountains are large enough to keep in sight from a lot of directions," Alaris murmured, after a long period of silence. The cold had begun to set in, and his breath curled in a visible wisp, even against the dimming skies. The flatlands left them with no shelter; only brief spots of partial insulation from an errant earth mound or group of trees.

"If it were more obvious, there would be no secret to hide," Bayer replied, scanning the horizon. To their right, he could see a faint red light shimmering in the wind, swaying. Immediately he set a trail after it, and Alaris followed suit.

As they neared – and it took a while for it to even seem 'near' – they could see the faint illumination of two half obelisks, leaning, ancient, with weather-beaten fissures along their surfaces. The red light was a nearly extinguished fire cage bashing against one of the stones, its torch blown to angry embers by the relentless winds. Between the crumbling pillars, leading to the mountain beyond, was a series of small, round stones, planted in the ground, barely visible through the grass.

"As if this were the difficult bit," Alaris scoffed, looking ruefully back over the deserted plain. "At least we've found it."

Bayer took in a deep breath. "Now let's find out what we're up against, and see if Jed was right."

They marched into the darkness, following the stone trail. The grass thinned and the wind grew sharper, while in front of them the mountain towered into infinite shadow. The stars were no longer visible. As the space before them opened into cold, dull rocks, a figure appeared from behind an outcrop, holding a veiled lantern. Barely lit by a thin sliver of unhindered light, the grizzled corsac fox gave them a warning glare from under his hood.

"Late in tonight," he growled.

"Better late in dark than in light," Alaris rumbled back, trying to disguise his voice.

The fox made a dismissive noise through his teeth and beckoned for them to come forward. As they approached the outcrop, Bayer caught a glint of metal in the rocks above them – a crossbow, with a sniper undoubtedly laying at its trigger, having watched them traverse the plain for some distance. The fox carried a lighter crossbow made for poison darts, and just under the folds of his tattered cape he saw a poison flask, with separate spouts for dipping darts and trailing the liquid onto blades. No chances, no mercy – death would protect their secrets, and now Alaris and Bayer's lives hinged on their infiltration. There would be no escape.

The fox grabbed their left pauldrons and inspected the symbols. The light wasn't great, but any imperfections in the design would be visible instantly. He flipped between the two and scoffed.

"These are a mess; I've killed people for marks that bad before. Where did you get them?"

Bayer laid a hand on his sword, fixing the fox with a glare of his own. "I've killed people for asking fewer questions about The Claw. You should know better."

The fox's eyes narrowed, and his hand slowly sunk to his own blade as he studied the two. After a second he shook his head and moved aside. "Fine. I'm not in the mood to clean up your sorry corpses tonight."

Quickly the two went inside, moving past the heavy curtain that concealed the cave's entrance. But far from being the cragged, tiny opening they were expecting, what met them past the threshold was more sinister than darkness.

The walls, although distorted over time, were smooth, with a faint blue sheen that rippled in the shade as they passed. Lambent blue dust lay in the interwoven gaps between the smooth stones. Ahead came the growing tremor of a thousand voices reverberating in a huge chamber. Four guards flanked the opening from the tunnel to the cavern and watched them pass with disregard, awaiting the meeting within. The voices rose, shaking the walls and floor.

The tunnel opened into a huge, cylindrical chamber not unlike an open-roofed cathedral, with passages and antechambers leading off in various directions from the central atrium. Fires roared at their gaping hearths around the walls, spreading the crisp heat and wavering orange light over the floor, and the hundreds of armoured beings within. Opposite them was a large stone platform, like a stage, currently loaded with dark wooden crates of varying sizes.

Amassed in the chamber were soldiers from all sovereigns, not just the white-clad Andarn troops they were expecting. Tremaine's golden armour could be seen throughout the assembly, as well as the deep blue of Pthiris, the orange of Al-Mayena and the dark red of Hadris: all of the northern nations. The black sheen of the Dhrakans, however, remained conspicuously absent. It was a relief in a way, but the enemy had been easier to recognise when they wore the same uniform.

Bayer and Alaris edged through the crowd as quietly as they could, trying to find a space to discuss their next step without being overheard. Individual conversations were difficult to hear anyway, given the din of the clamouring voices and loud celebration going on; there was an armoury on one side of the room and a bar at the other, and neither of these would be quiet places to begin with. They found a free section of wall and leant against it, both stunned to cold silence by the sheer numbers around them.

Alaris looked about them, his stare hard. "What is this?"

Bayer gritted his teeth. "Our hidden army."

The pangolin held a claw to his neck, studying some of the faces in the crowd. "I know these soldiers. I'm not sure if I see any commanders, though..." He scanned the horizon of armour to try and find colours or tabards that denoted seniority, but with the arena so tightly packed and the general milling of bodies within, it was tricky to discern anything other than the sovereign they were allegedly serving.

"We should split up and work our way around the room," he continued. "If someone recognises me, at least you'll have a chance at getting away."

Bayer was reluctant to agree, hoping instead he could protect Alaris, but he could see no better way of investigating. There may have been no safety here, but at least he was unknown.

Hesitantly, Bayer nodded and strode into the sea of warriors, working his way around the walls, listening closely to conversations that caught his ear.

It was a frustrating crush. Group conversations swayed and merged in armoured waves, like water disturbed by creatures underneath the surface. Bayer found himself weaving between bulky soldiers with increasing irritation, and had to hold himself back from lashing out when they would swing back or step in his way, clashing against his shoulders. Eventually he broke free and skulked around the edges of the groups, trying to look inconspicuous, and picking up whatever information he could.

Unfortunately, most of the soldiers appeared to be in the dark as well; many were asking similar questions about the 'final plan', or boasting about duties they'd carried out for Shadow's Claw and who they'd replace or kill once they were in power.

"Jed was right," he thought. *"But is this it? Is this army cohesive enough to overthrow the Senate?"*

A glint of dark blue armour caught his eye. A caracal soldier stood alone by the wall, her arms folded, watching the stage with a misanthropic countenance. Her armour was rounded, unusual amongst the angular or fluted designs popular in the southern sovereigns. A Pthiris armour set. Her cloudy green eyes were wide but disinterested, and she definitely seemed like she'd had her fill of company for the evening. The way she watched the others suggested more than an unwilling participant in company, perhaps a deeper resentment for her surroundings. Shared disdain could be a useful opener for some information. And if she *was* actually from Pthiris, then maybe he could find another way in to a conversation. He straightened himself and strode to her. She refused to acknowledge him as he approached, but he saw her grim expression hardening with each step. She probably expected a pick-up, and in a way, she wasn't wrong.

"Excuse me, you're from Pthiris, right?"

She threw him a dismissive scowl and rolled her eyes back to the stage. "Not interested. Piss off."

"Do you know a Commander Mai Enyart? A soldier, would have returned there about four years ago?"

"No, and I said piss off!" she growled, tensing against the wall. She turned to leave.

A cocky grin split Bayer's face. He felt low even putting on the act. "It's just that he said he'd never let a female into armour, because they'd be afraid to dirty their claws punching someone."

Her fist whipped round; he blocked it just in time. She launched a claw at his breastplate collar and pulled it, and him, towards her. "The *hell* did you just say?" she roared, teeth bared at his face. "I'll show you how dirty my claws

192

have been, Andarn maggot!"

Bayer held up his hands, his faux arrogance replaced with grave sincerity. "Right, I'm sorry, but you look like the only person who will give me the information I'm looking for – I'm new here, and nobody is talking. For what it's worth, I do honestly know a soldier in Pthiris called Enyart, or at least I do if he remained a soldier when he returned."

She glared at him for a few seconds, her dusky green eyes piercing with rage. "You're an ignorant son-of-a-bitch," she scoffed. "Did you honestly think you had to spout that chauvinist drivel with me? I'm a soldier, and you can damn well treat me like one from the beginning. If you ever try that again I'll be wearing your face as a gauntlet, so I can punch you every single time I take a swing." She pushed him roughly away using his breastplate and cracked her knuckles. "And believe me, it happens a lot. This isn't a place for ignorant rookies, and I don't take disrespect lightly. What do you want to know?"

Bayer felt very small, and was suddenly incredibly hot underneath his armour. That had been bad judgement on his part – he wasn't used to approaching female soldiers, especially ones so outspoken. He looked about for a second, trying to find some adequate words to respond with. "Look, I'm not a rookie," he retorted eventually. "I'm just new here."

"I don't care. This isn't some high-class secret society that shakes hands to pass gold around. Just another warfront."

"So we *are* going to war, not just creeping around stealing supplies? That's what I'd been doing. I thought we were just trying to make money selling secrets and weapons," he lied, attempting genuine confusion. "Do you think the Senate will put up a fight?"

She shrugged. "I've heard the two armies protecting it are supposed to be fighting each other, so I doubt they'll have any resistance to offer."

"But how are Andarn and Tremaine going to war? If you were going to do that, isn't it smarter to just take them down from the inside? We have a lot of soldiers here."

"It's not enough. Even if we get everyone an officer's position, the normal soldiers will still know they're being led around with a rotten carrot." She flicked dirt from her gauntlet. "Better for us to let them do it themselves. Give them enough of a push and they'll wipe each other out. Then we can take their places when there's fewer left to object, and they're demoralised from losing."

Bayer was on thin ice. Asking too many questions would destroy his illusion. She would be quick to notice it, and would probably kill him. He had to be subtle. "So you think there's a place for you at the top in all this?"

She shot him a sideways glance. "I'm a soldier, not an officer. I've no interest in taking up authority, only in righting injustices."

"You don't see this as taking up authority, making yourself an arbiter of a corrupt government?"

Her face broke in a hard scowl. "Don't patronise me. Once this is done I'm going home. The soldiers will be gone, and I'll be able to keep it safe, and help it become what it was always meant to be – peaceful and respected."

"I didn't realise Pthiris was so corrupt," he said, muted.

She shook her head with an exasperated laugh. "Idiot. I'm not from Pthiris. Pretentious snobs, the lot of them.

Too arrogant to involve themselves with anything other than preening their own tails. I'm from Kyrryk."

Bayer's eyes flared for a second. "You're... from here?"

"What, does that shock you? Am I too articulate, too clean, too well-fed?" She rounded on him. Even though she was his height she looked physically stronger, and certainly was far bolder and more aggressive. She pounded his armour with an accusing claw. "You think we're all destitute peasants? You Andarn braggarts are all the same, looking down on us from your whitewashed castle. Drag your face in the muck for a few seconds and you're no different from the rest of us. You're only in it for the money yourself – thieves aren't soldiers. You don't know anything."

Bayer swatted her claw away, glaring fiercely. "Look! I'm not making any accusations, and I'm not an Andarn soldier! I'm from Kyrryk too."

She stared at him in silence, and he returned the action coldly.

"I ran away after the war," he said, through his teeth.

She rolled her eyes. "After the war, huh? How pleasant for you to think it ever ended," she said bitterly. "Every day the soldiers marched around suppressing us to the brink of starvation. Any longer and we'd have become an empty vassal of Andarn's perversion. It was only when Kura came along that we banded together and started resisting. He taught us to fight again."

Bayer leant in darkly. "How do you know you're fighting for the right people? You'd let a stranger take you into battle against an entire continent's worth of armies?"

"Don't preach at me," she flared. "You might have suffered the battles, but the conflict stayed long afterwards.

You have *no* idea what we went through just trying to stay alive. The people I fight for are the ones left in the villages who have no hope. Kura's no stranger to our struggle – he's one of the old Kyrryk warlords, and one of the few with enough power to help us stand independently. He infiltrated the Andarn army upon their invasion and has been undermining them ever since, getting our soldiers into their ranks and placing Shadow's Claw members in the Senate. Without him we would have nothing. We've been laying traps for the Senate for years, organising raids and turning sovereigns against each other to distract from our presence. We even helped the Dhrakans invade and suppress Xayall, for all the good it did us. We started making a move at the same time, but they withdrew and disbanded before we could do anything."

Bayer's fists balled. "Do you really think this is the way forward?" he gnarled. "Do we need to start a war to end another?"

She flicked her hand dismissively, looking away. "I gave up trying to think about that. Kyrryk is so deep under Andarn's foot that the only way to get out is to remove them completely, and they won't go without a fight." She gestured to the soldiers standing around them. "We're from everywhere. The ones from Kyrryk are the ones fighting for what's left of our sovereign, the others are opportunists, anarchists. But they're opportunists who see the corruption and want to take it down. Nothing comes of sitting under a rock."

Bayer shook his head. "It won't work. You'll end up going down the same path hoping for a different destination, and sowing the seeds of another revolution under your feet. A government formed by violent activists is only going to collapse more quickly than one forged by diplomacy. You can't force understanding at the point of a sword."

She scowled at him. "Why are you here, then, thief? Is picking pockets too far beneath you?"

A roar burst from the crowd on the other side of the room, followed by a clamour of angry shouts.

Alaris had been caught.

Chapter Seventeen

The voices in the atrium hummed through the walls to the adjoining passageways. One larger, darker cave, barely lit, droned with the echoing cries. Several figures waited in the eerie, still gloom, performing a tense exchange.

The heavy padding of Anserisaur feet reverberated in the gloom. The creature stopped by the circle and its rider dismounted with a flourish.

"It's done," Haru hissed. "The Tremaine military will be mine upon my return." He listened at the echo of the rumbling mass beyond. "Raucous grunts. Soon they may be too drunk to rally."

His comment disappeared into the darkness, the hulking bear to his right saying nothing but narrowing his eyes with disdain, and the four young figures opposite them continuing with their work, assembling small metal components onto a larger, central piece. Behind them, another watched, his black muzzle rendering him almost invisible in the shade, his long dark jacket and high collar obscuring him even further. The wolverine's claws flicked deep in his pockets as he watched his metallic servants. A construction of silver and gold, it looked like a crossbow with bulbous, rounded guards for the handle that swept down where the wielder's arm would rest under the stock. At its front were two short blade-like protrusions with a hollow between them, and at its midsection was a spherical hollow framed by a matrix of gold metal. Behind the bladed tips, mounted along the weapon's body, were dozens of tiny gold needles pointing forwards, and on the swept metal stock a circular handle attached to a dial. It was alien, unlike anything Haru or Kura had ever seen.

"This takes time and precision," the wolverine rapped. "Or would you rather it explode in your faces and leave your rebellion headless, like the Dhraka?"

Haru flexed his claws and made a sucking sound through his teeth, staring at the ones putting his device together. They were young creatures, mostly from tree-dwelling species, and each of them had some metal augmentation or another, be it a hand, leg, eye or other part of the body. Astounding craftsmanship, but the frailty of the children they were attached to created a marked ghostliness to their additions, an echo of the emptiness they were fed with. But such was the nature of this technology: arcane, distant, and incredible.

As one the young animals stopped and stood up, their work complete. The wolverine removed his right hand from his pocket, revealing himself to be holding a metal box. His fingers twitched and flicked constantly, unable to remain still. He lifted his other hand and gave a series of rapid, unnaturally fast clicks, and from the shadows beyond came another young creature – a ferret girl, slender, with an ashen face. Her head sagged and her eyes were cold and blank, but in her arms she cradled a small cloth bundle which, when commanded by the wolverine, she unravelled. A short, silver staff, entwined with blue crystals along its handle, glinted in the light. Its sharp, spear-headed point gleaned with its expertly-hewn edge. Haru's eyes widened hungrily.

"This is it? This is the weapon?"

The wolverine took the rod and placed it gently within the chamber of the device on the floor. A few seconds later he opened the metal box and removed a small crystal orb, wrapped in twisted metal bands, and placed it into a mount in the stock. The metal let out an approving hum.

"This is a resonance cannon. It took some time to modify it for a non-resonator's use. It is in a state of constant activation, and as such your time to use it is limited. I can replace the crystal battery, but the structures within the staff cannot be reworked without the original author, or a resonator of equivalent ability."

"The first is dead, and the second soon will be," Kura rumbled.

The wolverine let out a disgusted snort. "You are wasting an opportunity. She could be controlled, in time."

"We do not have time, and I will take no more chances. We will succeed where Dhraka failed, and it will make no difference. Did you discover what they were searching for, other than the resonators?"

With a grimace, the mustelid shook his head. "Their interrogation was interrupted before they could uncover anything, and when the siege was broken none knew where Crawn had gone; no answers were left before the dragons fell into chaos. I only understand they were looking to control Xayall's crystal resources."

"We should have that in hand before long," Kura huffed into the darkness. "What happened to the relic found in the crystal, the black stone? Did the Dhrakans put it to good use?"

The wolverine's hands pulsed erratically. "They were able to extract the artefact from the stone with my assistance and equipment, but after that I was left behind, so I did not witness the final results. Given we're not currently in audience with it, a reasonable assumption is that the artefact was destroyed."

Kura's eyes narrowed, keeping a firm gaze on the wolverine. "Apparently so. I'm surprised you were able to escape, given your involvement." Haru folded his arms. "Can we guarantee it wasn't your equipment that failed them? What measures have you put in place to ensure this device won't go awry? Or the bombs? I've heard what these crystals can do."

The wolverine gestured to the young creatures around him; the ferret glanced up at him furtively, then stepped backwards. "These have been docile and obedient since their implementation with my technology. They may even be at your disposal, should you succeed. Do not be fooled – the pieces I make are delicate and precise, hence my need to retrieve the advanced prototype I sent with the Dhraka to Xayall. The weapon in front of you, though, is an investment in your victory. I hope it shall be returned with interest and protection."

Haru knelt down and ran his hands over the surface of the metal, breathing ravenously. "You've tested it?"

The wolverine regarded him with a derisive sneer. "It follows the same structure and mechanism as the other devices I've constructed. It's simply bigger. The parts are fully functional, so there is no reason that it should fail."

The mongoose lifted the weapon to brandish it, cradling the stock in his left hand. He gave the wolverine a stern glare. "If this doesn't work, I will flay you."

Kura let out a single, loud grunt that echoed through the chamber. "If that fails it will only matter to you. I have power enough to take down the Senate, and there is a whole army behind us. You place too much importance on your own role."

Haru reeled back, pointing the weapon at the shadowy bear. "Don't get arrogant with me, Kura," he seethed. "You would never have started a war against Tremaine alone. Your army is pitiful in comparison to the forces loyal to me. I gave your sovereign border disputes, murders, skirmishes, terrorist attacks – everything to unsettle the ones who weren't under your control. You may be leading the charge, but *I* am the one casting fear into the heart of Andarn to justify your battles!"

Kura loomed over the mongoose, claws flexed. "We will see how effective your weapon is when next to a creature that has natural resonance ability. If you fall, I will not avenge you, nor regret your loss. You have been useful, but do not consider yourself anywhere near as strong as I am. Be grateful you are still alive to crave the power you hold."

Before Haru could respond, cries rang out from the hall beyond.

"Sounds like your troops are getting fired up," the wolverine muttered.

Kura said nothing, but marched towards the veiled doorway leading to the stage in the domed chamber. Haru gave the dark scientist a wary look.

"You've survived this through our charity so far, Talos. The Dhrakans would have torn you to pieces fighting over you. Keep those crystals safe for me and I will ensure you will have everything you need."

The mongoose spun on his heel, the cannon-like device held tightly in his grasp, and followed Kura.

Talos grinned in the darkness and addressed his young companion, the ferret, who held a tiny mechanical bird in her hand. "Lucky for us we do not have to stay around once this is over. To the victor the spoils, eh, Feith?"

The ferret said nothing, but gazed solemnly at the bird.

Bayer pushed through the crowd, followed closely by the caracal, as a mob of soldiers wrestled Alaris onto the stage, piling on top of him. The pangolin kicked and elbowed, and threw a soldier clean off the platform with a wild swipe of his claw. More assailants clambered up to subdue him, and eventually, he was held, two soldiers at each limb and one with an arm crooked around his neck. As Bayer reached the centre of the room, he caught a desperate, warning glance from Alaris, and stopped, his hand tightly around the hilt of his sword.

The crowd began a slow chant: "Kill... kill... kill," rising in intensity. The soldier around Alaris' neck drew a sword and held the tip at the base of his throat, a goading smirk stirring the crowd into a baying frenzy. Just as he readied his arm to strike, a crack, like splitting rock, hit the room, and a pillar of stone burst from the stage, wrapping itself around the executioner's elbow, halting his strike.

Kura lifted his hand from the stone floor, revealing a deep red crystal embedded in his hand. As soon as Alaris saw the figure before him everything fell into place. General Kura Gallis. The corrupt officer Aeryn caught trying to smuggle weapons into Kyrryk two years ago, the one who had her imprisoned. The arbitrator of the conflicts and skirmishes all over Andarn.

"Settle down," Gallis boomed, his words rumbling over the room without even raising his voice. He stood to his full height and strode slowly, allowing his footsteps to echo over the murmuring currents of anticipation in his soldiers. Alaris could only watch, the sword still pressed against his windpipe.

Gallis stopped opposite him and grinned, a deliberate and terrifying expression well-constructed over years of menace. "Captain Alaris. I see you responded to my summons after all. How dedicated of you to find me here, instead of obeying my orders and remaining in Andarn."

"I never trusted you, Gallis," Alaris spat. "I should have guessed you were behind this after you squeezed out of your court-martial two years ago."

The grin disappeared from Kura's face. "Yes, I have your division to thank for that. I was disappointed that your she-wolf friend is no longer a fugitive. It seems we share our fortune in being granted exceptional pardons. A mutually beneficial form of corruption."

"Aeryn's exoneration is nothing like *your* disgusting exploitations," the pangolin growled. "You're trying to enslave the whole continent."

"They are already enslaved," Gallis muttered. "I will be an orchestrator of freedoms the likes of which Cadon has not seen for generations. It takes corruption to beat corruption, Captain. An honest creature will never prevail against a dishonest one, because he will never want to dirty his hands. The citizens are impatient, unruly, and quick to anger, but apathetic without a cause. They have no idea of their own power. Not one of them will ever have the means to stand up for themselves and change the country as is their birthright, because they are too far removed from the incestuous families of influence. Their ideas are ignored, their houses robbed, and their borders crushed every day by those who have and will always have the power."

The bear turned to his audience and cast a claw at Alaris. "This is an example of the ignorance that has let tyrants reign for centuries over this land. When Kyrryk fell into civil war, the Senate sought fit to police our battles with their own sense of justice. Can anyone tell me how a commander of a sovereign so rich, who has never set foot in this land, dare to think he knows what is best for this land and its people? The civil war was brutal, but it was *our* war, and it was necessary."

Murmurs swept over the hall. Bayer gnarled his teeth; behind him the caracal watched intently.

"War is never necessary," Alaris hissed. "All you'll do is spurn hatred from the ground, and then, like *you* did, it will rise against you and bury you. You will always fail."

Gallis' teeth glinted in the firelight. "We will tear apart anyone who stands in our way. They will fall."

Alaris roared defiantly. "Any warrior can attack a few soldiers at a time, but someone who stands in defence can protect thousands. Those who protect will always have the greater force, the stronger shields, the higher walls, the sharper swords. All you have is greed."

The bear's expression flickered with opportunity. "This creature thinks we are underprepared," he called over his consumed audience. "Many of you do not know why the war started. Like all wars, ultimately it was a struggle over power. A power that could end all battles in favour of whoever controls it." He strode to a pile of wooden crates behind Alaris and pulled from it a shimmering blue stone. "These crystals."

Gallis continued, eyes wide. "These were found in this very chamber by a creature that deserted my own household. He informed another warlord of his discovery, hoping to buy his way into to power and protection. Unfortunately for the deserter, I had sent trackers after him, under orders to kill without mercy. My executioners laid claim to the trove of crystals, and when the warlord appeared, *that* was the first conflict of the war. Allies and enemies alike marched onto the battlefield and rallied support from anywhere they could, until all factions had been either enlisted or neutralised. Chaos ravaged the land, destroyed the villages, killed thousands. And not a single being knew where the crystals had come from or how to use them. Except me."

He held out his claws, basking in the light of the flames. "I knew that this war could not be won alone, and that there were sovereigns eager to give anything for information on these strange crystals. I contacted Dhraka and informed them of the horde I was trying to defend, and immediately their commander sought to gain control of it. I am not one to be conquered or bought, and I forged an alliance instead.

We split the crystals and artefacts between us, and agreed to exchange munitions, diplomacy, and acts of espionage to further our agendas. They had access to technology that could awaken the crystals' true potential, and we had control of the resources."

"By that time, however, Kyrryk's war had spread beyond our walls and Andarn had blundered its way inside, thinking it a mere territory dispute. Luckily for us, their arrogance paved the way for their ignorance. I moved into hiding to protect the crystals, and the Dhrakans swore they would join us in a victory that would secure not only the fair representation of our people, and theirs, in the Senate, but for all people on Eeres. We were to become a utopia."

"The Dhrakans, however, were greedy, weak, and too ambitious. Their plan was always to decimate and conquer, not to subvert and rebuild. It was *our* network that enabled them to invade and lock down Xayall, but they were brought down by that single, pitiful city through poor leadership and inept battle tactics, blinded by the betrayals they made with their own avarice."

"If he knows about the resonance crystals, there's a chance he knows about Nazreal," Bayer thought, his body cold. *"Xayall will be next."*

"But we are still here!" Gallis roared. "We have survived! We are superior! Through years of subterfuge, we are ready to cut the head from the snake that has been constricting the lives of everyone under the Senate's dismal rule. Observe our arsenal."

Haru stepped forwards grandly. The device in his hand pulsed and whirred. He turned the dial on the side and the array of needles spun intricately. Raising the weapon aloft, he pointed at the wall above. With one pull of the trigger a shimmering orb of heat formed around the top, then ignited the air in front of it, causing an explosion of fire that streamed over the shocked soldiers. With a second flick of the dial, an icy blast surged from the cannon and froze three of the wall-mounted torches. Another twist, and a lightning bolt flared out, exploding the metal fitting and leaving a smouldering crater in the wall.

"This is only a small demonstration of our power," the mongoose bellowed triumphantly. "With these crystals, we are unstoppable."

Gallis turned to Alaris with a slavering grin. "And so you see, pangolin, we can attack as many of you as we like."

The colour drained from Bayer's face. He stepped back, half tripping. The caracal braced him with her arm, watching him carefully. She eyed her General suspiciously, looking back intermittently to check Bayer.

Gallis raised his fist skywards, and the soldiers raised theirs too, shouting as one in a fierce testimony to their leader's strength.

"We will be the ones who bring true unity to the world!" he roared. "The Shadow's Claw fights for all!"

"You fight for yourself!" Alaris bellowed, his voice strained by the wrenching of his neck. Kura grinned in sardonic expectation.

"Do tell, *Captain*."

"This isn't justice, it's murder!"

Gallis leant in, his breath hot, his teeth wet. "The Senate's executive order to dispatch Andarn troops into Kyrryk gave them license to murder hundreds of our people. They murder hundreds more each day with ignorance, ambivalence and neglect; not just in our sovereign, but in all sovereigns. As they persecute and criminalise us for defending our own land, they should be held responsible for their actions." He stood tall, leering coldly at the pangolin. "As will you be."

"I have done nothing but protect Andarn's citizens!"

Gallis' deep laugh punched the room. "You have indeed. An honourable and commendable soldier. Which is why it shall be a greater blow to the army's credibility when they discover how badly you betrayed your sovereign."

"I'm not joining you!" Alaris spat, resisting against the soldiers holding his arms.

"You have already done all you need to," Kura sneered. "I called you back to Andarn to have you arrested for plotting the murder of Councillor Mattok. Even being here now, nothing will change the verdict handed to you. Your fate is already in hand."

Alaris laughed. "That's ridiculous. You're creating a lie that needs more lies to support it. Better to kill me now."

"Your frantic denial will be a better testimony of guilt than your death, especially when faced with *overwhelming* evidence. We will succeed. We already have reports of your early desertion of Xayall and unexplained absence during the time of Mattok's death, and proof of your presence at his death is only a few drops of blood away." He leant in even closer, his barbarous eyes flaring. "And, as if this plan could not get any better, here you are in Kyrryk, having fled to escape scrutiny and trial. We may even be able to hold you responsible for the coup, given more time. You were going to be a scapegoat to pry us further into the military, but now you have become the perfect alibi for our complete absolution."

"You won't win!" Alaris barked. "You won't survive against the Senate's armies."

Gallis' massive paw closed around Alaris' neck. At the bear's will, a pulse of energy flashed from the red crystal and the stone restraining the soldier at Alaris' arm crumbled, then reformed around the pangolin's claws like stocks. With his trunk of an arm Gallis lifted Alaris into the air. The pangolin wrestled to try and slip free. His legs thrashed against Gallis' thick chest, but the bear's huge claw gripped tighter, trapping his throat with crushing strength.

"Such ambition for a creature so low, and so rare. Where did the pangolins go? Were they eaten into hiding, or do they travel the shady market squares, selling their scales one by one as phony medicine? Your sentence will be a fitting tribute to their scarcity."

The crowd jeered and bellowed; Bayer lunged forwards as Alaris was thrown back to the soldiers, who once again restrained him, this time with chains and manacles.

"Alaris!" Bayer cried, drowned by the cheers around him. The caracal pulled him back.

"Don't be stupid, you'll be killed!"

"Alaris!" he yelled, louder this time. As the soldier next to him turned his head in surprise, she wrenched Bayer from the centre of the crowd and pulled him into a side chamber.

"You're walking into death tonight, you idiot!" she hissed, slamming him against the chamber wall. "Why the hell are you so concerned about that spy anyway?"

He had no answer. She drew her sword, fixing him in a vehement glare. "You..."

"Hold your sword!" he hissed. "You have no idea what

you're supporting here! You're signing the death sentence for Eeres if their plan moves ahead!"

"Don't patronise me. The hell do you know about it?" she spat. "There's no-one else to fight for us. You're just trying to protect the Senate and its gold-lined pockets."

Bayer rolled his vambrace under her sword and pushed the blade away. "I don't work for the Senate!" he growled. "I don't work for anyone."

She threw her free arm out. "Great, that's a world of difference. You want to save him despite what he's done? What the hell's wrong with you?"

"Look!" he growled, "I was sent from Xayall to protect him, where he had been stationed after the Dhrakan invasion. He is one of the few people in this world worth protecting, and I can tell you where every single one of the others are too – inside Xayall, *and* in the Senate! What Andarn did to Kyrryk isn't what the Senate ordered – the soldiers were panicked, inexperienced, and greedy. *They're* the ones who should be held accountable, not a whole sovereign of innocent citizens. If Gallis puts his army into place then everyone will suffer exactly the same fate that we did. How many of these soldiers around you now have the interests of the world at heart? Would you trust them to look after your villages? All they have in their eyes is ambition and greed. A real soldier protects the weak and stands their ground – soldiers don't start wars, they *end them.* Gallis is the worst of any – he may even destroy the world if he gets too far, just like the Dhrakans tried to."

"Destroy the world – what do you mean?"

Bayer paused for a second. He had to earn her trust, and soon before the opportunity trickled away. "Those crystals, this enormous vault they discovered, is more dangerous than any politician, any general. They can't be controlled."

The soldiers began moving, gathering arms and armour.

"Ridiculous!" she scoffed. "How do you know?"

"I've seen it! Those tremors, months ago, do you know what they were? They found a city, thousands of years old, which held those same crystals. One person, one resonator, like Gallis, gained control of it for a few minutes and the world shook, and it would have crumbled to dust if it hadn't been stopped. Eeres *trembled*, do you remember that?" He grabbed her arm desperately. "They have no idea what they're doing! We have to stop them. You're wrong if you think the only way we can survive is to murder every seat of power that wrongs us." He balled his fist, his eyes not burning with anger, but determination. "Even if we lose those we love most, there are still a million others who need to be saved, lost in the dirt and darkness. I refuse to be fooled – this country needs to be healed, not dragged into war. The fighting won't end here. Gallis wants to march over every inch of land until it submits to his command. And do you really think the other sovereigns will be fooled into submitting their territory to a subversive, charlatan leader? They'll fight back, and the whole continent will be covered in death. It has to end."

"What would you do, then?" she shouted. "We're alone here!"

"No." He saw the fur on her neck stand on end as he fixed her with a ferocious stare. "No, we're not. We can still end this war, if we strike at the right places, at the right time. If you're with me, it'll double our chances."

She looked to the rallying troops in the adjoining

chamber, hearing the rising war chants that began shaking the stone around them. She shook her head, letting out a bitter laugh. "You don't even know their plan, and you're going to jump in head first. That's the dumbest strike I've ever heard of."

"Then tell me what you would do."

"*Tell* you? I would have killed you already!"

"Do it, then!" he barked. "Take a side! But either way, I'll be right, and you'll be left picking up the pieces of a world in chaos."

She paused with her sword brandished between his eyes. Her grip was strong; the tip barely even twitched. Her entire frame was rigid, strong, poised to strike. Only her eyes showed the faintest hint of hesitation. He said nothing, but kept staring her down. Her grip tightened on the sword. For a second her eyes flared with intensity, then they softened, and she let out a sigh.

"The army here is marching on the Senate, to storm the building and make it look like a coup," she muttered. "They will be disguised in Andarn and Tremaine colours. Meanwhile, other Claw agents have been instigating a war between Andarn and Tremaine, the battleground for which will be the mountain valley between here and Kyrryk. They're going to blow up the cliffs using crystals mounted into bombs and kill every single soldier loyal to the sovereigns, and the Senate's remaining protection."

Bayer balled his fist and raised it to his mouth. "We need to warn Jed Othera in Sinédrion," he said quickly. "They may be able to defend the Senate."

"What about the armies?" she said, not taking her eyes from him for a second. "You won't stop them from being crushed by the rockfall."

He stared back at her. "If I can free Alaris, he could stop the Andarn army from taking up the position to be ambushed and withdraw from the battle. I know he could."

She shook her head. "Pretty damn ambitious, if you ask me."

"I have no chances left to take," he replied gravely. "I have to believe in those who led me here, and in myself."

Her sword point remained steady at his head. "And me?"

"I believe you'll do what you need to do. If that's kill me, then so be it."

They stared ardently at each other for a few seconds more, then she lowered her sword. "I haven't ruled it out yet. For now I'll see your argument. I'd only go back home after this war is fought anyway, if I didn't die valiantly in battle. At least this way I might save other sovereigns from the same fate as ours before doing so."

Bayer let out a breath as relief like a cold fire washed over him.

"When we're through, I'll make sure Kyrryk is protected."

"It already is," she retorted, "by me. My name is Raede. Raede Faolan. Remember it, because I'm coming to find you when this is over."

"Good," Bayer said, looking into the chamber. "If you can get to the Senate before the army does, warn Jed that Shadow's Claw is coming. Tell him everything, and tell him I met you. My name is Bayer."

"We have an underground spy route to Sinédrion that I'll take. It's too small for the whole army to go through, but it's faster."

"Good. I'll free Alaris."

As he went to leave, she grabbed his shoulder. "Are you sure you can fight them? You saw what he can do, right?"

"I know," he replied. "He's strong, but I've fought a resonator before."

She grabbed his shoulder and wheeled him round. She was smiling, an expression that relished the battle ahead. "Good luck, Bayer."

He wheeled out of the chamber and into the atrium, where the soldiers were forming a loose muster near the weaponry. Their commanders were beginning to shape the ranks for battle; with luck they would be slow enough for Raede to get to Sinédrion before they even gathered pace. He looked to the stage. Gallis had Alaris captive, bound in stone manacles; he and Haru were talking amongst themselves. As Bayer pushed through the massing warriors, Gallis grabbed Alaris by the neck and began striding towards the soldiers at the side of the stage. As Bayer reached the platform, Haru cast him a surprised glare.

"What do you want?" the mongoose snapped.

Bayer froze, locking his eyes with Haru's. "I want to throw the traitor into chains," he growled, lacing his tone with as much slaver and bloodlust as he could muster. "I want his blood to carpet our march to victory."

Haru gave a sly grin as he watched Gallis toss the pangolin at the ravenous, baying soldiers. They wrestled him into submission and between the six of them carried him into a tunnel.

"Go ahead, join them," Haru sneered. "They're taking him to the Andarn outpost in Kyrryk."

Bayer leapt onto the stage. He glanced back as he passed Haru. One backhand swing of his sword would catch the mongoose in the nape of his neck, severing his spine. But Bayer was too exposed; neither he nor Alaris would survive, and the battle would still continue. Instead, he kept his grip on the sword handle and ran into the cavernous darkness the soldiers had marched Alaris through.

Chapter Eighteen

The Claw's minions had Alaris by the arms, legs, and tail, with the fifth soldier holding a blade under the scales at his neck to prevent him from resisting, and the last one carrying his double-handed sword. Alaris surmised that being co-operative at this point might buy him time, but he would still need to forge an escape plan quickly. With his claws still bound in stone, it would not be easy, and he didn't trust them not to kill him outright.

The group of soldiers entered the low-ceilinged antechamber which housed their steeds: several Anserisaurs and one Theriasaur, currently attached to a cart laden with the resonance bombs. The captors halted and looked for the next step of their plan.

"Let's load him on the cart," said the bandicoot holding Alaris' left leg.

The soldier with the sword, a possum, dismissed him with a scowl. "But we're taking these bombs to the mountains with the rest of them, we'd need another cart to take him to the outpost. I thought we had a prison wagon here."

A horned lizard, holding his right arm, tried to flex his shoulders under Alaris' weight. He held a dagger to the pangolin's neck, but it kept drifting away under the effort of keeping him detained. "That's on its way to the west, remember? Those kids we attacked."

The squirrel holding his right leg growled. "Great, nothing to put him in. We can't take him on an Anserisaur."

The bandicoot braced his arm against Alaris' knee, trying to keep hold of the heavy creature. Fully laden with armour, Alaris was not an easy cargo. "Can't we kill him here and just dump his body?"

The squirrel looked around. "I guess so. We can just slaughter the guys inside and plant his corpse later. It's not like the blood has to be his. Nobody will be able to tell."

"We still need a transport. He's a big bastard."

Alaris flexed his claws, listening intently. He could still do some damage with his tail and legs, but the dagger in his neck would finish him in an instant. If it faltered, even for a second, he could try to break free. He knew Bayer wouldn't willingly desert him, but he may have been in the same situation. He hoped the ocelot was safe.

"Hey, isn't he supposed to be arrested?" a voice reverberated from behind them.

The possum turned to face the newcomer. "What?"

Bayer strode up to them. "You can't kill him yet, he needs an arrest record. He's no good as a scapegoat if he's dead."

Bayer quickly scanned the room and Alaris' captors. If he attacked, they would have to drop Alaris before they could draw their weapons. He glanced at the iguana and his dagger quivering at Alaris' neck. If the others dropped him, the reptile would lose his grip, and would probably be too distracted to kill Alaris first. The skunk, fox, squirrel, and bandicoot had their weapons sheathed, and could be dealt with successively. The main wild card would be the possum holding Alaris' great sword.

The squirrel shrugged. "We can forge anything, it doesn't matter. It's cleaner if we do it this way."

Bayer saw the iguana's grip tighten on the dagger and quickly gestured to the bomb cart. "What about that? Kura said he was our absolution, an alibi. What if he was taken to the mountains in that, and made to pull the trigger that killed two armies? Any survivors will see him, and that gives belief to his work as the mastermind behind the whole thing. Then you can arrest and detain him, maybe kill him if you like, but everyone gets away clean, *and* you don't have to forge any paperwork – you can leave it to the real clerks." Bayer gave the possum a quick nudge. "Because who can be bothered with all that crap, right?"

Alaris twitched.

The possum thought for a moment, then gave a begrudging, but accepting nod. "It's not his order, but I suppose this wasn't really planned..." He pointed at the cart. "All right, put him in the—"

An elbow to the face sent him reeling. In the same movement Bayer drew his sword and cut down the skunk at Alaris' left arm. The others dropped the pangolin, who landed on his knees and rolled forwards, grabbing the iguana's arm with his bound hands and forcing him into a twisting throw. The lizard's shoulder made a gristly pop as he curled over; Alaris finished his roll standing, and gave a heavy heel-kick to the side of his head. The bandicoot rushed him, flailing a sword. Alaris blocked the strike to his shoulder with his heavy pauldron, then knocked the blade away with his stone cuffs and launched the soldier backwards with an upwards strike to his chin. The possum had torn Alaris' sword from his sheath and swung the blade towards him. The heavy blade cast a wide, untidy arc that skittered off the pangolin's scales. Alaris swept the sword's tip to the ground and hooked his arm under the crossguard, lodging it in place with his weight, and gave a mighty kick to the possum's knee, which buckled backwards.

Bayer swung again at the squirrel, who backed away desperately.

"HELP!" he shrieked. "Traitors in the stable!"

Bayer's sword met the squirrel's leg; he collapsed, and one more strike silenced him. He whirled round, just in time to see the fox hurtling towards him, blade pointed at his throat. Bayer blocked the thrust and slid his sword along the blade, raising his pommel to jab it in the fox's eye. The fox staggered, then a heavy blow to his forehead rendered him unconscious.

Ahead of him, he saw Alaris bring his blade crashing into the breastplate of the possum, and then down onto the shoulder plate of the bandicoot. The bandicoot crumpled, unconscious, and Alaris gave a heavy kick to the possum to knock him out where he landed as well. The room fell into an uneasy quiet. The squirrel's cry had gone unheard, probably too deep for the sentry out front to hear, and without the guards in the chamber to back them up. Alaris looked to Bayer with relief.

"Thank you."

Bayer nodded, moving to the pangolin's wrists impatiently. "We need you out of these." They looked around for solutions. Alaris saw a single-bladed axe leaning against a stable fence, and Bayer spotted a post maul in the opposite direction. He grabbed Alaris' wrists just as Alaris went to take the axe; the two of them ended up pulling against each other and Bayer slid over on the loose stone, before muttering embarrassed curses and running for the maul. They met again in the centre with their tools. Alaris knelt on the floor, resting his wrists on the ground, and cradled the axe between his claws, blade down against the rock binding his wrists. Bayer frowned.

"You trust me this much?"

"You saved my life, I don't care if you hit me once or twice to get me out of these. Just try to miss my head," came the impatient reply.

Bayer nodded, swung the maul behind him and stepped back. Telescoping the long hammer in his grip he swung it over his head, keeping his eye direct on the back of the axe head. He only needed one strike; the hammer slammed onto the axe and drove it through the stone, which split into three. Alaris prised one of the cuffs off, but the other remained on his left.

He stood up and ran for the cart; Bayer grabbed his shoulder.

"Wait, what's your plan?" he hissed.

"I'm taking these to the Senate. Maybe we'll have a chance to stop the Claw before they get there."

Bayer grabbed Alaris' shoulder again as the pangolin turned to mount the cart. "They're not using these to capture the Senate – they're going to blow up the armies on the other side of the mountain range. They've started a war between Andarn and Tremaine to cover their invasion of Sinédrion. You won't get there before their armies will."

Alaris balled his claws. "Damn it. I'll head to Andarn then, see if I can stop our advance. If I can get hold of Major Dion, I should be able to bring this to a halt pretty quickly."

Bayer nodded. "I'll follow their troops to the Senate and try to sabotage their weapon. I made a friend who went on ahead of The Claw. I hope she'll be able to give Sinédrion some warning."

The two clashed their forearms together.

"Be safe, Bayer."

"You too, Alaris. Ride well."

Bayer mounted the nearest Anserisaur while Alaris took control of the Theriasaur hauling the cart; they left, the heavy footsteps of their steeds rumbling through the shadows.

Chapter Nineteen

Unsettled quiet sat upon Andarn's streets. The marketplaces were desolate, with not even half of the usual vendors wallpapered along the squares.

Weaving between the few attendants of the skeleton market, two Anserisaurs raced towards the centre of the city, their footfalls echoing against the bleak walls. The wolves on their backs wore hard expressions, having ridden all through the night and the better part of the day. Nimbly avoiding errant pedestrians and carts, their single focus lay on the castles and spires ahead, and the barracks that lay before them. Kyru pulled alongside Aeryn.

"We can get through the gates again, right?"

"Right," she asserted. "I'm not waiting around."

"This place is too quiet," he muttered, glancing around.

She nodded. "We've only seen soldiers at the gates – the other patrols are completely missing. Usually that means an emergency briefing or muster. We had two while I was in service: once when the King's son went missing, and the other when we thought there was an invasion from Ohé to our North."

"I'm touched you went to the trouble, but that wasn't me," he replied, prompting a smile from her.

"No, you're a much greater delinquent than some lost traders."

Up ahead the familiar gates loomed into view, with its stern closure, and the single, edgy guard standing just before it. The skunk shuffled from one foot to the other, looking about.

The Anserisaurs veered to a halt by the iron barrier. Immediately Aeryn looked to the skunk guard, who started slightly at her stern glare.

"Stop jumping around like you need to relieve yourself and open the gate," she commanded. The soldier grimaced awkwardly.

"I'm sorry, there's a muster going on," he replied, stuttering. "Messengers are to report to the signal station at the northern gate, where your report will be dispatched appropriately."

Kyru pulled his Anserisaur over to him, looming, able to cast a shadow even with the overcast skies above. "It's for General Gallis," he growled. "You won't want to keep him waiting, especially today."

The skunk studied them both for a second, then looked within, fumbling with his spear as his teeth clicked together. "Damn it, this always happens to me," he murmured. "Just go ahead and be quick, please."

The gate slid open and the wolves kicked their mounts into action, springing forward into the heart of the city. The stately buildings they passed seemed shrunken in the grey light, their elegance muted by the emptiness and eerie quiet that coated the streets. Smoke plumed from their chimneys, the only evidence of life. The ornate stone cocoons dutifully hid their dwellers from the outside world.

"You think we'll find Alaris in all this?" Kyru called.

Aeryn kept her eyes ahead. The barracks were drifting into view above the walls. "We can stand with the signallers and supply co-ordinators at the rear of the muster till the briefing's done. If we can get to Major-General Dion we should find out where he is. If we're lucky, Alaris will be right there."

Kyru sucked the air through his teeth. "All right, I trust you. I'm not sure how effective warning him of traitors is going to be at this point. Any potential threats will be right next to him already. At the very least, maybe we can get him surrounded by *his* troops, and not someone else's."

"That's what I'm hoping."

They broke into the arena adjoining the barracks and ground to a sudden halt. Immediately before them, ranked all the way up to the front steps of the military headquarters, were thousands of Andarn troops, all standing to attention. At their forefront, addressing them on the steps, stood the hunched but animated figure of Grand Councillor Vol. Behind him stood his high-ranking officers, including Dion. The jaguar stood proudly, his impressive stature making him taller than all of the other commanders.

"Vol…" Aeryn scoffed, leaping from the Anserisaur as soon as she caught sight of him. She had been brought before him during her false arrest – once you were guilty in his eyes, he could not be otherwise convinced, despite her eventual acquittal. He'd have no issue recognising her and arresting them both in front of the whole brigade simply because he objected to their presence. She pulled Kyru from his mount quickly, and they assimilated themselves into the supply corps at the back of the arena. Vol paced up and down the stage while his Generals, Majors, and Brigadiers all stood silently behind him.

"He's your military commander?" Kyru clicked. "Looks as useful as a bag of rotten potatoes."

Aeryn rolled her head. "Don't get me started. He's our Representative, supposedly, but anchors himself so deep within the city walls it's a wonder he even sees daylight. The only battles he's seen are spats between diplomats. He's only been in one engagement before, and he sat in a tent waiting for it to finish. Spends his time ordering others to strategise while he discusses 'logistics' and 'prospects' for Andarn. He has no idea what he's doing."

Vol came to an abrupt halt at the centre of the stage.

"Soldiers of Andarn, our war has begun!" he shouted, his voice straining to carry over the huge array of troops. "Tremaine, our so-called 'sister' state, has been pushing against our boundaries and our freedoms for too long. It has taken our land, our trade, and piece-by-piece, our freedom. For those of you that have not heard, two nights ago, we received word that the 17th Expeditionary Troop, our training company for budding young pages, squires…" He spent a few seconds adjusting his jaw, as if the words were stuck in the bottom of his mouth, tethered by quelling emotions. "…was brutally attacked. The soldiers at their guard were murdered, and the children are missing."

A deep murmur of anger rippled across the gathered army like a wave, turning to one another and uttering curses or statements of disbelief.

"Why would they do that?" Aeryn exhaled, watching Vol carefully.

The coati continued his address. "It is this unrepentant act of violence, this despicable transgression against our bright future, that has given us no choice but to fight against them. Unsatisfied with the capture of our innocent children and murder of our troops, they have accused us of the assassination of their own First Prince. In response, they are mobilising an army to deny us access to the Senate. They *know* they are in the wrong for their unspeakable crimes but wish to cover their tracks and further assault us. We will not be terrorised, and we will not surrender. Their attacks against us have gone far enough." He threw a fist out to the soldiers. "We will march forth and meet them with our teeth bared and our blades sharp! Today we march against Tremaine's army and strip them of their esteem! Nothing shall overpower our brilliant and mighty sovereign! For Andarn!"

He raised his fist high with his war cry. About a third of the soldiers responded; by the disappointment pulling Vol's expression to the floor, he had expected far more. Most of the troops remained serious, uncommitted to the war Vol was driving them into. It seemed many didn't share the passion with which he hated Tremaine. Major-General Dion in particular remained pointedly unmoved.

Vol pulled at his cuffs and raised his nose with a deep sniff, as if inhaling some unknown substance that would invigorate himself and his soldiers.

"As Representative it is not common for me to leave the city, but this time… due to the gravity of the crimes against us, I will be on the field with you." He stepped forward, like he was some grand presentation. The gesture didn't go unrewarded, as many soldiers nodded their heads in approval; others looked around in confusion. Aeryn's eyebrows hit the inside of her helmet; Kyru responded with a shrug.

Vol's voice was louder but still held a slight quaver. "You, soldiers of Andarn's First, Second, and Fifth Battalions, shall comprise the force meeting Tremaine on the north-western road to the Senate. We are not sure where we will come to engage their troops, but we will be ready. Scouts have them currently positioned heading south towards Eminent Valley, so we can expect their numbers to be strong, in tight formation, and to encounter them quickly. Major-General Dion will be in command of the line." He glanced mordantly at the jaguar, who folded his arms. "He is an excellent and competent leader." He looked back to the soldiers before him and cleared his throat. "Meanwhile, a smaller force of the Sixth and Seventh Battalions has already been diverted from the occupation of Kyrryk, led by General Gallis, to defend the Senate. We do not know if Tremaine has already sent troops there, but, if necessary, we will see to them first and then assist with the battle in the Valley from behind, and encircle them."

He let in a great breath, and a frown darkened his face. "For too long we have hidden behind polite diplomacy and crippling appeasements to Tremaine, and we are fully prepared to defend our right to sovereignty. It has never been our intent to go to war, but Tremaine's desperation is now out of control, and we must force them back. We are reluctant to again be the arbiters of peace, but it is necessary for the entire world, one that cannot govern itself cordially. Be prepared, for this may be a savage battle. However, we have superior numbers, greater experience, and a greater cause. We are justice in this world – there is no way that we can lose. Commanders, to your posts!"

Aeryn nudged Kyru, and the two began snaking their way towards Dion, through the assembling soldiers.

As the troops began forming in front of their Lieutenants and Captains, Vol turned to Dion, who was about to leap from the stairs and join his regiment, and stepped in front of him. With a low grunt, the jaguar stiffened and tensed, summoning as courteous a face as his obvious distaste would allow him.

"This is dangerous, Councillor," Dion warned. "Andarn may never recover from this if we fail, and Tremaine may not if we succeed. Is it not worth turning the other cheek and extending our soldiers in their aid, instead of across their throats?"

Vol's look of authority faded slightly, but his eyes locked Dion's with a fiery glare. "We have given aid enough, and this time they have taken the offensive. Fear not, though; we will not fail, Major-General. Gallis has been very thorough in explaining the tactics with me, and I trust him to the hilt."

The jaguar looked out over the soldiers. "I have to admire your presence. That will make a difference to the troops. And that Gallis' command could be so quickly resumed after such a long absence from domestic affairs I am surprised," he mused. "He only left Andarn a few days back, is that not correct? I imagine he barely had time to see the borders before he returned." Dion folded his arms.

Vol dismissed Dion's query with a wave. "It was below usual procedure, but how he conducts his matters is of no importance to me – what counts is that he was here to advise as soon as word hit us." The coati lifted his head to stare along his stubby muzzle at Dion, pompous satisfaction ebbing into his toothed smile. "We will put an end to Tremaine's oppression."

Dion raised an eyebrow. "Do you not think they have reason to be aggressive, Councillor? Our history is not one to be extolled."

"Tremaine is violent and greedy," Vol started, "and they always have been, sending their trashy refugees over here."

Dion pulled his chin tuft in suspicious contemplation. "Pardon my impertinence, but are you sure Gallis can be trusted with such an assurance of victory, seeing as he has yet to bring a twenty-year war and occupation to a close in all of his service?"

Vol stood on his toes, trying to make himself look as big as possible in front of the imposing jaguar. "I do not like your tone, Major-General. Might I remind you that your sworn duty is to *me* as commander and I will not suffer any kind of insubordination? Tremaine has humiliated us for the last time in front of the other sovereigns and I will not stand for it any longer!"

"Humiliation?" Dion growled, towering over the Representative. "What pride is there in bickering each other into the ground like toothless old badgers? A battle is only noble when the cause is, and a statesman's self-esteem is not." He flexed his claws. "I am lucky enough to have the power to remove myself from command if I so wish, but many of my soldiers are not. I fight for their protection and their honour; I would expect the Grand Commander of the army to do no less, not only for each and every soldier dressed in his colours but also for the very land he should *promise* to have them return to." He leant in, his voice calm, cold, and resonant. "I know that it is in gilded rooms far removed from the battlefield that both war and victory are declared. Any commander worth his banner remembers with honour those who bloody their spears in their leader's name and lie dying in the mud for sixty yards of barren territory."

Vol glowered, a fleck of panic in his eyes. "If resigning your command is so easy for you then perhaps you should be relieved of it!" he squeaked. "I have no need of such pompous dissenters under my rule."

Dion's eyes flared. "Your 'rule', Councillor? I am surprised to hear one use such a strong word. I was under the impression that your role as *Representative* was more co-operative."

Vol's mouth twitched a few times as if to speak, but he only managed a low grumble.

Dion stood tall, looking down his muzzle at Vol. "At least your military guise is not subject to such terms. It heartens me that you have such faith in your single, albeit currently absent, General Gallis and his assurances of victory. If you do not wish for me to personally guard you at the battle against Tremaine, however, then I would be glad to take whatever punishment you see fit." He drew his sabre and presented the hilt to his commander. "A deserting soldier is better dead than becoming a potential enemy, isn't that correct?"

Vol looked ill. He weakly shoved the sword handle

away. "No need for such dramatics, Major-General," he muttered.

Dion slid the sword into his scabbard. "Very well. Did the Senate have no response to our intention to go to war? I was under the impression negotiations were being mediated personally by Sinédrion."

Vol's face grew even more sallow. "We-we haven't the time to react with diplomacy; it's past all that ridiculousness now. Tremaine stepped over the line and now we're going to teach them a lesson for it. B-but this isn't a time to talk about procedure. I'll see you on the battle line." He marched off, his pace quickening to a clumsy half-run as he passed the borders of the barracks' stone frontage.

Dion rolled his neck, cricking a vertebra with a satisfying pop. A nimble figure appeared at his side, a slender golden tiger with piercing blue eyes. Dion turned to his Lieutenant with grim foreboding.

"Skye; honourable warriors are a dying breed in this city. We need to protect the few we can trust. This entire affair is irregular, and hellishly deceptive."

Just as Skye was about to speak up, the two wolves raced to a halt behind them. Dion's eyes widened at the sight of his ex-Lieutenant Aeryn, and he almost looked relieved. "Aeryn Lleyandi!" the jaguar boomed. "What ill fate brings you to our barracks on such a dismal day?"

Aeryn stepped forwards, giving a heartfelt salute to her former comrades. Skye punched her playfully on the arm.

"Hey, you can finally get me that drink you promised!" she cheered, launching into a sideways hug.

Aeryn smiled, but wrested the cat from her to address the commander. "Hopefully soon. Major-General, I apologise for the impatience, but we need to see Alaris urgently. There's a conspiracy in the military, and he – everyone – could be in danger."

Dion raised a stern eyebrow. "That we already are, Lleyandi. You have heard we are at war?"

She nodded. "Seems very extreme to me, but I've been in some unusual circumstances lately," she replied. Dion nodded in agreement.

"I think we all have been, whether we were aware of it or not. But as for your inquiry, I'm afraid Alaris is absent. He left for an undisclosed assignment several days ago and I have no knowledge of where he went."

Kyru gave a dismissive growl. "He left? Damn…"

Dion looked to the three of them pressingly. "I cannot leave my troops to die." He leant in, and in a growling whisper spoke to Aeryn. "Lleyandi, you and your concomitant have experience with disobedience. You need to inform Sinédrion of our mobilisation and implore them to intervene. This is not a war for survival; it is a war of vanity. For now I must obey my orders and help protect the soldiers who have no choice but to march against each other, and delay as long as I can, but I will not hesitate to withdraw as soon as Sinédrion appears."

Aeryn nodded and gave him a firm salute. Kyru bowed quickly.

"Skye!" Dion barked to his Lieutenant with a purposeful stare. "Accompany them to the Senate. You will need to take the road through Kyrryk, or you risk getting trampled by Tremaine's army. Return immediately, understand?"

"Yes, Major-General!" With no hesitation she saluted, and the three of them ran for the mounts at the back of the courtyard. Dion glanced at the clouds above, despairing the low, grey ceiling above, then moved to the head of the ranks.

Chapter Twenty

The Theriasaur's feet thundered in its run; behind Alaris the cart shuddered and rattled, bouncing into every crest and trough along the unsteady road. He'd ridden through the night to cross over Andarn's borders down the path he'd taken to Kyrryk with Bayer, the only safe direct route he knew. He had to get to the city before the troops left. He had proof now, and then he could march the army to Sinédrion and give it proper protection. Jed was right, he kept repeating in his head. He was right and a war was about to tear through Cadon, unless he could somehow reach Dion and stop it. The resonance bombs foretold a devastating fate for anyone who opposed Shadow's Claw, and signalled that there were more powers at work that could reuse the ancient and terrifying technology from Nazreal. If this war started it would be won quickly and brutally, and not by the right side. There may not even be a land left to rule.

He stopped at no checkpoints; there was no time, and

he would be under suspicion from both his own army and the Claw, even if they were currently mobilising elsewhere. There was nobody he could trust until he reached Dion. He could only guess that when the Claw had taken the Senate some sort of message would be sent across the continent for the machine to start tightening its chokehold on the sovereigns and sabotage his old command.

He took a few deep breaths, focusing his mind on building rage, sending fire through his veins. Gallis would pay. The only army to find a victory would be the one that turned back and walked away, and Alaris would be there to send them home.

Shadow's Claw would *not* win.

He pounded the reins; the tough leather whipped either side of the Theriasaur, which shook its head and kept onwards, pummelling the ground.

The city drew near; he knew this land well. Rounding a bend three Anserisaurs stormed along the road towards him. As they drew closer at unassailable speed he recognised their riders, and quickly hauled back on the reins. His Theriasaur thrashed its head but slowed, its momentum churning up loose dirt as it skidded to a heavy canter. Aeryn, Kyru, and Skye, recognised him too, and ground to a stop right by his vehicle.

"Alaris!" Aeryn half-cried, half-sighed. "You scared the daylights out of me when Dion said you'd disappeared."

Skye shot him a relieved salute. "Captain!" she chirruped. "We've got some nasty developments here and could really use you."

"I know," Alaris replied darkly. He gestured to the cart behind him. Kyru pulled his Anserisaur over to see them.

Instantly he identified the hue of the resonance materials inside the canisters.

"What the hell are they?" he growled.

"Bombs," Alaris hissed. "They've started a war and are going to blow up both the Andarn and Tremaine armies; I need to get back and warn Dion!"

Skye shook her head. "They've all gone; they're already on their way. We were on our way to the Senate to warn them about the war so they could stop it."

Alaris looked back at the bombs. "I know where they'll be converging. Continue to the Senate if you have to, but be careful – they're going to launch an assault there too. They have a really powerful elemental weapon. Bayer followed their troops to sabotage it and take out the Prince of Tremaine, who's wielding it. I'd suggest making him your target. The other resonator is General Gallis."

Aeryn and Skye looked at him with stunned silence.

"That sickening excuse for a General is a *resonator*?!" Aeryn seethed.

Alaris nodded. "Don't take him lightly: he's strong and merciless."

A new fire raged in Aeryn's eyes. She looked to Kyru urgently. He reciprocated with an equally determined look.

"We'll take him down," she snarled.

Kyru nodded, clashing his gauntlets together. "Agreed. We've done it once before. No better therapy than combat, right?"

The pangolin's face darkened. "Be careful. I'll head off the two armies and get them to Sinédrion as soon as I can."

Skye moved her steed to the side of Alaris' cart. "Captain, I'll escort you. If something happens at least one of us will need to get word to Dion."

He gave a nod of approval, and the four of them exchanged glances. "Good luck," he said gravely but sincerely.

"You too," Aeryn replied.

Each of them gave parting waves and kicked their steeds into gear, shaking the ground beneath their feet as they began their final runs to their destinations.

Chapter Twenty-One

The city of Sinédrion lay in the distance, it usual brilliance dimmed by overcast skies. The huge dome of the Senate building stood proudly at its centre, like an eminent tree in a field of golden-brown. The streets, laid out in a circular web, directed focus to the sentinel structure, a constant reminder of the presence and authority protected by the walls, and that governed their every move. An ominous, oppressive shadow to some; to others, a bastion of justice.

Right now, to the hungry eyes watching it from the forested hills, it presented an opportunity, a promise desperate to be fulfilled, and a gateway to a world where nothing would ever be too far from reach.

Haru stood with arms folded at the head of his army, waiting impatiently. His square-ended, split-to-the-neck cloak of gold and black rippled in the timid breeze over his vermillion robes. His golden helmet, an open sallet with a snub visor and a three-pronged crown of silver wrapped around its circumference, reflected his army in its polished, unmarred surface. Despite the crown still signifying his older position of Third Seat Prince, it was a testament to the climb he made to gain power. The world would finally be his to exact control over. There would be no more pandering to elder brothers, no more ridiculous council proposals and debates, no greater hierarchy than his. Now that he was the new Second Seat Prince and had the Tremaine military under his command, taking the sovereign would be easy. And with Sinédrion in front of him, he would take hold of both at once. Even Kura, the vicious creature he aligned with, would be no threat. All it needed was a little time and the right opportunity. He would have no fear. His appetite for power was too great.

The resonance device hummed in his grip. He could feel the low vibration with every inch of his body. The hairs on his neck stood on end, an electric taste bounced from his teeth. *This* was power.

Something large moved behind him. He turned to see Kura striding purposefully towards where he stood.

"Are your troops ready?" the bear growled.

Haru let out a wry scoff. "We've been waiting for you, Kura. Any news of your scapegoat?"

"What happens to him now is inconsequential."

The mongoose gave him a look askance. "So you won't force him to stand trial?"

"Don't waste my time, Haru," Kura spat. "He will serve his purpose either way. He already shoulders the blame."

"Are you sure?" Haru hissed. "What if someone investigated and found him dead before he reached Kyrryk?"

Kura's voice rumbled like thunder; not angry, but terrifying in its control. "How many of these soldiers would you trust with a secret? If I murdered him in front of them, it would escape in drunken boasts and damage our alibi. A group of six soldiers has less to say than a chamber of thousands. The *idea* of him as a traitor was all I needed; he was going to be apprehended after my summons in Andarn but he saved us a journey by coming directly to Kyrryk. If he had discovered us and escaped, it would be my word and that of every single Shadow's Claw operative against his. If he stood trial as an honourable soldier, his guilt would be proven by our evidence. If, and this is most likely, he was killed by our men, there is nobody left to defend him, and all of the evidence will point to his corpse. Whatever the means, the end result is that I will stand as a flag to rally behind in the name of integrity. My scenario is perfect."

Haru gritted his teeth, tightening his claws around the cannon's handle. "And of course, with you here, there is no way we can fail."

"I know my power," Kura boomed. "You have held yours for all of a few hours. I am not our weakness."

He raised his massive arm and thrust it forwards. Behind them, a ripple of short commands barked through the trees, and an army rose to its feet.

It took them little time to reach the city's southern entrance. The fulvous walls were suspiciously quiet, with no guards along its battlements. The gate was closed, dark and austere. Further back in the ranks of troops, Bayer felt his stomach rise. He wouldn't make it to kill either Kura or Haru from here, especially if they were in control of their powers; he'd have to chance it out in the battle, if it came to one. He hoped Raede had made it here safely, and in time. The silent gates gave no clue as to their current allegiance.

Kura flexed his claws, scanning the wall.

"We had guards here."

Haru glanced around quickly. "Maybe they're taking care of the other patrols."

The bear made a deep, guttural snarl. "We will not wait long."

Just as he was about to motion for a section of troops to skirt around to one of the other gates, a tall figure stood at the edge of the wall above them, holding a pair of short-handled twin axes which he brandished at his sides. The stag's imposing stance made his already formidable antlers appear as if to reach into the sky, holding up the clouds.

"General Gallis," Jed called down. "Your arrival is unwelcome."

Kura froze. "Jed Othera," he spat. "Your presence is unexpected. And temporary."

The stag stared at the army waiting to assault him. "You will not pass these gates. Your revolution is over, and you will be brought to justice for your crimes against the people and the Senate," he upbraided. "Prince Haru, it will be my duty to arrest you for the same crimes. If you do not surrender, we will take you."

Haru gave a shrill laugh. "You wish, Othera! You have no idea of the power facing you!"

Jed remained unwavering at the apex of the gate. "We will defend this city, and the right of our people, to the end."

Kura clenched his fists. "Then we shall make it a quick one."

He planted his feet squarely on the ground and, teeth

clenched, raised his arms. A deafening rumble shook the earth; the road between Kura and the gate rose and split in a tearing column. The shockwave punched along the ground until it hit the gatehouse. Jed quickly leapt aside as the huge barrier surged upwards. The force of the bear's resonance travelled up and along the wall, rending the stone from its earthen seal. The entire gatehouse exploded outwards, showering the surrounding area with chunks of rent brick. The wooden gates collapsed forwards. Within the city, the formation of Sinédrion guards stood bewildered but firm, their pikes undeterred from the target they had been warned of.

"Soldiers, advance!" Kura roared, drawing a large, curved sword from his belt and raising it high into the air. With a unison warcry, the Shadow's Claw army began its march.

Jed appeared again at the wall. "Sinédrion!" he bellowed. "Advance to the gate, quickly! Do not let them enter!"

Haru swung the resonance cannon up to Jed's position and pulled the trigger. A bolt of blue-green energy streaked from the clawed barrel and sliced along the wall underneath the stag. He leapt clear, but the stone that had been struck only inches from him smoked and bubbled.

Kura laid his sword across the device, snarling. "Don't squander the power on a single target. I will take care of Othera; you focus on getting our troops past the wall."

"I am not *support*!" Haru hissed. "I am the head of this army, and I will not be reduced to—"

Kura grabbed him by the throat. "If you are a leader, then LEAD! Take your army into the city and stop whining like a child!" He thrust the mongoose forwards; Haru stopped for a second, his hands tremorous, eyes glazed. He could kill him right now.

Cries from the wall shook him to his senses. Ahead, the Sinédrion soldiers were taking their positions. A rank of archers formed at the other end of the bridge straddling the internal moat. The tips of their longbows aligned in the distance like a platoon of shark fins.

Kura turned to his army. "Quick advance! To the wall!"

The Sinédrion archers drew their bows.

Haru wrenched the dial on the side of the cannon; the crystal battery inside shone with a pale, silver-blue lustre. He aimed at the sky.

A distant whipping sound caught their ears; the Sinédrion archers had loosed their arrows. Haru held out his arm. "HOLD!" he screamed. "Arrows!" The soldiers behind him loosened their rank and lowered their heads, bracing themselves for an incoming volley.

Holding the cannon up high, he saw the shafts black against the sky. He grabbed hold of a handle on the gun's side and twisted it outwards; the barrel spiralled outwards into a wide funnel, and he pulled the trigger.

A vortex of howling wind erupted from the cannon to meet the descending arrows. It whipped across them like an invisible shield, flinging them off in wild trajectories, breaking on the stone road. Some still pierced the wind to land amongst the soldiers behind him, and several more made their mark, too sharp and narrow for the wind to catch.

The mongoose grinned hungrily, twisting the dial again. The crystal hummed and turned a violent yellow. Aiming now at the Sinédrion defence, he broke into a run as he yanked the trigger down. A fiery heat wave billowed from the gun and rolled forwards, rippling the air. Unable to retreat, the front line tried to duck away, but most were hit head-on by the scorching wave. The armour deflected the brunt of it, but their eyes, faces, hands; anything exposed was singed and smouldered. Wooden pike shafts blackened with the heat.

"CHARGE!"

Haru fell to one side as the Claw soldiers began a running advance behind him.

In the middle ranks, Bayer found himself sandwiched in by soldiers. He would have to break free when they breached the walls. He tried to see where Jed had gone, but could not. Over to the left, Kura had walked to the city wall and held his palms against it. The stone folded outwards, creating a tall archway that he and Haru then disappeared through.

Yells and screams split the air, blade met blade and splintered wood. The Claw's soldiers began spreading around the breach in the walls. Bayer used the outward movement to edge his way closer, but fighters were already piling through. On the other side, Sinédrion soldiers tried to block the wounded wall, to no avail.

Bayer couldn't reach them. The other gates would be closed. And where was Raede?

More shouts from the line ahead. Bayer turned to see a plume of red fire spread like blood over the Sinédrion soldiers. The whole line buckled and swayed trying to avoid it. Those in combat were trapped by spears and shields, others by the troops behind them. The rear ranks broke formation and moved right, retreating from Haru's fiery cascade. The Claw soldiers broke through the remaining defenders, mounted the remains of the wall breach and entered the city. The line of archers retreated ahead of them to the nearby buildings. More archers stationed on rooftops began to hail arrows onto the invading troops. Bayer dodged and ducked as best as he could, trying to separate from the main force and assist Jed. The field was already chaotic. Every turn he tried to make threw him into blades or armour, and Jed remained out of sight.

The Sinédrion soldiers who had been blocking the broken gate had fallen back to the rear of the bridge, or were defending the road that circled the inner wall. More troops were hurrying to cover Kura's second breach. Bayer barely dodged an arrow that whizzed past his shoulder, slamming into the chestplate of the soldier behind him. He clambered over the wall with barely any space to move. The crush of plated warriors driving into each other had forced the infantry into a ridge at the apex of battle. Not all of the bodies standing were alive, having no space to fall.

A fleck of light to the left, further in the city, caught his eye. Haru was heading towards the western gate. Bayer's target. He had to break away.

Edging sideways, parrying blows from both sides, he inched closer to the bridge's wall, aiming to traverse the platform to the city itself. He leapt up and began a sprint, just as more Sinédrion guards ran to the bridge. One raised a throwing spear and cast it at Bayer. Stuck between leaping body-first into a heaving mass of armour or diving into the moat, he had no choice but to twist his body to try and evade it. It missed injuring him but struck the plating on the back and side of his left leg. The weight of the spear wrenched his leg sideways, toppling him into the water.

He hit the surface like an anchor and felt himself plummet down into the punishingly cold depths of the moat. The light disappeared. Frantically he pulled at the spear but the point was caught between plates, and he sank further. With one last twist he pried it free, freeing his legs to kick. Still heavy, he didn't climb. He wrestled at his right pauldron, eventually tearing the leather buckle free; the armour was just big enough to squeeze his arms out and, desperately, he swam upwards. Blinded by the water, his arm scraped a wooden beam. He grabbed it and launched himself in the direction he hoped was up, and felt the light swell around him. Just a few more feet until freedom.

He flailed around for another beam as his chest burnt and spasmed. His claws raked splinters from one but failed to bite, and he was falling too quickly to grab it again. He kicked further, and finally reached it. With one last effort he broke the water's surface and felt the air hit his face. Above him the soldiers yelled and armour clashed. He pushed himself towards the moat's inner edge, nearest the city, and hugged the wall, trying to find an exit. His pace was painfully slow as he tried to avoid catching the eye of soldiers either side of the walls.

Some way up towards the western side of the city he found a stairway leading to the street. He dragged himself up and quickly looked around. The battle lines were rough but distinct, with the Claw pressing the advance. Sinédrion's soldiers were well-equipped and fought hard, but had been broken too quickly by Haru's elemental weapon. For now, Bayer was further than their advance. If he were seen here, he'd be in for a hard fight alone. As he stood, the ground rumbled, and a building near the battlefront collapsed, billowing dust. A volley of flame licked the air.

The archers had been scattered. The besieged soldiers split in two as Shadow's Claw pushed further ahead. Their second column had now reached the gate outside and forced its advance to bolster the Claw's vanguard.

Sinédrion's defensive line began a retreat to the Senate. Bayer broke into a run, hoping to head off Haru and Kura with them.

Chapter Twenty-Two

Two armies faced each other, neither moving, a length of valley between them. The path between Andarn and Tremaine passed by the forked mountain ridges, at the centre of which lay Kyrryk. Treacherous, impassable cliffs were part of the reason Kyrryk had been vital as a path to the north, until its collapse. It meant a harder, longer, circuitous route. Currently those travel grievances meant nothing, as even this trail now faced its own obstacle.

"The battle should not be here," Dion grumbled, looking up at the cliffs. "We've lost all ability to flank." On the other side, a wide river engorged with winter rains from the north, washed mottled blues and greens along its path. "Only room to move forwards. And we're too close to Andarn. If we fail, the only place we can retreat to is our city, and they'll be upon us."

One of his other Lieutenants, a marmot, jabbed the butt of his spear into the ground. "Then we'll have to make sure we don't retreat, right, sir?"

Dion said nothing. That they might be denied even the opportunity to retreat was his greatest worry. There were too many good soldiers here, and the cause unworthy of such a sacrifice. It was a sorry sign that the Tremaine army looked as rushed into the conflict as Andarn, but both were unwilling to back down from the aggressive acts that each other had apparently made.

"It has become a very convenient war," the jaguar said idly, resting his claws on the pommel of his enormous bastard sword. Councillor Vol had been pacing back and forth in front of his troops for a good ten minutes on the back of his Anserisaur. Dion had given up following him after the first few circuits, as the coati found excuses to delay what would be his order to advance. It was one of the few times the jaguar had been grateful for the incompetence and reticence of his military commander.

Eventually, Vol drew up to the jaguar, only just about at eye level with the muscular feline despite being on his steed. "Well, Major-General," he croaked, clearing his throat, "what would your recommendation be?"

Dion cleared his throat to hide a derisive snort. "Councillor, it would be my recommendation that we begin a parlay with the Tremaine officers to assess the terms of battle. That is, unless you have another strategy in mind or wish to forego the chance for us both to turn around."

Vol cleared his throat again, pulling at the armour around his neck. It was made for him when he first took office: a few years younger, and a few degrees fitter. "Well, yes, I can see that being logical. I mean… what is your diagnostic of the field; do you think we have an advantage?"

"I thought you said Gallis' plan was guaranteed," Dion

growled deeply. He flexed his claws. "We won't know absolutely until we test Tremaine's mettle. There is no adequate placement for archers here with the valley so narrow, and on a bend. Sir, after you." He gestured forwards, and Vol, with difficulty, steered his Anserisaur towards the Tremaine line. Two Andarn flag-bearers marched alongside them.

Upon seeing the Andarn dignitaries move, the Tremaine commander, a female monitor lizard, rode to meet them with two of her soldiers and a flag-bearer. The closer the two groups came to the middle, the more tense Vol became. Dion could hear him seething as they came together. Dion and the monitor exchanged salutes. Vol did not; being a Councillor he did not technically have to, but his arrogance was further compounded by his poor diplomatic skills and xenophobia.

"I am Commander Artija." The lizard spoke directly to Dion. "Do you have terms for us, Andarn? We will not walk from your borders without repayment for your assassination of Prince Lyris. You have gone too far, you must realise this."

Vol interrupted Dion's expression of sorrow for the loss of the Prince. "We do not know who murdered your prince; there were no soldiers in Tremaine outside of our embassy and all of them were accounted for, at least until you imprisoned them," he said, severity rising in his inflections. "But one lavish prince is nothing compared to the hundreds of honourable lives we have lost at your borders. Return the children and we can consider negotiations for your safe retreat out of our lands."

Artija's tongue flicked curtly. "We have none of your

children, and we have found no evidence that Tremaine soldiers were involved. Our estimation is that it was a bandit raid from Kyrryk."

Vol pointed a shaking claw at her. "You dare mock our victims? The survivors warned us, and our sentries verified Tremaine soldiers among the dead! Why else would they be there?"

Dion slapped Vol's hand away and addressed Artija. "What we are here to address, Commander, is whether there are any conditions to which we can arrange an armistice."

She gave Vol a sharp, disgusted look. "That depends on receipt of our terms. I am authorised to demand a full, Tremaine-led investigation into the murder of our Prince and access to your military records. We also seek compensation for the families of our slain soldiers and further demand that all Andarn troops withdraw from our borders to a distance of at least ten miles, to give us a safe zone at ours."

Councillor Vol saw red immediately. "Impudence!" he spat. "You just want more of our land for yourselves; if we withdrew ten miles from our borders we'd lose a third of our farm lands! We've incurred enough indecency and thieving behaviour from your undisciplined and greedy soldiers! Give us back the land that is rightfully ours, and find the children, and we'll consider letting you keep your legs right here!"

Artija straightened, stiffening, and glared directly at Vol. "Enough. This concludes our parlay. There will be no terms. If you are left standing, we will talk again. Until then, our blades shall transfer this argument." She gave a curt salute, which Dion repaid, and then turned back to her troops.

Vol bristled, shaking his shoulders. "Vile, savage sovereign," he hissed. "Troops, to arms!" He raised his arm, fist clenched. "Prepare to advance!"

The soldiers hoisted their spears to their shoulders, ready to march. Dion ran to the far edge of his line, by the river, while Vol galloped quickly to the rear.

"Andarn!" Dion yelled. "Advance pikes!"

Polearm spikes arced down from their ordered position to aim at the enemy. The soldiers in white clashed their swords and axes against shields and armour in rhythmic bursts, filling the air with a menacing drumbeat. The Tremaine army beat their shields in reply, and the unison rumbling of armour shook the valley. The flags of both sovereigns' forces trembled in the wind.

As Vol stood at the back of his battalions with his retinue, a rumbling of heavy gallops swept across the valley. A Theriasaur and Anserisaur stampeded past him, pounding around the narrow left flank to the front lines. Taking a second to observe their trajectory, he saw the Anserisaur heading for Dion, and the large, rhino-like Theriasaur headed directly for the Tremaine army.

"What on Eeres is this?" he muttered, and wrangled his mount to follow.

He saw a tiger dismount directly in front of commander Dion. Immediately, he heard the jaguar roar: "Andarn, HOLD!" His sergeants echoed his command and within seconds the entire block had halted. The Tremaine army maintained their intimidating armour clashes and began a slow march forwards.

Vol whipped his steed into action, and almost fell from it as he arrived in his bluster. "Major-General Dion, what is the meaning of this?"

Skye ignored him, busy imploring Dion to withdraw by recounting Alaris' information to him.

"Where are they?" Dion rumbled. Skye shrugged.

"We don't know. We only know they're in the mountain somewhere," she replied.

Vol thrashed the reins of his steed. "DION! I *demand* an explanation for this interruption!" he yelled.

The jaguar threw him a vicious snarl. "Quiet, idiot!" He looked ahead to where Alaris was riding, trying to flank the Tremaine soldiers along the river. He broke into a run to follow the pangolin.

Alaris held his arms up to the spears brandished at him in confusion, looking like a bizarre single-cavalryman strike. "I'm not trying to attack you!" he implored. "I'm looking for Captain Ibarruri! I need to see him!"

His presence had disrupted the Tremaine line, which now progressed in an uneven wedge towards Andarn while the soldiers he passed turned to try and defend against him. Sergeants broke from their lines to circle Alaris, aiming their long-handled axes at his chest. The pangolin kept craning his neck, trying to catch sight of his friend. Within a few seconds, a call came from further up the line.

"Alaris! Soldiers, stand down!"

The soldier that greeted him was not who he was expecting. One of Rowan's Lieutenants, a sleek and well-equipped ferret named Vendrell, pushed through the line. He held his wrist-mounted crossbow above him, trying to keep it undamaged, almost losing his satchel of bolts in the crush.

Vendrell sprinted down the ranks, his rapier clashing at

his side. He broke through the circle of axe blades, throwing them away from their target. "I said stand *down*! Fall back in line, all of you! Alaris, what the hell are you doing?"

Alaris dismounted and gave Vendrell a thankful handshake as the soldiers dispersed. "It's good to see you, Ven. Where's Rowan?"

The ferret froze. "He's… he's dead, Alaris."

Alaris stared at him blankly. "What? Don't be ridiculous, I need him."

Vendrell's shoulders sunk. "He is, Alaris. I'm sorry."

The pangolin shook his head, stepping forwards. "No, you're wrong; he can't be dead. I haven't seen him yet."

"No, listen, Alaris. He was killed with Prince Lyris a night ago by Andarn soldiers. He—"

Alaris grabbed Vendrell by the shoulders and looked about to protest. His eyes were wide and glistening, his jaw clenched. His shaking claws rattled on the ferret's golden armour. "Ven… you…" he said quietly, through heavy, unsteady breathing. "Who killed him?"

Vendrell hung his head. "Andarn soldiers. They stormed through the parade and killed the Prince's guard. Rowan was… one of them. I couldn't… I wasn't able to stop them."

Dion skidded to a halt by Alaris, with Skye just behind. "Hiryu!" he bellowed, clapping the scaled creature on the back. "Glad you could join us!"

The Tremaine army had now stopped, as the monitor lizard Artija broke from her position to ascertain the bizarre behaviour her enemy was displaying and pounded towards her disrupted right flank.

Alaris had no reply for Dion's greeting, still stock-still

from Vendrell's news. Skye watched her captain with concern; he looked just about to crush the slim Lieutenant. A second later he released his claws and turned to Dion, eyes desperate and piercing.

"The Lieutenants informed me of our situation," Dion continued. "I will order the troops to withdraw."

Alaris locked eyes with him. "Get them all out. Get everyone away," he said through careful, seething breaths. "They killed Rowan." He tried to focus. He knew the army would be nearby, ready to trigger the bombs that had already been planted. Alaris had unhitched the stolen cart behind Andarn's line, unwilling to risk them being set off by the combat. He didn't even know where the saboteurs were, and his head kept swimming with Vendrell's words.

The Major-General spun on his heel just as Commander Artija arrived.

"What is this, defection or surrender?" she barked. "You're making a mockery of military tactics."

"Commander," Vendrell began, "we need to—"

Screams rang behind them. Soldiers on the Tremaine line had been killed. Instantly, Dion saw a pair of Andarn archers disappearing behind the cliff's edge. And, over Tremaine's line, Tremaine archers were taking aim at Andarn's infantry. Their arrows loosed and hit home, killing two and wounding another. Still by his formation, Vol raised his sword; his shrill cry burned into their ears.

"Advance!"

Alaris leapt onto the Theriasaur, slammed his heels into the creature's tough back. It let out a deep bellow and thundered along Tremaine's battle line, snapping the few spears that dared to point at it.

Dion cannoned towards Vol. He grabbed the harness of the coati's reptilian mount, hauling it off course, and gave a roar at his troops. "HOLD!"

They kept moving.

"I said HOLD!" he bellowed again. Some of the troops looked to one another in confusion, then between Vol and Dion. The line slowed.

"You've been removed from command, insubordinate brute!" Vol spat. "Let go of me and fight if you want to retain your rank and honour!"

Dion bared his teeth. "There is no honour fighting for you."

Skye ran to meet him. Dion ripped off his gauntlets. "Lieutenant Skye, with me! Climb the rocks!"

He sprinted off, skirting around the infantry lines ranks to the rock face behind them.

Vendrell yelled for his lines to halt their advance and tried to plead with Artija; she was already re-joining her battlefront in lieu of Andarn's renewed charge, and charging Vol.

Assessing his choices, Vendrell sprinted past his own troops, following Alaris' trail of broken spears to the cliffs.

Chapter Twenty-Three

D ust and screams filled Sinédrion's air. Aeryn and Kyru's mounts pounded through the trees, aiming for the northern gate, away from the fighting. They would never force an entrance through the troops, so their quickest and safest gamble was to gain entry through the gate most likely to be open for civilian or dignitary evacuation.

The wolves sped across the cold winter ground, eventually breaking through the forest's cover to see the city's northern gates, and the steady, hurried train of civilians being ushered along the road. Several companies of guards kept watchful eyes on the outer edges of the city in case the fighting began to spill further, or the attacking forces opened a second front. Troops kept the pedestrians moving quickly, even though most were laden with as many possessions and provisions as they could carry. Carts and carriages had become makeshift ambulances for the wounded and infirm, heading for anywhere safe between here and Pthiris, further north.

"Damn it, they're already here," Kyru growled.

Aeryn and Kyru steered their sleek Anserisaurs to the road, racing alongside the refugees in the opposite direction. Many flinched away, or leapt in panic.

The guards thought so too. Blades came to meet them at the gates.

"Hold! You cannot enter!" the otter sergeant yelled.

Kyru took point, pushing his Anserisaur as close to the guard as he could. "We need to see Jed Othera. We know who's conducting the siege and may be able to help him."

The otter pointed back at the city. "It's too late; nobody enters. Councillor Othera is already at the front line. The fate of our city is up to them now."

Aeryn rode to Kyru's side, her bow already in hand. "He may not be able to do this alone. We've come from Xayall and Andarn; the weapons and the warriors they're using are the same used against us in our siege. If you don't let us in now, he might lose the chance to exploit their weakness."

The guards looked to one another and their sergeant. The refugees were still coming through. Soon they would be fighting off the invaders from the civilian's sides, and they were vulnerable enough with the southern part of their city under the enemy's blade. He brandished his spear at them. "I have to get my people to safety. If you want to risk dying then go. And if you stop even one of Sinédrion's citizens from escaping you'll be held accountable with a blade in your skull, am I clear?"

Kyru gave him a salute. "Thank you, sir. We won't let your city fall."

With a kick of their heels, they raced into Sinédrion's heart. Kyru gave Aeryn a sideways look as they ran. "Let's hope they're similar enough to Faria or Vionaika for us to make a difference," he muttered.

"I didn't lie," she replied, smiling slightly. "It's not a huge advantage, but if we can at least take out their crystals, we'll even the field a little more."

Bayer hugged the walls as he followed the trails of fire and rumbles of stone barrelling towards the Senate building. Rooftop archers supported their commander as they could, until an impact to their building shook cracks through the stone. The Sinédrion troops were being driven back while the Claw troops advanced, led by Haru, barrelling along the main streets with a wild, elemental whip thrashing at its head.

A strange, caustic smell caught on the wind. Bayer could see smoke, but the buildings weren't on fire. Perhaps an abandoned hearth was burning over. Something familiar about it peppered his memory, like the painful scent of Xayall's siege. Haru's scorching flame shouldn't be that powerful, though…

He put it out of mind and shadowed the main street as best he could, trying not to be sighted by archers or regrouping soldiers that would end him before he could prove his allegiance.

A flash of gold between buildings stopped him in his tracks – he finally saw Jed holding his own against Kura's powerful onslaughts. The stag leapt, rolled, parried everything he could, but was still on the retreat. The Senate building was close behind; once Jed passed these few buildings, only open ground remained before the bear reached the dome. No cover, no alternate route, just a dash for safety, or devastation. The cries of the Claw's army rang ever closer down the main street.

Just as Bayer rounded the next alley to start a sideways run at Haru, he was met by the backs of Sinédrion soldiers, poised behind a huge wooden palisade the entire width of the street. He dove across the alley and quickly checked around the other side of the building. More soldiers, this time with wider palisades, looked to block the main street.

A great impact shook the ground; Bayer just managed to stay his balance. Jed landed heavily on his feet just inside the plaza. He had barely been on the ground a second, when he gave a bellowing command: "Now!"

The soldiers sprang into action. The wooden palisades charged into place, blocking off the side streets. Kura turned; Haru still sprinted ahead. Sinédrion soldiers appeared at the rooftops and unfurled crates of caltrops onto the stone.

Standing in the plaza were three huge ballistae, aimed directly at the invading troops. On each one was a large smouldering clay orb.

"Hold!" Kura cried.

Haru looked up, too late. In blinding quick sequence the three ballistae loosed their shots and the clay projectiles flew into the street. The first two exploded in the midst of the attackers, billowing flame and splattering burning oil through the screaming, fleeing troops. The third exploded just above the ground, showering the Claw soldiers with red-hot sand, searing, seizing up their armour, choking their breath. More palisades moved into place in the side streets, cordoning off the flames, blocking their retreat to anywhere but back towards the walls. The attackers ground to a halt and backed away, pulling any injured they could reach into the safe area further back.

Kura whirled round as a pair of grenades flew towards him. In a split second he hit the ground. Immediately afterwards came the flash and explosion, and Bayer saw nothing else. The soldiers leapt clear of the impact that hit their palisades; segments of wood broke free and spiralled away.

Bayer ran to Jed, who watched the wood grimly. His armour had a large dent in the breastplate, but he seemed otherwise unscathed.

"Well done, Kanjita. You and Faolan returned your intelligence just in time."

"Your soldiers work quickly," Bayer replied, not considering his return halfway through a siege he was supposed to have prevented to be deemed punctual.

"I take siege defence drills seriously," the stag said darkly, not taking his eyes from the front palisades. Behind them, the Sinédrion guards stationed at the other gates were running into place to flank the soldiers in the streets.

"Where did Raede—?"

"Commander Othera!" the cry rang from behind the palisade. The two wooden barriers parted and Jed stepped through. Where the grenade had fallen, the stone had warped, bubbled and blackened by the explosion.

"Advance on the Shadow's forces; halt their attack. The rest of you, get away from—"

The black rock split and shattered. Stone fragments flew out like cannonballs, crushing soldiers, wounding buildings. At the centre stood Kura, his eyes aflame with rage, teeth bared, jaws wet. He slammed his feet into the ground, creating small wedges of stone under them. In an instant he rocketed forwards, the stone propelling him along at blistering speed. His claws raked the ground either side of him, gathering it into rocky gauntlets.

His speed took him into a flying leap for Jed, who raised his axes and braced his antlers to meet the brunt of the bear's attack. The bear brought his claws crashing into the stag's axes, which sparked, but held. Kura headbutted Jed, tore his claws from the axes and began punching wildly, salivating and roaring. Bayer ran to assist, but a shower of icy needles rained across his path and he twisted to a halt. Haru wore a vicious grin, his clothing ragged and covered in the remnants of the burning sand. His battered helmet had not protected the tips of his ears, which were singed and raw.

He pulled the trigger again, launching a second volley of ice shards at Bayer. The feline dodged away but the barrage followed his path as fast as he moved. He spiralled round, closing distance on the mongoose in an arc. With the cat upon him, the prince drew his needle-like sword at the last second, barely giving Bayer enough time to parry.

The Shadow's Claw soldiers who had evaded the sand trap pushed their way through the flames, while the second battalion braced their advance from the rear, punching into the newly reformed Sinédrion lines. The defence bulged outwards, almost splitting into the plaza. The roar of soldiers shook the air. Those at the heart of the siege's shifting crush screamed, stabbed, tore off limbs with the desperate swings of their weapons. The dead fell and became steps for inflicting higher wounds, or a brace to push against the attackers. The ground turned dark with churned up earth, mixed with the blood seeping through its cracks.

Jed threw Kura off, then rounded on him with a swift strike to the back with his axe. Kura blocked the swing with his hefty right arm, then brought his left in for a swipe at the stag's neck. He jumped back, but as soon as he did, Kura send a column of stone erupting from the ground to slam into his chest, knocking him to the floor. The bear tore chunks of rock from the ground and began hurling them at Jed's body. The stag rolled free just in time, one of the boulders landing inches from his left antler.

Haru leapt back and aimed his device right at Bayer. A stream of flame gushed from the barrel. Bayer careened backwards; even though the flame missed him, the heat was painful enough, scorching the fur on his right arm. Before he could recover, Haru swung round and blasted the backs of the Sinédrion troops. The soldiers collapsed and the line slipped closer to the Senate. More soldiers massed from the other gates, but The Claw's mercenaries still challenged their numbers.

Kura slammed his fist into the ground. An enormous crack split the plaza, opening up a trench just behind the Sinédrion line, isolating the supplemental troops trying to bolster their comrades. The rocks grew higher, then snapped at the centre and collapsed, trapping or crushing those underneath. He gave a deep laugh, then launched another attack on Jed.

"I'll murder every one of you!" he roared. "Your army will be nothing but *dust!*"

While Kura continued his barrage, Bayer leapt at Haru

again; more sprays of flame forced him to retreat. The mongoose laughed shrilly, turning again to the soldiers he'd burned just a second ago. As he turned, a flash of blue charged in from his left, bulldozing him to the floor, sending the device spinning out of his hand. Raede had her sword drawn, aimed at Haru's chest. He groaned and whimpered, casting his hand around for the device he'd lost.

Bayer ran for it. A rumble stopped him in his tracks. Jagged stones burst from the ground, surrounding the device and separating Raede from Haru.

"Get up or I'll eat you," Kura boomed.

Haru choked out an apology, clambering over to the cannon. Kura sucked the stone back to his open palms like a river of sand, then cast out more rolling blades of rock to cover Haru.

Arrows streaked between them. Aeryn and Kyru approached at speed on their Anserisaurs. Kyru held his double-ended volgue to his right side in both hands, ready for a running strike.

The bear glanced around for a moment, his breath rasping from his throat, saliva frothing from his open jaw. His claws twitched and shook. As the wolves almost reached him he let out a roar of anger, then swung his fists high into the air and slammed them to the floor. The ground he stood on rocketed forwards and upwards, a giant column of stone that drew from the plaza's pavement and arced towards the Senate building. The end of the pillar flattened out like a hammer and burst through the ancient wooden beams, throwing him inside. Haru scrabbled up the stone and sprinted along in pursuit.

Jed leapt onto the stone. "We have to protect the

Representatives!"

Aeryn, Kyru, Bayer, and Raede surrounded the pillar. "They didn't *leave*?" Kyru bayed.

"We didn't have enough time to get them out, and we had underestimated their destructive ability."

They climbed the stone, following the bear's destruction to the Senate.

Chapter Twenty-Four

*A*laris raced behind the Tremaine flank, and the banner-bearers at the back, his mount shaking stones loose from the ground.

Something raked off his back: an arrow from the Claw's archers positioned on the ridge above. Another shot whistled in, this time scraping his breastplate just below his chin. A third shot hit the Theriasaur in the neck. It reared and threw its head, throwing Alaris from his saddle as they rounded a bend. He slammed into the rock, curling up as much as he could to shield himself from the impact. Although his scales were hard his armour constricted him: he couldn't fully roll. He felt the rock slam into his right side; he twisted and slid over it, checking himself for blood. Nothing, but he could tell something had broken. Watching for more arrows, he saw the archer disappeared. He hauled himself up, pain coursing through his right half, and lurched for his sword, cast onto the path.

The Theriasaur had dispersed the team of sappers

planning to blow up the river's bank to flood the battlefield. They had leapt clear when the reptile charged through, scrabbling to return to their positions.

Alaris raised his sword and stumbled towards them, growling intensely. Two were armed and drew their swords as the third shakily tried to attach the bombs to a match cord. The swordsmen: a lemur and a stoat, advanced on him. Alaris reversed his blade and held it behind him in a low guard. They both lunged for him: the lemur aiming for his head and the stoat thrusting at his leg. Alaris swept the blade over his head and shifted his body – he blocked the headshot and avoided the thrust, then slammed the lemur in the chestplate with his sword and swung the pommel into his shoulder. The lemur tripped backwards. One more heavy jab from Alaris caved in the breastplate and the lemur dropped his weapon, struggling to free himself before he suffocated.

The stoat swung for his back with a yell. Alaris barely parried it, but a dull thud hit the creature's back. The stoat screamed and arced, dropping his sword. Vendrell loaded another bolt onto his crossbow.

They marched on the sapper, a quokka, whose hands were shaking so much he kept dropping the match cord. Alaris thrust the point of his sword into the ground beside the fumbling animal. The quokka yelped and slid aside, giving him a fearful, panicked leer.

"Leave," Alaris rumbled.

The quokka looked about; the lemur was already helping the stoat escape. "I didn't—"

Alaris raised his sword. In that instant, the quokka spun on his heels and vanished into the cliffs. The pangolin turned his attention to the cliffs behind him where the archer had been, and saw the body crumpled at the foot of the rock face, a crossbow bolt in his head.

He gave Vendrell a thankful nod and the two ascended the slope.

The stones were cold, rough, and uneven, with loose slate threatening to spill careless travellers onto the floor below, but their claws found traction, pushing them fast and fervently to find the remaining sappers.

It didn't take long. They ducked behind a stony outcrop.

Shadow's Claw had dug out a trench near the cliff's edge, creating a higher wall of rock collapse into the valley. Alaris peered round the corner and caught sight of a cheetah's shoulder hoisting a bow. The cat shuffled, nervous.

"He's not back yet; should I check?" came a whispered voice.

"I don't care. You know him, he's probably scarpered already," was the gruff response. "This is more important. We'll only be here another minute."

"*My thoughts exactly,*" Alaris thought ruefully. He readied his sword and prepared to jump out.

A roar barrelled along the half-tunnel. Confused yells rang out; Alaris could see the cheetah readying his bow. Taking no chances, he jumped and ran, bringing his pommel crashing into the archer's shoulder. The cat crumpled under the impact; one kick to his head knocked him out cold. Vendrell loosed a bolt at one of the other soldiers.

Dion and Skye were tearing through from the other direction. He'd dispatched the two other archers already (with an arrow lodged in his right pauldron) and had pummelled the creatures nearest him into the ground with devastating efficiency. Alaris caught another sapper in the stomach with the flat of his hefty blade, striking him to the floor, then bashed the pommel into his head, knocking him unconscious.

"Is this it; have we stopped them?" Dion asked, breathing heavily and looking about at the carnage he'd wrought.

"We took down the ones at the river's edge," Alaris glowered, dropping his sword to examine the sapper's bombs. They'd been buried fairly deeply; the only visible sign remaining a long match cord laid in gunpowder, threaded into a divot on the ground: the bed where the bomb lay.

He brushed the gunpowder away and gave the match a cautious tug. As he did, it revealed a fuse that trailed all the way along the mountain ridge.

"How many are there?" the jaguar grunted, tearing through a third piece of match; not all of the bombs had been strung together yet.

"Doesn't matter," Alaris replied, "as long as we stopped them. Even one would be enough to kill the soldiers below. This was planned for complete annihilation."

Dion cracked his knuckles. "Which may happen yet, Hiryu, unless we can pull our armies apart."

Alaris held the match in his claws. There were so many soldiers down there. Many he knew, even more that he didn't. And the one life that he had wanted to save most wasn't even in the world any more. He sat back on his haunches.

"He's... really gone."

Vendrell laid a hand on his shoulder. "I'm sorry."

Alaris clutched the match tightly. Right now he didn't really care if it blew him up, but... Skye, Dion and Vendrell, they didn't deserve it. Nor did the troops below. He stood up.

"I have an idea."

Metal tore into metal, splintered wood, rent flesh by the cliff's base. Commanders bellowed for their troops to push harder into their opposers, and the soldiers fed into the pulsing crush of armour as their comrades fell beneath them. Both sides pushed their shields walls and thrust their pikes with equal casualties on both sides, but neither of the leaders were willing to concede ground. Vol's helmet wore a large gash and his leg armour had been dented considerably, but he still shook with rage and bloody-mindedness as he faced his enemies. He bled from his teeth. His troops had disengaged to rearrange their block, trying to tighten their lines into a spearhead to split Tremaine's polearms. Tremaine's lines directly opposite were bolstering their centre.

Vol raised his sword once more. "Andarn, adva—"

A deep explosion from behind Tremaine's ranks halted his command. The shockwave burst through the valley, shaking loose small rocks and slate from the cliffs above. The soldiers looked about in worry.

Vol lifted his sword again to repeat his order when he heard confused cries ring from ahead. Artija, much more intact than her Andarn counterpart, wrenched the reins of her Anserisaur and trotted quickly to the rear of her command. The soldiers kept glancing behind them, and soon the blast's consequences became apparent to the Andarn troops as well. The levee had broken upstream and the river had split.

Vol raised his hand a third time to renew the advance when another interruption cut him off.

Alaris stood at the head of the cliff with Dion, Skye, and Vendrell around him.

"Soldiers of Tremaine and Andarn, this is not your war!" Dion boomed. "You have been made to eliminate each other so that both of your sovereigns could be taken over!"

Skye and Vendrell held up two of the sappers, captured, but unconscious, in each of the army's colours.

Alaris took a deep breath and gave his address. "These mercenaries, part of the Shadow's Claw cult, has infiltrated your armies and conducted atrocities under both your names to increase their power, to goad you into hatred and mistrust. And here, at the apex of your commanders' fury, they were going to bury you under this mountain."

Agitated murmurs rippled through the ranks. The Tremaine soldiers edged away from the water, and the Andarn troops stepped back to give them space as they began to crowd around the cliff base. Vol threw his sword on the ground.

"This is preposterous!" he screamed. "We've seen their defiance and hatred against us! We know—"

"You know *nothing!*" Alaris roared. His voice rattled the valley, silencing the coati at once.

The pangolin cast an accusing claw at Vol, whose jaw ground so tight it looked like it might snap under the strain.

"You were so quick to blame Tremaine without question that you played directly into their hands. You were looking for an excuse to wage war to satisfy your disgusting prejudices and fearful greed!" he shouted. "You never bothered to seek the truth." He addressed the soldiers, "Your leaders have been played for fools, and we... we have lost so many friends through their ignorance."

Alaris cast the point of his sword over the rocks behind him. "Around here is proof that you were all to be killed. We found the bombs that Shadow's Claw were using to bring this mountainside on top of you, for no crime other than loyalty to your sovereign, and for trying to defend yourselves from the misguided will of ignorant superiors and tricksters." He nodded to Skye and Vendrell, who ran around to the path behind Andarn. "That way is safe. We will show you the real battle."

Vol stared in disbelief as both ranks of troops began filing out of the valley, following the path shown to them by the Lieutenants. He stammered, tried to find the words to bring his power back. The Andarn soldiers gave him withering stares and the Tremaine soldiers pushed roughly past him as he sat alone on his mount, the river's dark waters swirling slowly around him.

Chapter Twenty-Five

Kura's stone beam rammed through the wall of the domed Senate, high up in the building's structure. Haru had disappeared from sight, following the fervid warlord inside. Jed led the chase, with Aeryn and Kyru just behind, and Bayer and Raede following on. All had their weapons drawn, their focus on the jagged opening ahead.

As they crossed the stone arc's narrow crest, Bayer saw something shimmering to their left on the roof of the dome.

Haru.

"Run!" he yelled, pushing ahead. They saw at the last second; Jed made a leap for the Senate wall as Haru fired his device. The green bolt lashed the stone at the centre of the group just behind Aeryn and Kyru. The stone cracked and sparked. The two wolves felt it move and made a mad jump for the hole, landing inside. Bayer and Raede stalled short of the blast. They only had a second before Haru recharged his shot, and now Shadow's Claw troops were mounting the stone in pursuit.

"Go!" she yelled. Bayer stepped across quickly, then swung round and directed his sword at Haru, who, although aiming again for Raede, saw the ocelot and fled around the dome's large wooden buttresses. He glanced back to the caracal.

"Get him!" she barked. "I'll hold off the soldiers."

She spun and swung her sword into a high guard as the line of soldiers climbed to face her. It shook uneasily with their footsteps. Bayer turned to the roof and began climbing towards the glass at its centre.

Chief Senator Tyrone sat at his desk in the Senate's highest floor, churlishly scribbling on parchments and scrolls for ratification at the next meeting. Shelves towered over him, overflowing with endless volumes of bound papers and crusty books. A fire cracked and spit quietly opposite him. Two of his aides stood nervously either side of the aged, hulking badger, whose face was close enough to the desk that he could well have been signing with his nose. The aides, an anteater and an armadillo, flinched and fidgeted at the muffled sounds of battle coming from outside.

"Your Eminence," the armadillo aide squeaked to the Councillor, while giving her partner a sideways glance. "Might I suggest we find a safer place to stay? There are guards down in the lobbies who might be—"

"I can't hear anything worth bothering about," the wizened badger huffed, violently scrawling his signature across a paper as if it had caused him deep personal affront.

The anteater echoed the armadillo's concern. "There was that large crash a few minutes ago, Your Eminence. You don't suppose that they're inside?"

The badger paused. Immediately the two straightened. "I will not leave. If we do not continue our duties even in the hardest of times, the world is truly lost. Walls may crumble to dust, but anyone's resolve can be made eternal by their choices and how they are reflected in their legacy. Is that clear?"

The aides nodded, allowing themselves to relax a little after expecting a far more cantankerous tirade.

"However," the badger barked, "should you find yourselves insecure, you may patrol the corridors to ensure we are still as safe as we have always been."

The anteater let out a sigh and gave a subtle nod to the door. They both gave Tyrone a bow as they made their way outside. Pulling open the door, they started at something approaching them along the large corridor. Tyrone cast a wary eye towards the doorway, his hand hovering above the papers. As his aides tried to duck from the oncoming force, a large claw struck the anteater, punching him clean into the opposite wall. The armadillo ducked under the second claw and ran for her partner, dragging him away as Kura's rabid visage loomed in the doorway; his claws raked deep gashes in the wooden frame.

"High Councillor Tyrone," he growled, his voice more of a quake in the walls than an utterance from his mouth.

The old badger didn't stand, but kept signing paperwork. His hands were shaking. "I do not know you," he replied, his voice hoarse but firm.

Kura had reached his desk. "No, but I know you," he rasped. "So fitting that the head of this corrupt and belligerent company of boors is such a crumbled, wizened mismanager. Do you even move, or has your gold-fed backside been permanently attached to your throne to save time on your graceless Senate ratifications?"

Tyrone took the next sheet of paper. "There is no throne here. We lead through the voices of the many."

The badger felt an immense grip around his neck. Huge, muscular claws clamped on his windpipe, lifted him from his seat.

"Whose voices, Tyrone?" Kura growled. "The 'many' of the streets, or the 'many' of your gilded corridors? Those Councillors you so proudly describe grovel into their position by appeasing fops, merchants, and cowards, whose money entitles them to hide away from the world's injustices. And in turn they deal *more* injustices that separate them from what they fear most – truth."

Tyrone, his body hanging helplessly in Kura's grasp, raised a frail arm to pull at the bear's wrist. His mouth gaped, his eyes widened and rolled back into his head.

Kura's teeth glinted in his enraged grimace. "I am the truth. The servant of the oppressed, the judge of the ignorant, and…" He brought his other fist up to Tyrone's pulsing, quivering chest, and slammed his claws deep into his ribcage. With one, swift movement, he clenched them tight shut and twisted his wrist. A series of soft cracks, and Tyrone's arms fell limp. "…executioner of the corrupt."

He held his kill for a few seconds, watching the life drain from Tyrone's eyes. His face split into a grin, and a short, deep laugh rumbled in his throat. "The new era begins."

Movement behind him. The bear turned just in time to drop his kill and block the dual axes with his armoured wrists. He gave Jed a blunt kick to the chest and jumped away to the room's far corner. Aeryn and Kyru entered after Jed, who kept his eyes fixed on the hulking, smiling General. Kura licked his teeth. "Your persistence will be in vain. Your army will be crushed, and your precious, vindictive leaders will be overturned from within."

Jed remained firm, his axes gleaming in the light of the fire. "Your plan and attack force is in tatters. You underestimated the strength of those who fight honestly, and those who know true tyranny when it comes to bite them."

Kura shook his head. "The Shadow's Claw has ignited the voice of the forgotten. We will lead them to your homes, pull you into the streets, kill you, and replace you with those who understand what it means to have suffered." Kura's eyes hardened with ire. "You will not destroy another country like my own."

The bear lunged towards the hearth. His claw slammed into the stone chimney and the tiles erupted outwards, showering the room with flaming logs, embers, ash, and brick. Aeryn and Kyru ducked away; Jed crouched down, shielding himself with his armour and axes. When they stood, Kura had formed the brick into a hole and escaped. They ran to the gap. Directly below them was the huge Senate chamber and the platform where the Council sat facing the amphitheatre of delegates – they shared a central chimney with Tyrone's office. Kura's explosion had smashed the walkway above the stage and collapsed the brick tower.

The bear had disappeared. Jed sprinted for the door; Aeryn and Kyru followed. They rounded the huge circular passageway and came to the nearest door leading to the Senate's upper gallery. They paused by it for a second as Aeryn readied her bow and Kyru prepared his weapons, then pushed quickly through.

The door's heavy creak resonated in the eerily dormant chamber. Kyru's armour rattled as he circled the upper balcony. Aeryn scanned the room for signs of the bear, bow half-drawn. The sudden quiet made her ears flatten momentarily against her skull.

Kyru descended the sloping aisle and peered over the edge to see the stalls below.

"Kyru, behind you!"

He didn't even look but dived aside, and the stone column that burst through the floor pulverised the wooden platform to splinters where he'd stood.

Aeryn launched two quick arrows at the bear. Kura swirled his claws on the stone beside him, drawing it round him like a cape, and the arrows skittered away. Jed and Kyru swept down the spiral stairs on either side of the upper gallery, advancing on Kura's shell. Kura kept his canopy blocking Aeryn from shooting him, but saw Kyru and slammed his foot into the ground, sending a ripple of brick under his feet, disarming his run. He then swung round and punched the stone behind him; spikes shot out from the thin wall, straight at Jed. They were too weak, however, and broke against Jed's heavy frame and hardened axes.

With the stag inches away behind his thin stone veil, Kura wrought the marble floor into his hand with a great twist, then slammed his hand into the ground. Jagged tendrils of rock spiralled from around him, thrashing upwards and out, splitting wooden seats and smashing the wooden panels of the balcony. Jed leapt back as a vine scraped his flank; Kyru ducked and wove past those that flew his way. Aeryn was relatively safe above them, but the gallery's wooden floor shook, and with each strut that broke her footing became more uneven.

Kura wore a salivating grin, visible between the whips and undulations of his living stone barrier. His back hunched and swelled with his increasingly heavy breaths. As the arm he'd planted in the floor began to twitch at the elbow, his grin folded into a grimace and he clenched his other fist.

"Your attacks are weakening, Gallis," Jed yelled, swinging at a stone vine that came too close. "It is only a matter of time now."

Kura's eyes flared. "I never weaken!" He raised his other fist, glowering at Jed, and then threw his weight behind it, slamming it into the floor.

The tree-like limbs whipped upwards and then crashed down, smashing through the wooden stalls, sending splinters and debris flying everywhere. Kyru rolled to the outer edge of the room. Aeryn took shelter between benches, and Jed had escaped being crushed thanks to the low overhang above him, blocking Kura's attack short.

Jed immediately ducked under the branch and dashed at Kura. Kura hauled his body backwards, his hands still stuck in the floor, and the vines whipped drunkenly backwards, lashing the stag's legs and sweeping him to the floor. Aeryn shot another arrow towards him; the instant that Kura saw it, the stone reacted to his momentary panic and an angular wave of stone burst in front of him, shattering the arrow.

Kyru began his attack, leaping over the vines, his volgue

raised and aimed directly at the bear's neck. Jed picked himself up to see more serpentine tendrils rising behind the wolf, this time pointed at him like lances. They lunged forwards. Jed leapt to his feet and crashed into Kyru, knocking him away.

Stone spikes erupted from the floor where Kyru had been advancing. Both they and the spears impacted Jed. Blood spattered the broken ground.

Bayer climbed the dome to its glass apex, sword held by his side. He turned the blade slowly in his hand, stalking his target. The noise of the battle below and the breeze coursing over the building made it difficult to hear any movement, and the faint smell of char and dust masked any potential scent. Taking this as a clue, Bayer followed the wind's path, thinking Haru would be coy enough to hide downwind to ambush him.

Below, he could hear Raede shouting as she clashed with soldiers trying to assail the building. He hoped to disable Haru quickly enough to support her.

From the wide circle of chimney stacks around the central glass dome, smoke escaped into the sky in diminishing waves, the fires below dwindling with few to tend them. If he and the others failed, there would be nobody left standing who knew the truth, and all of their efforts would be overwritten by a dark, tyrannical chapter of Cadon's history.

He peered over the top of the Senate roof's highest step, scouring the edges for Haru. Had he found a way back inside?

A nearby clink of metal against brick pricked his ears. He turned, blade up, poised to strike. From behind the chimney Haru leant out, loosing a bolt of green energy towards Bayer. The ocelot swept his right leg backwards, twisting his body to the side just in time for the beam to sweep past his chest. Haru cursed and fired another, weaker beam, but Bayer was already on the move. He strafed and circled around, trying to keep the stone chimney between them. Haru backed away, bringing himself towards the exposed centre of the dome to give himself a vantage point from which to strike anywhere Bayer moved. Bayer sensed his disadvantage but tightened his grip on his sword and he kept his run strong, trying to circle around and outpace Haru's elemental bursts. If he kept the pressure on, there was a chance he could close distance between volleys.

A rumble beneath them shook the roof. One of the chimney stacks buckled and shifted down a few feet, as if broken at its middle. Haru looked at the glass beneath him, catching a movement in his peripheral vision. Bayer took his chance and lunged forwards. Haru mishandled the gun's controls and instead of firing it, closed his finger on the rigid trigger guard. In a panic he pressed harder but nothing happened. Bayer was upon him. To defend, the mongoose thrust the end of the gun into Bayer's chest, ramming him several times with its metal barrel. Bayer grabbed the top of it with his free hand and tried to wrest it from Haru's grasp, then brought his sword up to slam it into his face. Haru pulled his body into the gun and hunched over it; Bayer's sword crashed against his backplate, tearing his cloak. Haru thrashed about and leapt at Bayer, trying to sink his needle teeth into the ocelot's face. Bayer recoiled, letting go of the gun to land a punch on Haru with his now-free hand. Haru was knocked back, but kept hold of the gun. In a second he checked his hold and found the trigger. He fired but Bayer, being so close, had less distance to clear and the shot burst past his left flank.

Just as Bayer brought his sword round for another swing, a series of impacts below them rocked the roof. The wood trembled, both of them nearly losing their footing. Haru glanced through the glass at the writhing stone mass beneath them and cracked a gleeful smirk.

"You're finished!"

Behind him, a figure sprinted up the roof.

The stone arms hung motionless as Kura examined his target.

The mass of spines was almost too dense to see through in the clouds of dust formed by the transforming stone and crushing impacts, and as it cleared, the grim silhouette of the impaled figure stood before them.

One of the spikes had grazed the side of Jed's face, missing his eye by inches. He was pierced at the right thigh, his left foot, and through the top of his left shoulder. He was still standing, and glared into Kura's nest; through ragged, bloody breaths he spat his determination.

The bear's triumphant grin fell into a twitching sneer.

Aeryn loosed an arrow at the unmoving cage; it skittered through the gap and clashed against the bear's greave. Kura growled and threw Jed free with the stone, hurling him into the wall. Immediately he directed his spiralling limbs towards Aeryn. She ran around the outer ring of the chamber as they scraped the wall above and pounded into the stalls. Their movement was sluggish, but the pursuit was relentless and their strength devastating. Meanwhile, Kyru swung at the stone protecting Kura, thrusting his volgue through the gaps, trying to slash his legs and give Aeryn a chance to dodge. Kura, unable to move his hands, roared at him and stamped his foot, forcing more stone into a barrier around him. When the arms lashing at Aeryn slowed she loosed an arrow; in her hurry it flew too high, but it was enough to distract him. Kyru increased his attacks, slamming his shield into the rock and using the vines as a step to thrust his blade over the top of the rocky curtain.

Kura shook with rage, his jaw gaping in gnarled frustration. His breaths had escalated to harsh, ragged growls; spots in his eyes blossomed with blood. He drew his fists together under the stone and raised his arms, dragging a column of rock beneath them, then plunged it into the ground.

Above, Raede barrelled straight for Haru with her blade drawn. He aimed the resonance cannon at her just as Bayer cast a lunging strike at the mongoose.

Pillars of stone erupted from the floor of the Senate chamber like a colossal wave; debris flew high into the air, thrown up and through the roof. The rolling tide of devastating towers burst forwards, annihilating the once-pristine meeting hall of the Senate in an indiscriminate barrage of force.

Outside, the ground quaked; ripples thundered along the

ground, dislodging paving stones, tripping soldiers in the heat of the battle. The fighting paused and all eyes fell on the Senate. The Shadow's Claw soldiers started backing away from the rumbling dome as the ground shook once again; their spear points still aimed at the Sinédrion defenders, who were trapped between them and the pulsating, splitting building. Root-like ridges surged from under the plaza, breaking the battle lines.

Aeryn and Kyru barely had time to react. The eruption nearest Kura hit highest, breaking the stone arms. Jed's body was thrown again into the air; another stone caught an antler and snapped it in two.

Kyru ducked underneath a bench sent spinning through the air by the stone onslaught, but a pillar directly underneath him caught his leg, casting him into the stalls further back. He disappeared between the rows, and a torrent of pillars raced past him, masking his landing place. Aeryn sprinted from her position on the upper level to try and reach him but a stone eruption burst through the floor, catching her in the side, lifting her up and tossing her to the ground floor stalls. Her bow clattered to the stone.

The glass dome tore apart with the debris Kura flung through it.

Haru tripped backwards, a plank of wood flying right by his face. Bayer barely jumped clear from his attempted attack on Haru as the fight below erupted through the roof. Raede, too far into her advance, raised her arms to shield herself and lost her footing as the glass broke beneath her. She dropped instantly. Desperately she grabbed the dome's wooden frame and braced her arms around it, fighting against the weight of her armour. Haru readied the gun again.

Bayer ran towards him. Haru twisted his body and fired.

The green bolt hit Bayer's right arm. He felt a searing, burning pain, and a loss of weight from his right side. He lost his balance and stumbled. His sword clattered to the roof, his severed lower arm still gripping the handle. He fell to his knees, eyes wide, the intense ache creeping further up his shoulder, into his neck.

Below them, the bombardment of stone stopped. Kura dispersed his shield to examine his attackers. He could see nothing as the reverberations of his assault slowly subsided into an eerie calm, painted only by the echoing battle from outside.

The rubble twitched on his far left. Kyru lurched upwards from under a wooden bench and shoved it away. Aeryn appeared on the ground, bruised but stable. Her shattered bow lay a few feet in front of her.

Kura's eyes flared, his teeth ground together.

"*Vermin!*" he spat. "Cockroaches!"

Kyru gave a dusty laugh. "You'd be surprised what we can survive." He readied his volgue and Aeryn drew her dagger.

Above them Haru picked himself up and strode triumphantly to Bayer. He kicked the ocelot's severed limb down the roof; it and the sword careened to the ground.

"You were nothing. You have always *been* nothing." The mongoose let out a shrill, cruel laugh. "Less than nothing! What is a warrior who doesn't even have his sword arm?"

Bayer's breath heaved from his body. His voice rasped.

"Faster."

He sprang from his kneeling position and streamed to Haru, who didn't even have time to pull the trigger. Bayer grabbed the Prince's jaw with his remaining left arm as he ran past, digging his claws into his flesh, and tore up and backwards. Haru toppled back, dropping the cannon, flipped sideways and over by his jawbone. Bayer tightened his grip for the final part of his throw, a vicious twist that snapped both Haru's jaw and neck. The mongoose let out a strangled, wet gasp, his eyes desperately wide. His fingers twitched for a few seconds, then fell still. Blood oozed from his mouth.

Bayer looked to the cannon, now just behind him, resting on a bare section of wood. As his vision blurred he felt himself fall forwards again, onto his knees, but he stopped short of the gaping hole in the roof. A metal-clad arm reached across his chest and hauled him upright, while a familiar gauntlet reached for the cannon. Raede shook him; his vision returned slightly.

"Bayer! Come on."

He nodded vaguely. "The cannon. It's all we have."

"I know."

She supported him as they walked to the edge of the hole that Kura had blown in the roof.

Kura let out a deep growl. "You are all fools."

The room began to shake. A deep hum grew steadily louder, closer, from under their feet. The debris trembled.

Aeryn clenched the dagger tightly. Kyru whirled his volgue, breaking into a run.

Bayer and Raede tightened their hands on the gun, and together pulled the trigger.

A thick green blast whistled directly down onto the bear, lancing his left side. The beam continued for another second, slicing through his ribcage. His mouth gaped open. As the beam dissipated, a shadow leapt at him from his right and plunged a blade up into his eye, while another sweeping strike from a large, flattened blade slashed open his neck.

His head twisted as Kyru drew the volgue out of his throat and the weight of Aeryn hanging on the dagger in his eye tore him downwards. As she let go he collapsed. A gruff, guttural sigh escaped his dead maw, and the room descended into silence.

A spasm of pain washed over Bayer; he dropped the cannon and Raede did too, opting to catch him instead. The gold device spun and twisted in the air as it fell, before smashing on the rocks, to reveal the silver crystal rod embedded within.

Aeryn and Kyru both looked up, and immediately ran for the roof.

Chapter Twenty-Six

S oft white light drifted into the room, filtered by the flowing, almost ethereally white curtains veiling the window. Bayer had drifted in and out of slumber for some time, but his eyes were finally focusing enough for him to keep them open, and the dizzying haze that swirled around his head flowed away to reside as a dryness in his throat. He looked to his left and found himself facing a wooden screen. It was very quiet, quieter than he would have expected from a hospital ward in the Senate after such a fierce battle.

Something kept tickling his ear. He tried swinging his right arm to scratch it but found it unbalanced, unwieldy, and his bicep felt unusually swollen. He checked to see if he'd fallen asleep on it, and a chilling wave flooded through him as he remembered the extent of his injuries. An oozing, bandaged stump just above his elbow was all that was left. It twitched with the strain of him lifting it, the muscles severed and distorted. He could feel tingling sensations and movement below the end of the stump, like the ghost of his forearm was in spasm, but when he tried to touch the end of it all he felt was horrific, burning pain. He stifled a scream, his teeth clamped shut so tight he thought he might break his jaw. After a few seconds it subsided and he relaxed back in bed, breathing heavily. A cold sweat crept down his back and legs.

He lay in bed for a few minutes more, staring at the stone ceiling and the wooden beams running along its length. Eventually growing restlessness forced him to swing himself upright, and he carefully balanced on the edge of the bed. He took deep breaths to steady himself, fighting against dehydration. Next to his bed sat a small chest, on top of which was his shirt, torn and burnt. He pulled it carefully over his arm and head, then rose to his feet.

The ward wasn't as long as he thought, only four beds wide before reaching a corridor at the edge. There were two other residents, both of whom were in a deep sleep. Bayer shuffled his way into a walk, moving unevenly, trying to accustom himself to the shift in his balance. He must have been separated from the main casualties; there was no way that so few in Sinédrion required hospital treatment.

When he reached the window at the corridor he saw why everything seemed so out of place. He wasn't in Sinédrion. The city beyond him was full of golden sandstone buildings and grey spires. Narrow sentry towers sat along the wall that bordered the city, and he could see grey mountain peaks in the distance.

A nurse marmot marched towards him. He put a hand out to stop her advance, thinking she was going to wrestle him back into bed, and he wavered, almost falling. She took his arm and he instinctively clenched his fist, grunting irritably. He had not long escaped the need for this kind of support.

"I'm fine," he hissed. "Where am I?"

The marmot rolled her eyes. "You're in Tremaine. You were brought here from Sinédrion as their hospitals were over capacity. I'll take you somewhere to sit down and get you some water; you need a drink."

Reluctantly, Bayer allowed himself to be led to a seating area nearby and made to sit. He leant back in the chair while she walked away. Around him echoed the sounds of the sick, dying, and healing; muted, but distracting. He began tapping his foot and watching for the nurse to return. The cold sweat washed over him again and the pain in his right arm swelled. He pressed his hand against his shoulder and held it tightly, hunched over, rocking slightly.

Was this it? Was he useless again already?

"Is this for you?" came a voice.

Slowly he unfurled, and his eyes met with a set of blue armour. He looked up, and Raede was standing above him, having taken the tankard of water from the nurse.

"You look like you need it," she continued.

Bayer nodded and took it, sipping at first, then taking huge gulps. He finished it within seconds, and kept looking at the tankard as if there should have been more within it. His desperation was mortifying, and he hated the way she was still looking at him.

"Glad to see someone I know," he murmured.

"Liar," she hissed, sitting heavily in the chair next to him. "You look like you want to die."

"I'm a little tired right now," he replied, gripping the tankard tightly.

Her eyes caught his in a sideways glance. "You looked like you wanted to die before; now you just look like you've lost your reason to."

Bayer managed a weak smile and raised the tankard to catch a few more dregs on his tongue. "Didn't *want* to die, but was ready to."

She cracked her knuckles. "I think it's more heroic to live, to be honest. You can't climb a mountain by jumping off halfway and hoping to fly to the top."

He nodded faintly, and stared into the empty tankard. Images of his journey from Kyrryk to Xayall and back again, flowed through his mind. He had been driven out by war, then drawn back by the same war fought in a different land. In his youth it had been all he wanted to fight and protect, to be strong, and be the one whose sword blocked the blades held towards the ones who deserved to be protected. Now his injuries were unable to be ignored, would he fall back and let someone else, someone he might not even know, fight in his place? How could he trust them to be as strong, to keep looking in the right direction? He all but deserted Faria when things became difficult, just like he ran from Kyrryk after his family was killed. He had nowhere to run now. It just felt so… final.

"Hope you're as good with a sword in your left arm as you are with your right," Raede said, giving him a playful jostle. "Maybe you don't even need one, with the way you killed the Prince."

He gave a bitter laugh, then froze as her words sunk in. It was meant as a joke, but a quiet energy buzzed just underneath his skin. He had relied so much on his strength and sword skills, assuming that was the only way to defend

298

against another warrior. Bayer had never believed in diplomacy and refuted the idea that a country could ever be completely unified. His devotion to protection had been to select individuals, not institutions. But the world was full of people worth protecting. If everybody had thought like him, there would be so few left now, and all in isolation from each other.

"You're right, I don't think I'll need it," he said eventually.

"What do you mean?"

He turned the tankard over. "I think my sword can be put to better use in someone else's hands. It's too easy an excuse to kill, and I think we've lost enough lives for now."

She shrugged. "So you're retiring?"

He smiled. "No, far from it. Just learning to fight in a different way." He looked to her and she looked quickly away. He thought he saw the semblance of a smile on her face too, but by the time she looked back she wore her usual, steady indifference.

"Your pangolin friend is here, by the way."

Bayer's ears pricked up. "Alaris? When did he get here?"

"He's been here almost as long as you have. He…" she paused, watching Bayer for a second, "…lost someone."

Chapter Twenty-Seven

The colours outside were soft, muted. Even the blue sky overhead was a gentle, quiet shade, with thin white clouds drifting silently overhead. The pale grass rippled and twitched in the breeze on the hillside graveyard. The cemetery, far enough from the centre of the city, wasn't disturbed by the noise, but the whole sovereign had been in soulful mourning since the loss of two of its Princes, and the dozens of soldiers caught in the conflict on both sides.

Other creatures walked respectfully between the headstones to pay their respects, but one figure sat hunched in front of a particular grave, and had been there for longer than anyone knew. Alaris sat back slightly from the headstone, his head low, and looked at the carving he'd etched into the corner of the marker with his claws. It had taken him a long time, but nobody had called on him to stop. It was a small caricature of a meerkat, smiling, with closed eyes.

"You don't know what I'd give for you to make a stupid

comment right now."

The breeze was cold, sometimes uncomfortably so, but he didn't react. It soothed him, in a strange way. A punishment, maybe, or some kind of penance. He wasn't sure, but with it he could both feel and quantify the hurt, and even though he couldn't stop his legs or arms from shaking when the sun disappeared, he welcomed it as an accompaniment to his aching loss.

He traced a claw across the ground in front of him, weaving its sharp point between the grass blades. He could hear footsteps, but didn't turn to look – the cemetery had a lot of visitors right now. Many soldiers had lost their lives, but most of them had been honoured in the funeral of Lyris, and placed in more honourable gravesites. Rowan had always requested different treatment. He didn't consider himself a hero; he felt it would lead people to disappointment if he ever made a mistake. '*Heroes should always be admired; I'm not always an admirable person. I don't do outlandish things for justice. I just… do what I can*', he'd said.

"Missed the point, didn't you?" Alaris croaked quietly.

The footsteps behind him had stopped, but he could see a shadow to his right, and recognised its owner. He pulled his claw back into his lap.

"Alaris," Bayer said quietly. "I'm sorry."

Alaris shook his head. "It's a risk we all take."

Bayer and Raede stood in silence behind him for a while. After a few seconds Raede placed her hand on Bayer's shoulder and walked to another headstone some way down the hill, then leant on it and folded her arms, patiently on guard.

"I didn't believe it at first," the pangolin breathed. "He

couldn't be dead. Why would he be dead? He's not done that before. I got so angry. Killed so many Claw agents. And once the battle was over I rushed here because it couldn't be true, it had to be a mistake. Then… then I realised I was thinking irrationally, that I can't just come here and fix it. I'd even started believing that someone had just looked in the wrong place and he was sat quietly by himself in a room somewhere. But…" he let out a whisper of a laugh. "He was never quiet, or sat still. I still expect to see him somewhere, among these streets, even here. It doesn't feel real. I didn't see it. I don't… I don't know what to think. But…" Alaris focused on his friend's name etched into the headstone's smooth surface. The gold lettering shone in the light; steady, permanent. "I'll… really miss him."

He sat in silence for a second, then let out a strained laugh. "Stupid bastard tells me to be careful and then gets himself killed in his own city. I mean, come on, how is that fair? I risked *everything* in this mission, got through and he just… gets killed? Just like that, without me even able to come back and tell him that I'm safe? Taken down by cowards. It's stupid."

Bayer said nothing as Alaris raked his claws into the ground, sinking his head further towards the gravestone. His voice rose as he spoke. "He was a good soldier, and a good friend. *My* friend. He didn't deserve it. I've seen… I've seen soldiers die, ones I've known, but him… he was… Damn it, why couldn't I have been there?"

Bayer bowed his head, holding his arm, trying to quell the tremoring spikes of pain that shot from where it had been severed.

Alaris threw the grass he'd torn from the ground and

cast it into the wind. "He was supposed to be here!" he cried. "I had so much left to say…"

Bayer clutched his arm even more tightly. He could see a shadow of himself mourning his younger brother in Alaris' grief.

The pangolin looked to the sky, his eyes closed. He breathed deeply for a moment, then sighed. "We were going to, uh…" He pulled at his neck with his claws, as if trying to pluck the words free from being strangled in his throat. "We had talked about joining our regiments together, a sort of combined army between Andarn and Tremaine. Not a free one, but a united one. One that didn't have political allegiances, and stood for the protection of the citizens. After all this… it seems like a bad idea, doesn't it?"

Bayer sighed. "Nobody's going to trust any army right now, let alone an unaffiliated one. Shadow's Claw has done more than kill; it's riven the Senate. We'll be lucky if any of the sovereigns are on speaking terms for a long time, especially with the Senate itself in tatters."

Alaris pulled at his claws. "Is this what Kyrryk was like? Did I really not understand what was happening there?" He let out a pained sigh. "I feel so stupid. Makes me just want to run off and disappear. Do you still feel that way about Xayall?"

Bayer shrugged. "Yes and no. I won't be going back as Faria's bodyguard, but I don't want to isolate myself from the world any more. I won't be able to help anyone if I do that. The injustices and cruelties won't ever stop without someone to stand against them. It's futile to just shout at the world while you have some degree of power to change it."

Alaris drew his arms around himself a little more. "I got

complacent. As much as I knew it might happen, Andarn and Tremaine were always so strong that nobody stood against us. Xayall was the first I saw of what I would call 'real' warfare, and we were lucky to have some incredible power supporting us. It's easy to avoid conflict when you're part of such a large military system. I… don't want to put anyone in that situation again. I want… Rowan back."

"At least the place to start… might be between his army and yours, given that he meant so much to you."

Alaris nodded, almost imperceptibly. "Yeah. I just… wasn't supposed to be alone."

Bayer knew those words well. He'd lived them for a long time. He stepped forwards and laid his hand on Alaris' shoulder. "You won't be. There are many others who have lost friends, brothers, sisters… Tell them about Rowan and what you wanted to do together." He smiled, distant but warm. "You would be surprised how much people need to hear that. I'll do all I can for you whenever you need it, and you'll always have Aeryn and Faria, too. They won't abandon you."

Alaris stood up, laying his claws on Rowan's headstone, and pressing his head against it. "I'll come back soon, Rowan. I don't want to leave, but… there's a lot to clean up. Thank you…" He took a deep breath and let out a slow, controlled sigh. "Thank you for being my friend. It was… a true honour."

He straightened and let his claws slide from the polished stone, then slowly, gradually, stepped back and turned to see Bayer. His eyes glistened with sadness, but the pangolin lifted his arm and placed it around Bayer's shoulder, and together they walked down the hill to where Raede waited.

Chapter Twenty-Eight

*S*ix weeks passed. Since the removal of Andarn's troops from Xayall, the rebuild had been significantly slowed, and with the Senate in tatters, there had been little administrative help from them. The winter, although generally mild, saw supplies stretched to their thinnest in years. Now, however, with the sun hanging higher in the sky and the temperature warming, the farmlands were recovering well and the first lines of diplomatic communication had begun to reopen.

The death of Tyrone and disappearance of many minor councillors and representatives caused many positions in the Senate to be left open. Of those who had ties to the Claw, some were arrested, but others merely vanished, and not always peacefully. Elections and recommendations were coming, but slowly, and a certain degree of chaos was still being smothered as smaller groups vied for power in the wake of the huge military divisions.

Even after his injuries, Jed had refused to abandon his

position as Sinédrion's Representative and governed from his bed – Faria had received several letters from him keeping the Representatives updated as to the reconstruction of the Senate. He was grossly in favour of re-establishing and streamlining the Senate's hierarchy, but could not force the sovereigns to remove anyone from office. Undoing the destruction that had already been wrought was hard work and nowhere near complete. The Claw had infiltrated all levels of authority, or at best displaced them, and the new appointments had a lot to learn on the job. He and the remaining senior Representatives, Councillors, and Senate officers were tutors as much as they could be, and retained the hope that widespread inexperience would not lead to further conflict.

Having left her wheelchair behind a few weeks ago, Faria found walking a little easier, but at the moment she could only venture between one place of rest to another, and relied on a cane. She pushed herself further each time, and swallowed the dizziness and aching fatigue that tried to hold her body to ransom. She pushed herself to do daily therapeutic exercises once she convinced the doctors she was not in need of overprotection. They had been so used to dealing with her father's frailty, and while she respected the caution with which they'd treated him, she had no choice but to become stronger, and quickly.

She had not yet touched another crystal after the last one exploded in her hand. They frightened her now. Physical training was all she could focus on to try and curb her fears. If she could hold herself up without feeling sick or passing out, she could start to think of using her powers again, or learn to cope without them.

She sat outside in the arena with Aeryn, as Kyru and Kier trained in front of them. The gentle sunlight spread warmly against her fur, and she sniffed the fresh, light air. She looked back at the Tor at a window about halfway up. Every time she went outside she looked back at it, hoping, almost expecting Tierenan to be leaning out of it, giving her a wave or yelling to her about the amazing clouds, or how much better the sun is in Skyria because the trees made it sparkle instead of just shine. Thinking of his little dialogues made her smile greatly; she missed his sense of optimism intensely right now, one the world sorely needed but was rarely granted.

Before, where she would sink into the vacuum of sadness his injuries created, now she steadied herself with determination to find a way to heal him. She'd had a lot of time to reflect on those feelings, and this, one of the brightest and warmest days of spring so far, would have had him basking in the sun next to her. He hadn't moved since the night of the attempted coup, and there had been left no clue as to how Barra had managed to rouse him into action again. Despite the haunting memory of his reactivation as a weapon of war, Faria swore she would learn all she could about resonance healing, and give Skyria everything they needed to help him recover.

She looked to the sky again just as Aeryn gave her a gentle nudge.

"Here we go."

Kyru had made a bet with Kier that the fox couldn't strike him with his resonance powers engaged. Despite Kier's reluctance to take part, eventually Kyru convinced him it would be a good training opportunity for them both, as they had no idea how many other resonators existed or how they would fight. Finding a weakness would be imperative, and Faria would not be up to combat too soon.

"No enemy is insurmountable," Kyru had said firmly, knowing all too well they were only a hair's breadth away from being killed by Kura. The wolf chambered his fists, standing opposite Kier, who had forgone his armour in place of a more formal coat, to match Faria's diplomatic attire.

"You don't mind getting that dirty?" Kyru asked.

Kier shook his head. "I'm not as clean-cut as you think," he retorted. Kyru broke a sly smile.

"All right, whenever you're ready."

Kier nodded once, then vanished, leaving only a small, almost imperceptible cushion of sand billowing from where he'd stood.

Kyru turned his head, watching for something; neither Faria nor Aeryn could see it. Suddenly he spun round and gave a low swing of his left arm away from his body, a body block, and threw his right fist into a punch straight ahead of him. Instantly Kier appeared, stumbling back in shock. He tumbled back and rolled over his shoulder, cradling his stomach.

"How... did you know?" he croaked eventually.

Kyru rubbed his right shoulder while stretching his rotator cuff. "I couldn't see you, but I could follow your trail in the sand. Only just, but it was enough. You were almost too fast."

Kier pulled himself to his feet, leaning on his thighs. "The punch, I mean – you blocked it without seeing me."

The wolf shrugged. "Well, you're too polite to go all out

from the beginning. You're also too polite to hit me in the face or knock me out with a roundhouse, too worried about my dignity to trip me, so I figured you'd be going for a gut-check for show. Next time, don't hold back." He held out his hand for the fox to shake. "Besides, there are advantages to being hit."

Kier tilted his head quizzically. At that moment they were met by Aeryn and Faria. The female fox held her walking cane tightly. "Are you all right?" she asked Kier. "That was quite a hit you took."

Kyru and Aeryn bumped fists before he walked back to a position to fight again, both their tails bristling with immense satisfaction.

"Er, yes, Faria. I'm fine," Kier replied. "Thank you."

She looked up at his ears, and the shards of white crystal that hung elegantly from them. "When I'm doing better, would you mind showing me how you use your resonance?"

He rubbed the back of his neck, a smile creeping onto his face despite his best efforts to keep his composure. "Oh yes, of course."

Her face lit up in response, but something caught her attention behind him, coming from the entrance of the arena. He turned to see what she'd spotted: a sizeable deputation of troops approaching, in gold and brown Sinédrion armour. At the forefront was Jed, enormous in stature and marching boldly, his bright red cape billowing behind him. Beside him, in robes of purple, black, and gold, Bayer looked more regal than he ever had before. The sleeve of his amputated right arm was slit open; within it a ribbon of crimson, ruffled silk, that shimmered like blood.

Faria clasped her hands together, alight with pleasure at

seeing her former bodyguard again. Kier froze upon seeing his friend. On their reaction, which Bayer had been expecting but was incapable of handling nonetheless, the ocelot looked away, earning a brief glance from Raede, who marched alongside him.

When they reached Faria's party, both of the foxes gave a deep bow to Jed, who returned the gesture in kind, lowering his head respectfully. Faria was still smiling at Bayer, but her expression faded upon seeing his arm. Kier's hands were gripped tightly in front of him. He was stiff and awkward, and kept looking to the ocelot, but the relief in his eyes escaped even with his efforts to suppress it in front of esteemed formality.

Jed looked to Faria. "Your Imperial Majesty, I am Jed Othera, Representative of Sinédrion and Acting High Councillor of the Cadon Senate. We have already been in contact, but it is an honour to finally meet you in person."

She bowed her head in thanks. "My Lord and Representative, I am honoured to have you as our guest in Xayall, and I would like to personally thank you for tending to my friend Bayer. He means a lot to us."

"I can see why. He is a loyal and capable soldier. None of us may be here if it weren't for him, and all who helped defend Sinédrion that day." He gave a deep, acknowledging nod to Aeryn and Kyru, who both saluted back. "If I may request a meeting at your convenience to discuss changes to be made to the Senate, I would be most grateful."

"Of course," Faria replied. She looked to Aeryn and Kyru, who flanked the stag to escort him to the meeting hall in the Tor. As they and Jed's entourage left, Bayer and Raede remained, facing Kier and Faria. There was a brief but reflective silence as they regarded each other.

"I'm glad you're safe, Bayer," Faria said eventually, in a comforted sigh.

"Thank you, Faria," he replied. "Alaris sends his apologies, by the way – he is busy arranging a troop exchange between Tremaine and Andarn, and setting up a task force to uncover the crimes that went on around the borders so they can be remapped."

"Is everything stable?" she asked tentatively. He shrugged.

"It's hard to say. The cave that Shadow's Claw gathered in before the siege was completely ransacked before we could return, and the children that went missing prior to the battles haven't been found yet. That's part of what they're searching for." He took a breath and looked around for a second. "Faria, I... wanted to ask permission to leave your service."

She nodded, the grip on her cane tightening to give away the expectation of his question. "You never had to ask, Bayer. You've always been free. It meant the world to me that you returned after the siege, but I had always wondered if you might find a greater meaning for yourself outside of the city."

"It's not a greater meaning as such," he replied. "Being here truly saved me, even though I didn't see it previously. There is nothing that will ever change how much Xayall means to me, and the people within it." He looked to Kier. "But I did find a new path that I want to take. Well, an old one, I suppose. Just one I will be walking myself rather than waiting for someone else to do for me."

Kier's expression softened. Not a smile, but it wasn't

sad. Bayer's chest swelled with purpose as he delivered his news. "I'm going to rebuild Kyrryk, along with Raede. Together we'll find its strength, and be an ally to you in the Senate."

Faria and Kier looked to one another, then back to Bayer.

"We will help you however we can," Faria said proudly. "I'm really happy for you." She stepped towards Raede, who bowed smartly. "I am Faria Arc'hantael, Empress of Xayall. It's lovely to meet you."

Raede smiled. "It's a privilege to meet you, Your Imperial Majesty. I am Raede Faolan, formerly of the Pthiris Guard and Shadow's Claw. Bayer informed me of the struggles you have faced. It would be a disservice not to support you in your fight to save the world from itself."

While Faria and Raede talked, Bayer and Kier clasped their left hands together and pulled each other into an embrace.

"It's good to see you," Kier said, muffled by the huge, wing-like epaulettes on the ocelot's shoulders.

"Told you I'd come back," Bayer replied. "Well, most of me did."

Kier frowned. "Are you doing all right?"

"Yeah," the ocelot replied, with a slightly sharp, bitter, laugh. "You don't realise what you miss when it's not there. But... it's fitting, I guess. If I can't hold a sword it will mean more to the people I'm trying to unite."

"It doesn't make you weak, though. You know that, right?"

Bayer gave him a dull look. "Yes, I do, but thank you. I had considered getting a prosthetic from Skyria, or an artisan one from here, but…" He looked to the sky for a moment, and the white clouds that moved briskly overhead, brushing the sun's rays like a hand over the water. "I have no reason to hide my history, not the old or the new. Maybe once I've rebuilt Kyrryk I'll take one, or maybe I won't ever need it again. We'll see."

Kier smiled. "All right. Just don't forget about us. We'll send you aid whenever you need, and escorts or retainers, and—"

Bayer halted the fox's ramble with a hand on his shoulder, and a warm smile. "It's fine, Kier. Thank you."

Kier placed a hand on Bayer's shoulder too, and looked about to pull him to another hug when the ocelot flicked him on the ear. Kier flinched and shook his head, looking put out.

"Pain in the arse," he sulked.

Bayer ignored him, but smiled wider. "You remember our bet, right?" Kier tilted his head, searching for an answer. Bayer slyly indicated Raede.

"I told you I'd bring back a companion. You keep your end of the deal?"

Kier looked around quickly, a little flustered. "Well, er, it's been going well. I mean, we've shared lots of meetings and she knows about my resonance and—"

Bayer smiled again. "Good. That's all I needed to know."

Chapter Twenty-Nine

Nazreal's barren, rocky zenith in the desert loomed under the drifting, unquiet clouds. At the gates, four soldiers stood in Xayall armour, near their makeshift shelter beside them. They were silent, stoic, and disquieted. The air around Nazreal smelt of death. The land itself seemed now to be aware of the city's presence: a sense of fear, and an alienating feeling of rejection blew in the sand that swirled around its base and crawled up the walls.

The giant metal doorway, now devoid of its resonance lock, had been pushed closed, albeit not completely. Missing the power that once held them in place, they sagged under their own weight, groaning and rattling ominously like a decaying monster. The soldiers exchanged uncomfortable looks with each deathly creak. It was not something to get used to.

Below, four more soldiers ascended the steep staircase towards the group, flecks of white and silver visible under the cloaks that rippled in the wind. As the squad reached the apex of their climb, the four Xayall guards signalled their relief with a thankful salute, and began their descent without a single word. The new soldiers took their positions and waited, keeping watchful eyes on the Xyall patrol's downward climb.

Once the previous detachment could be seen traversing the desert plains back towards Xayall, the Andarn patrol quickly spun round and forced open the huge metal gates. The dull slabs wailed open in a slumberous, low yawn. Two of the guards entered, skirting scattered debris.

"Are you sure nobody was in here?" the wolf hissed. "What are we even looking for?"

His partner, a lithe elk, ducked under a rocky outcrop. "If it's still around, I'm told it looks like two spears joined together. They might have taken it, I don't know."

The wolf dropped his shoulders, exasperated. His voice pitched high as he kicked a stone down a nearby crevice. "So we're here for nothing?"

"Keep looking," the elk hissed.

The wolf wouldn't relent. "If it's not here do we just sit at the gates like lemons and wait? What are we going back for if it's all over?" He picked up a rock and cast it into the darkness. "I mean, is this even an official order? Who are we even working for?"

The elk whirled round. "You'll find out when we get back to Kyrryk, idiot! Now shut up and—"

A noise.

The wolf froze, brandishing his spear to the shadows.

The noise again. A hollow, distant noise, echoing around the desolate city.

"What... is that?" the wolf rasped. "Is it... is that the

wind?"

Nearer this time, the noise came again. A shuffling, dragging sound. Weeping closer. A shape stumbled in the darkness before them.

And then, it screamed.

Acknowledgements

This book took me a lot longer than I was anticipating. Having it finally complete is a huge relief, and gives me renewed encouragement to keep pushing further. I absolutely want it to be less than five and a half years before completing Book Three!

To that end I have a lot of people to thank for helping keep me myself and maintain my faith in my abilities. My wife Madison has allowed me so much freedom to relax and create, which has been absolutely invaluable. Even just in this last year I've made so many friends through cosplay that naming them all will require a whole other volume, but they've been insurmountably encouraging on a creative and a personal level. Aaron, Meghan, Kenta, Amanda, Roger, Jenna, Sergei, Way, Tabitha, Jenny and Chris, Cami and Matt, Rusty, Lee, Raven, Will, Samuel, John, McKenna, Anna, Jordan, Gordon, Tj, James, Chris B, Shay, Trey, Moose, Burnice and Ashley, Sarah, Brandon, Mr. Freeze Pony, and the entirety of the 105th Squad, thank you SO MUCH for giving me a place to be myself unapologetically, and providing me so many tools and occasions to let my creative side escape in some of the most fulfilling ways possible.

My friends and family in the UK are incredibly special to me. Huge thanks to my parents Coral and Rob, who are still as excited to hear how I've been doing one time from the next; my older sister Dulcie and her husband Matt, who work unbelievably hard and helped inspire me to push myself to finishing my own creations. My younger sister Venetia has drawing wonderful concept art for the major characters and I get blown away each time, and had given me plenty of opportunity to geek out and be weird, along with her awesome boyfriend Simon. I also have to give special thanks to Lawrence, for a seemingly routine conversation in a coffee shop that helped me unlock this book's potential. Without that transition this would have been so much harder to complete, and may not even have been finished yet. Awesome friend Jeremy remains an inspiration in dedication, ability, and damn good luck. Su-Yang has been incredible for talking and just de-stressing generally, which I did not fully appreciate the value of until I'd experienced so many long days and short nights. Dan, my oldest friend, still gives me the ability to smile through remembering crazy adventures, and the promise of creating some enormous project in future. To Paul, who remains my constant goal for the kind of person I want to be as I grow older, thank you for remaining such a wonderful friend and resilient person.

Dan, Ashley, Maggie, and Matt are four more friends I have to give mention to, for giving me a place to feel welcome when I first moved to the States. I don't know if I would have survived here without your help and friendship. Thank you to each and all of you.

This list is getting long, but some of the most important

thanks are yet to come. Sara-Jayne Slack, the driving force behind Inspired Quill, has been unendingly patient and dedicated to all of the authors and seeing their work brought to life. She has been instrumental in so much of this process, and I owe her and IQ immeasurable thanks.

The beautiful cover art is by Katie Hofgard, whose talents are incredible and immense. There aren't enough words in the book to describe how much the art means to me and how much I immerse myself further into the world every time I see it. I've thanked her a lot via email already, but once more (until the next time), thank you so, so much.

There are fans who have taken time to write to me and connect with the characters on a deeper level than I was ever expecting. Jonathan, Chloe, Phillip, Michael, Nich, Cameron, Joseph, Marshall, Malefic-Maelor, thank you so very much for all of your communication, encouragement, and for indulging in the fruits of my imagination. I am eternally grateful. Also huge thanks to David, who told me about reading *Legacy* to his three children, and moved me with stories of how they'd pretend to be the characters in the playground. As a slave to imagination games in primary school myself, this completely blew me away.

Finally, great thanks go to you for reading this page right now. Either you are someone I've already mentioned, or you have the book, or you're at least interested in it enough to check this bit out. For giving me consideration, for even looking at a small title like this, it means the world to me.

Thank you, everyone.

About the Author

Hugo lives in Raleigh, North Carolina. He was born in Chichester, UK, and lived there until the age of 26, moving to the USA to live with his wife.

Along with writing, Hugo has a passion for stage acting, voice acting, stage combat, and anime. He has performed in several professional theatre productions, as well as a few documentaries, and was an extra in *The Young Victoria*. Intermittently he has led stage combat workshops for the Chichester Festival Youth Theatre, Chichester College and The Point Youth Theatre in Eastleigh.

He constructs his own anime, fandom, and Steampunk costumes and regularly attends any conventions he can. He has an enormous array of soundtracks from anime, films and video games. Music is one of his biggest inspirations, with various favourite tracks responsible for the majority of the Resonance Tetralogy storyline.

Find the author via their website:
www.hugorjackson.com
Or tweet at them: @PhoenixTheBlade

More From This Author

Legacy

Book 1 of the Resonance Tetralogy

Her power is unmeasured. Her abilities untested. Her destiny inescapable.

When her father goes missing, Faria has to rely on her own strength to brave the world that attacks her at every turn. Friends and guardians rally by her to help save her father and reveal the mysteries of the ruined city, while the dark legacy of an ancient cataclysm wraps its claws around her fate... and her past. She soon realises that this is not the beginning, nor anywhere near the end. A titanic war spanning thousands of years unfolds around her, one that could yet cost the lives of everyone on Eeres.

Legacy is character-driven epic fantasy action forged in an exciting and intricate plot that reaches deep into the Resonance world's history.

Paperback ISBN: 978-1-908600-22-6
eBook ISBN: 978-1-908600-23-3

Available from all major online and offline outlets.

CPSIA information can be obtained at www.ICGtesting.com
Printed in the USA
LVOW07s1619130916

504435LV00001B/21/P